PRAISE FOR
Widow's Walk

"... In the inspiring novel *Widow's Walk*, a church community discovers the power of compassion, faith, and coming together to heal broken hearts."

—*Foreword Reviews*

★ ★ ★

"Jane Willan's *Widow's Walk* takes readers on a journey of hope through the eyes of people in a small coastal town in Downeast Maine. She balances a fast-paced story with a lot of heart for every character, handling each one with tenderness."

—Maren C. Tirabassi, former Poet Laureate of Portsmouth, NH

★ ★ ★

"A heartwarming tale of second chances and spiritual awakening."

– Mary Karnes, acclaimed author of the *Wedding Planner Mystery Series*

★ ★ ★

"*Widow's Walk* is a refreshingly honest portrayal of faith lived out in the messiness of real life, weaving humor throughout without diminishing the profound spiritual questions at its heart. It's exactly the kind of honest, hope-filled narrative our world needs."

–Rev. Nicole Grant Yonkman, the first woman senior minister of the historic First Church in Windsor, CT

★ ★ ★

"Willan crafts a tale with unexpected twists and turns that do not shy away from reality, while also granting us a glimpse at the possibilities for change, redemption, and ultimately, love."

–Rev. Kathy Cunliffe, former Senior Pastor of the First Congregational Church of Wallingford, Connecticut.

Widow's Walk

A Novel

JANE WILLAN

Sibylline Press

Sibylline Press
Distributed to the trade by Publishers Group West

Copyright © 2025 by Jane Willan

All Rights Reserved. Published in the United States by Sibylline Press, an imprint of All Things Book LLC, California. Sibylline Press is dedicated to publishing the brilliant work of women authors ages 50 and older.

www.sibyllinepress.com

Distributed to the trade by Publishers Group West
ISBN Trade: 9781960573452
eBook ISBN: 9781960573513

Library of Congress Control Number: 2025933366

Cover Design: Alicia Feltman
Book Production: Aaron Laughlin

To Reverend Martha Everhard

Widow's Walk

A Novel

JANE WILLAN

*You are no more strangers and foreigners
but fellow citizens with the saints of God.*

Ephesians 2:19

CHAPTER ONE

"And whose nitwit idea was this?" Betty Hardacre snapped, her orthopedic shoes sinking into sand. Betty was the chair of the Episcopal Church Women. She prided herself on upholding the parish's long-standing traditions.

Pastor Miranda McCurdy looked up from the grill where she tended to the sizzling barbecue. As the first woman to lead St. Gabriel-by-the-Sea in 180 years, she was used to resistance. "Not a fan of wings?" She flipped a drumette, aiming for that sweet spot between crispy and burnt.

"It doesn't matter if I like chicken wings," Betty said, facing Miranda across the grill. "And no, I don't care for them. But that's not the point. We've always had bratwurst at the Feast of St. Gabriel. Bratwurst, Pastor. Not chicken."

"Changing things up a bit can be good." Miranda adjusted the heat for one last crisping blast. Before becoming a priest, Miranda had been head chef at a top Boston restaurant, The Pellegrino. To her, cooking and ministry were two sides of the same coin—both nourished the soul. She took pride in feeding her congregation spiritual sustenance and, when the need arose, the comfort of a few heavy carbs.

"This isn't a five-star restaurant, you know." Betty turned and stomped away toward the badminton game where Harry Hopkins, senior warden at St. Gabe's, had just lobbed the shuttlecock over the net to the cheers of his team. Miranda sighed, her gaze drifting across the beach. The clear, crisp autumn light bathed the scene, her congregation scattered across the beach in small groups, savoring the last church picnic of the season. As tradition dictated, St. Gabe's members had come to worship in Hawaiian shirts and flip-flops, then migrated to Sparrow Town beach after the final "amen."

Now they awaited the first chicken wings from the grill. St. Gabe's congregation shared their priest's love for food. Miranda's first year had been a whirlwind of potlucks, pancake breakfasts, and post-worship coffee hours laden with lemon squares, cookies, and cream pies. Did church people crave the reassurance that good food offered? Did a cheesy casserole or a basket of warm dinner rolls give them needed sustenance in the same manner as an inspiring sermon or a rousing hymn? She wasn't sure, but she did know that she needed to cut back on her own calorie consumption. And soon.

Fresh from seminary a year ago, Miranda had thought herself ready for anything. Then came Betty. The older woman's weekly office visits brought a litany of complaints, all circling one theme: change. Betty bristled at Miranda's preaching, theology, and casual attire. She railed against the smallest alterations—from kitchen towel organization to banning plastic at potlucks—as if each were a seismic shift in church doctrine. Underlying it all was Betty's unspoken objection: Miranda's audacity to be a female priest.

Miranda flipped a few chicken wings and dabbed each one with sauce.

"Did you learn to grill at that fancy restaurant in Boston?" Harry walked up to her, badminton racket in hand.

"Nope," she replied, smiling. "I owe it all to Famous Bill's Burgers. My first real job. Ninth grade. I worked the grill, washed dishes, and, on a busy night, waitressed."

Harry laughed. "So, you didn't start at the top?"

"Not by a long shot."

"Well, that's probably good." He gazed at the water for a moment and then turned back to her. "Don't give Betty Hardacre a second thought. Everyone loves you here at St. Gabe's. Betty is just Betty."

"I suppose." She appreciated Harry's support, probably more than he realized.

"Did Colville tell you someone tried to pick the lock on the side door last night?" Colville Duby, the church sexton, had cleaned and polished St. Gabe's for the past forty years.

Miranda pushed back her chef's hat, eyebrows raised. The crime rate in Sparrow was exceptionally low. Most of its citizens left their doors unlocked at night.

"How do you know? Was the lock broken?"

"Not broken. Scratched up pretty bad." Harry reached into the pocket of his yellow and green Bermuda shorts and withdrew a small red pocket knife in a plastic sandwich bag. "Found this. On the sidewalk in front of the door."

She turned the knife over in her hand. "But they didn't get in?"

Harry shook his head. "Tried hard enough."

"If you're picking a lock with your knife, would you drop it right in front of the door?"

"Could've gotten scared and run off." Harry shrugged.

"Maybe they needed a place to sleep. I hate to think of someone coming to the church for help and finding nothing but a locked door." She flipped a few of the chicken wings.

Harry was a good person, but Miranda figured he wouldn't have much sympathy for a trespasser, no matter how needy. "Did you report it?"

"First thing tomorrow. The police will want this." He slid the sandwich-bagged knife into his pocket. "Looking forward to that chicken." He gave her a nod and wandered back to the badminton game. She mopped more of the thick, flavorful sauce onto the wings. *Where salty meets sweet and true love is the result*, the food critic had said when her sauce won *Yankee Magazine*'s Best of Barbecue, 2015. She paused for a moment. Had it really been eight years since the award? Time was funny. In one way, eight years was a snap of the fingers; in another, a hundred lifetimes.

Thinking back on that year, 2015, made Miranda's throat tighten, but only for a moment. Until then, life had seemed straightforward, predictable. An ordinary day meant kissing her husband Jason goodbye from the stoop of their apartment, then power walking the ten blocks to The Pellegrino. There, she would eagerly pull on her chef's whites and begin the demanding yet exhilarating dinner shift. Life was perfect. Until it wasn't. Until the world turned upside down. And nothing was ever the same again.

"We need those wings, Pastor," Ramona Duncan said, stepping up to the grill. Ramona was the vice-chairperson of the Thanksgiving Committee and the owner of Down-the-Drain-Plumbers. Miranda hoped the straightforward and sensible woman would bring a more lighthearted mood to the contentious Thanksgiving Committee.

"Almost ready," she said. The meat thermometer read one-hundred and sixty-seven degrees, which was perfect. She piled the wings onto a platter and handed it off to Ramona.

"St. Gabe's is lucky to get a pastor who was a famous chef at a fancy restaurant in New York City," Ramona said.

"Boston," she corrected. "And maybe not famous. But fancy, yes."

"First woman head chef on the East Coast. Isn't that right?"

"Not the very first, but one of a few." Miranda scraped down the grill and reduced the heat.

"Must be quite a change—from the big city to Sparrow." Ramona passed the loaded chicken platter to Myra Jenkins, who rushed it over to the table. A cheer went up from those waiting.

Miranda pulled another bowl of marinating chicken out of the cooler at her feet and deftly lined the grill with wings. She was moving chicken faster for the annual church picnic than on a busy night at The Pellegrino.

"You like it, though, don't you?" Ramona licked her fingers.

Parishioners sometimes worried that the small coastal town of Sparrow, Maine, might one day dissatisfy her, that she would beat a path back to the city, to her old life as a chef, abandoning the good people of St. Gabe's.

"Are you kidding?" She basted the chicken, her movements relaxed and contented. "I love it here." And she did. How could you not love a place where the mountains were only a pleasant drive to the west, and the beach a short stroll to the east?

Sometimes she missed the city: crowded sidewalks, boutique shopping, the gleaming Hancock Tower. Boston's energy, even with its grit and traffic, was absent in this bucolic town. When nostalgia struck, she'd retreat to the rectory's tiny kitchen, cooking to soothe her urban cravings. Cooking was good for everything—almost.

A breeze lifted Miranda's curly, chestnut fringe. She wiped sweat from her brow, round cheeks flushed from the grill's heat. Her loose shirt settled over her soft, curvy frame as she adjusted the temperature. "Do you know Gordon Ramsay, that TV chef?" Ramona asked.

Everyone in Sparrow assumed she was best friends with Ramsay, Rachael Ray, and that tattooed guy from *Diners, Drive-ins, and Dives*.

"I met him once," Miranda answered. "Insufferably smug, but brilliant." Miranda looked up to see a man in a gray suit striding across the beach, his leather shoes slipping in the sand. He scowled at his phone, oblivious to sand and waves. The perfect September day went unnoticed as he fixated on the small screen.

His outfit—dress shirt, jacket, and pressed pants—was not really beach attire. "Excuse me." He stopped in front of the grill. "I'm looking for Pastor McCurdy?" His voice reminded her of a person talking to customer service—tense politeness edging toward annoyance.

Ramona smirked.

"I'm Pastor McCurdy," she said. His piercing blue eyes locked onto hers as the sea breeze ruffled his salt-and-pepper hair. Miranda suddenly became self-conscious in her floppy chef's hat, Hawaiian shirt, and baggy shorts.

"Oh. Right. I just thought—"

"That the pastor would look different? A man, perhaps?" She was determined to shake off her discomfort, and being a bit cynical was the quickest way she knew to do it.

"No. Certainly not. I was thrown off by the chef's hat and Hawaiian shirt."

"Don't forget the Bermuda shorts," Ramona added. "And flip-flops."

"Fair enough." Miranda turned back to the grill and flipped a few sizzling drumettes. "And I don't imagine you're here for chicken and potato salad, so how can I help?"

"I'm Adam McClain. My great-aunt is Lucy McClain." He looked around the beach at the crowd of church members. "She told me she would be here after church."

"I don't think she is." Miranda cast a concerned glance across the beach. Lucy rarely missed a church social event.

"I didn't see her in the choir this morning," Ramona said.

"That's odd." Miranda frowned. "Lucy's usually so reliable. I hope everything's alright."

Adam, now sweating in his immaculate gray suit, fixed his gaze on the grill. "You know," he said, "chicken needs at least twenty minutes of high heat."

"Really?"

"Are you using a meat thermometer?" he asked.

"Oh. So a meat thermometer is a good thing?"

"You should always use a meat thermometer with chicken. The temperature should reach 165 degrees at a minimum." He scanned the grill top again. "And you really have to be careful when you cover the chicken in sauce like that; it's even harder to tell if it's thoroughly cooked."

"You don't say?" She gave him a long look. He was around her age, late thirties, with striking features. His chiseled jawline and straight nose gave him a classically handsome profile. Dark hair, neatly styled, framed his face, while intense blue eyes caught the sunlight. Miranda found herself oddly drawn to him, despite his obvious arrogance. But as he continued to mansplain, his condescending tone grated on her nerves, bringing on a mixture of outrage and unwelcome attraction. She was appalled at herself for finding such a rude person appealing, but there was no denying the pull she felt.

"Speaking of cooking, Lucy usually brings her famous potato salad to these events," Miranda said. "I'm really getting worried now."

"McClain?" Ramona interjected, looking thoughtful. "Pat and Nancy McClain are your parents, right?"

Adam slipped his phone into his coat pocket and gave Ramona a quick smile, which made his face less tense. A cute smile, especially for a guy who showed up at the beach in fancy shoes, a suit, and tie.

"My parents," he said.

"I do their plumbing." Ramona identified everyone by their plumbing. "Is it true that they've sold their house on Lincoln Street?"

"A month ago. Moved to Portugal."

"No!" Ramona gave him a skeptical look. "They left the country?" Clearly, Ramona would never consider the life of an ex-pat.

"They told me they were looking for life's next big adventure." The faint disapproval in his voice had returned and made Miranda think that *adventure* might not be Adam's top priority.

"I wonder what kind of plumbing they have over there," Ramona mused. "Tell your folks they can call me for advice anytime. I've heard European toilets can be tricky."

"I'll tell them," Adam replied, his voice solemn.

Miranda liked that he took Ramona seriously—a woman who took plumbing seriously.

"With your parents so far away, who's checking on Lucy?" Ramona asked.

"Her care has fallen to me," Adam replied, a trace of fatigue in his voice. "Of course," he quickly added, "I'm glad to do it. She's meant a lot to me over the years."

"You should stay and eat," Ramona told him. "The pastor here makes really good sauce."

"Did they teach you how to barbecue at seminary?" He turned back to Miranda.

She noticed that his voice was serious, but his eyes smiled. "Yes," she replied, with an equally straight face. "The Sacramental Nature of Grilling. Required for graduation."

"And chicken wings are biblical, I assume?"

"Everything," she said, "is biblical. If you look hard enough."

"I don't doubt it." His eyes smiled.

"So you're checking on Lucy?" Ramona interrupted.

"Yes and no." Adam gazed out at the ocean for a moment. "My aunt is pretty independent, and I live in Portland, so it's not like I can head to Sparrow all the time."

"Don't worry," Ramona said. "I'll be over at her house this week. Downstairs toilet. Leaky flange."

"I do call her weekly and I set her up with a ride-share app." He met Miranda's gaze. "Sounds a little weak, huh?"

"Not at all." She flipped a wing that had started to smoke. "Ride-share might give Lucy some much-needed independence. And don't underestimate the amount of stress and exhaustion that comes with caretaking."

"Thanks for saying that." His smile revealed a slightly crooked front tooth.

Miranda liked the hint of imperfection in his otherwise polished appearance.

"My mother wasn't happy about the ride-share app." He loosened his tie.

"Well, mothers." They both laughed. "Actually, it's a good idea. Lucy's been talking about needing to get around more." She paused. "So you haven't heard from her at all today?"

"No. And I need to find her." A nod to Ramona. "Thanks for the plumbing intel." Turning back to Miranda. "Pastor Miranda, nice to meet you. Perhaps our paths will cross again."

"If you need help checking on Lucy, just give me a call. I'm happy to stop by her place."

Their eyes met in a moment of unspoken connection.

"Thanks. I appreciate that."

Her mind raced for the perfect thing to say, but the words eluded her. Instead, she re-focused on flipping the chicken wings on the grill, trying to ignore the fluttery feeling in her stomach. She looked up and watched him walk toward the parking lot, his polished shoes slipping in the sand the entire way.

★ ★ ★

Miranda's muscles ached as if she'd just finished a long shift at The Pellegrino. She'd waved off rides, opting to walk the five blocks home from Sparrow Beach, hoping to stretch out her soreness.

She was grateful for the rectory—a cozy bungalow on a quiet lane. Close enough to the beach to hear the waves at night, but far enough from the church to dodge calls about forgotten keys or broken boilers. More private than most Episcopal rectories.

She pushed open the screen door, kicking off her flip-flops and dropping her beach bag in the front room. The house was modest but perfect, especially the kitchen. The recent upgrade, funded by the vestry—the elected body managing the parish's finances and operations—included a new gas range that made her inner chef sing. Miranda headed straight for it, already planning dinner despite her exhaustion.

"Hey Howard," she said into the empty house. "I'm home."

The aroma of fresh grounds filled the air as she poured water into the carafe. Despite the early evening hour, she craved the warmth and comfort of a cup of coffee. A chill from the ocean breeze had seeped into her bones, and fatigue weighed on her eyelids. Coffee would ward off both the cold and the temptation of an ill-timed nap.

"Time to wake up, Howard," she called out. She turned on the overhead kitchen light and crossed the room. A miniature hobbit house, complete with a round door and windows, sat in the warmest corner of the kitchen. The snug house was home to Howard, Miranda's fourteen-ounce African pygmy hedgehog.

Miranda had adopted Howard a year ago, just before moving to Sparrow. A classmate from divinity school, headed for an Arizona parish, had needed a new home for Howard. High temperatures give hedgehogs heatstroke, and air conditioning sends them into hibernation. Miranda found a spot for the four-toed Howard and his hobbit house in her 2009 Honda Accord. They headed for Maine together.

Her phone buzzed.

I'm in Sparrow. You live here?? Text me your address. Tony

CHAPTER TWO

"Everything you loved about The Pellegrino, you'll love about the new restaurant."

She had forgotten how compelling Tony Barici could be in his egocentric-yet-charming way. He was the result of DNA that coded for handsome features, olive skin, and perfect teeth. Add in lots of money, a prep school education, summers on Martha's Vineyard, and you had Tony. His parents owned The Pellegrino. Mr. and Mrs. Barici might have pulled themselves up through years of hard work and sacrifice but had handed their youngest son everything. He hadn't started his restaurant career like Miranda had: working the grill and scrubbing pans at Famous Bill's Burgers.

"It's just like The Pellegrino. Except maybe, less Old World. More contemporary." Tony leaned forward on the loveseat. "So? What do you think?"

Miranda grabbed a corkscrew and picked up the bottle of wine that Tony had offered. *Prunotto Barbaresco*.

"I suppose you liberated this from the restaurant's wine cellar?" She wanted to slow down this conversation. Her two worlds were crashing with Tony sitting here in the rectory offering her a job as a head chef. A job, she had to admit, that was at least a little exciting.

He shrugged. "What can I say? It's my restaurant."

"As I recall, your mother owns the place." Miranda pulled out the cork and then filled his glass and then her own. "Or has that changed?" She knew that Mr. Barici had passed away a year after she left for seminary. "I'm sorry about your dad. He was a great guy."

"Thanks," Tony said, his voice serious for once. "Dad was a legend."

"I think your mom is the legend. Your dad was the—" Miranda thought for a moment. "The *momentum*." They sat in silence for a moment, sipping wine. "How's your mom doing?" Miranda found herself kicking into pastor mode.

"Good. She works too hard, so I am taking over the new restaurant. I'll manage the Seattle site, and if all goes well—eventually, it really will be mine. That's why I want you there. You'll make it work."

"I left the restaurant business." She sat back and swirled the wine in her glass. She had always liked Prunotto Barbaresco. Red berries, smoky vanilla, silky, extra dry. "I'm a priest now."

"I never understood why you threw away such a great career. You were the best."

"This is a great career."

"But a priest? You don't seem like the type."

"I'm not bad at it." She sipped the smoky berry flavor. "It fits me. Anyway, it's my life now."

Tony cocked an eyebrow. "A little town in northern Maine? You were such a city girl."

"I know. Go figure." She held Tony's gaze, hoping to disguise that he had caught her off guard. And that she was interested in the job. At least a little. Which scared her. She felt settled here in Sparrow. Like she was home.

She reached over and flipped on the table lamp. Warm yellow light filled the room. Maybe, she told herself, she was only interested because leaving Sparrow meant that all the stress and expectations of the priesthood would disappear, vanish into the chaos and noise of a kitchen slammed for the dinner hour. The coffee table between them was covered with books and notes—the flotsam and jetsam of her prep for Carl Quincy's funeral the day before. A near disaster at the graveside. She had stepped backward, sinking one of her two-inch heels into the soft dirt, which made her pitch sideways. Her arms flailed helplessly, and her prayer book went flying. Only a last-minute save by the funeral director had prevented her from joining Carl in the grave.

"I belong in the pulpit," she said, voice firm. "Not in the kitchen."

"You're sure?"

Was she sure? Flipping chicken on the grill that afternoon had rekindled something. Miranda had experienced, at least for a moment, an old and deep satisfaction: the pleasure of cooking. Not just cooking, but the whole picture: creating a menu, mixing a sauce, choosing ingredients, all coming together with the response to her food. Sometimes she wanted nothing more than to step into a crazy, busy kitchen, tie on an apron, and start prepping for the next shift.

Tony stood up and stretched. He began to pace around the small room as if trying to puzzle something out. "But is this place really a life? I mean, like, sure. It's quaint here. Beautiful scenery. I'll give you that. But they must roll up the sidewalks at nine o'clock."

"Five o'clock." She pushed aside her eulogy notes and placed her wine glass on the table. "When do you open?"

"Early January. I'd want you onsite at least a month ahead. December. The sooner, the better."

She mentally reviewed her calendar. Advent. The children's pageant. The Christmas Fair. Greening of the church. The Candlelight Christmas Eve service. She would miss it all. St. Gabe's would carry on though. Without her. Her chest tightened. But beneath everything, a flicker. Of what? Relief. She shoved the feeling away. "This is my home," she said firmly. "These people. This church."

Tony sank into the loveseat, legs sprawled. He laced his fingers behind his head.

"But why?" His eyebrows quirked up. "All that talent, wasted in this backwater?"

"Sparrow is far from being a backwater." Defensiveness rose in her voice.

"I just meant—" Tony sat up. "My God, what's that noise? Do you have mice?" Tony looked like he was about to jump up on the coffee table.

"It's Howard," she said.

"Your boyfriend makes noise like that?"

"Howard isn't my boyfriend. He's my hedgehog." The pudgy, spiny little hedgehog grunted and snorted like a baby pig. He loved to scurry across the hardwood floors and burrow underneath the throw rugs. At the moment, he was rooting through her recycling bin, indulging his love of shredded paper. "He's nocturnal so he runs around after dark."

"Oh." Tony lifted his feet as if Howard was about to scramble up his pant leg. "Kind of loud, isn't it?"

"Howard's a noisy little guy."

"So you're out here in the boonies with nothing but a hedgehog for a friend." He put his feet up on the coffee table, his left heel squarely on top of the Episcopal prayer book.

Miranda pictured Adam McClain. His crisp gray suit. That polished, worldly handsomeness. A man who cared for his elderly great aunt. She couldn't imagine Adam with his feet on a coffee table. Let alone a prayer book. "What do you want? Is it the money?"

Miranda hesitated.

"I'll pay you twice what you're making right now."

"You don't even know what I make now." She kept her voice neutral. Never would she let Tony know just how broke she was. She had taken a leave of absence from the restaurant during Jason's illness. With his life insurance going to medical bills, she had started depending on credit cards for everything from rent to groceries. Then three years of seminary meant a frightening student loan, the payments which now appeared every month like a bad dream. She took a sip of wine and forced her face into a look of cheerful disinterest.

Tony stood and stretched. "Double," he repeated. "And all the freedom you want to write your own ticket. Menu, staff, everything. It'll all be yours. Your little kingdom."

"Queendom."

"Whatever."

Miranda followed him out onto the front stoop.

Tony slid his hands into his perfectly pressed khakis. The platinum watch on his wrist caught the light. "The offer's on the table," he said. He let the words hang in the air. "But not forever."

She watched him walk down the flagstone path to his car and remembered how Jason hadn't liked Tony. Too smooth. Silver spoon in his mouth. Jason had grown up fighting for scraps. He had worked through art school, lived off ramen noodles, and paid for his little sister's prom dress.

Tony opened the door of the cherry-red Mercedes convertible. He turned back, one arm resting on the smooth fabric of the closed top. "Head chef. In an amazing new restaurant." He slid into the leather seat and lowered the window with a soft whir. "Let me know." Miranda zipped her hoodie, pulling the sleeves over her cold hands. The whispery sound of the waves on the beach told her the tide was going out.

The Mercedes purred to life. Twin beams sliced through the darkness, revealing Cricket Lane's border of hydrangeas. Muted blue and pink clusters nodded in the headlights' glare. "I won't hold the job forever." Tires crunched on gravel as he pulled away.

CHAPTER THREE

Miranda stood at the altar. The folds of her white chasuble fell around her plump frame and brushed the tops of her pink Converse sneakers. She held aloft the silver communion plate mounded with round wafers. But then, just as she was about to recite the Words of Institution, the unconsecrated host turned into a stack of burgers with double cheese and mayo on the side.

She bolted upright in bed.

Light from the streetlamp seeped in around the edges of the window blind, and the bells at St. Gabe's chimed the hour. Three o'clock. Too early to get up and make coffee, but then, slim chance of falling asleep again.

She flung the covers off and sat on the edge of her bed. Howard snuffled boisterously from the front room. Being nocturnal, he threw a little party every night—hedgehog style. The festivities included pushing crinkle balls down the hall, nosing under throw rugs, and skittering across the kitchen's tile floor. By the time the sun rose in the morning, he could be found, curled up and exhausted, in his Hobbit house, snoring his little hedgehog snore. An entire existence composed of eat, play, sleep, and eat again. Not a bad life, she often thought.

The phone glowed with text messages. One from Myra Crabtree asking for Miranda's barbecue sauce recipe. Another from the local nursing home requesting a worship service on Tuesday. And Colville Duby reporting a light on in the Youth Room. Odd, she thought. There was no youth meeting yesterday—all the kids had been at the picnic. She clicked off and dropped her phone on the bed.

"Howard," Miranda called out into the dark house. "Want a treat?"

A series of grunts and snuffles, and he scurried in, fat, bristly, adorable. He stopped on the braided throw rug and waited. His twitching snout turned upward. Miranda opened the drawer of her nightstand and pulled out a plastic container. She popped the lid and tossed him an insectivore snack: eight different insects and worms compressed into one pellet. She tried not to think of what she had just touched. Howard grabbed the pellet and darted under the bed.

She stood and pulled Jason's old fisherman-knit sweater over her pajamas. The stretched-out wool, bobbled with pilling, comforted her. Jason had been tall with a lanky swimmer's body, and the sweater reached her knees. She had given it to him a few months before he died. He had lost weight and often shook with cold. She had tried everything—heated throws, fleece blankets—but he reacted angrily to being wrapped up in a blanket, and she didn't blame him. The heavy wool sweater kept him warm, and he had worn it almost every day until that final week when he lay in bed, too sick to care anymore.

Miranda padded across the chilly kitchen tiles and settled into the snug window seat of the small breakfast nook. She tucked her knees up to her chest, smoothed the sweater over them, and buried her toes in its hem. The eerie brightness of the moonlight illuminated the kitchen.

She stared at her phone and told herself not to do it.

She did it anyway.

She clicked on the "Recordings" tab and scrolled down to November 22, 2010, 11:27 a.m. Jason's last voicemail, left for her just before everything changed. Before the medical professionals revealed the reason for his exhaustion, the frightening episodes of slurred speech, and unsteady walk. This voicemail was sent during those blissfully ignorant and peaceful days, when neither of them had ever heard of Amyotrophic Lateral Sclerosis, ALS, or Lou Gehrig's Disease.

He had called her from the hospital parking garage. He wanted her to text a grocery list because he planned to stop at Whole Foods on the way home, or could she bring leftovers from the dinner shift? And he wanted her to stop worrying. And he loved her. And the parking garage at Mass General was way too expensive.

She had intended to go with him to his appointment so they could hear the results of his EMG together. But on the way, her phone had buzzed. The Pellegrino. Could she come into the restaurant? A crisis with the wine vendor. She had jumped out of the car at the next red light and hailed a cab. Hours later, she came home to find Jason sitting on the couch, tears streaming down his face.

★ ★ ★

Miranda leaned her forehead against the cold windowpane and gazed out at the side yard. The potting shed, hydrangea bush, and overturned wheelbarrow took on ghostly shapes, shadowed humps in the moonlight. She had told Dr. Michaels, her therapist in seminary, that she had stopped replaying the recording. Stopped returning to the world of Jason. It was a lie, but she couldn't admit to him that after two years of therapy, she still clung to a fifty-seven-second recording as if it were the last life preserver on the *Titanic*.

"Have you considered deleting it from your phone?" Dr. Michaels had asked. "Doing so might open you up to new people, new experiences." Miranda couldn't bring herself to tell him that she had no intention of ever deleting Jason's voice. But she did try to listen to it less often, like a smoker cutting back on cigarettes—not quitting altogether but doing it less frequently.

Dr. Michaels had been right. Listening less often had helped her stay grounded in the present. And things were better, for the most part. Then, without warning, something—a voice, a song, the smell of autumn leaves—brought Jason walking back into the room, as if he had never left. During the light of day, she could handle even the most visceral onslaught of memory. But late at night, in the darkness, memory meant a storm of grief.

Miranda usually rose from bed with the rising moon and, without turning on any lights, she would listen to Jason's voice. She would see his hazel eyes again and remember how they closed when he laughed, how his fingertips brushed her forehead and pushed her hair back just before he kissed her. His smile. His laugh. His cough. His huddled shape under the hospital blanket. Body bag zipped. Wheeled away. *Jason.*

She tapped the screen, closed her eyes, and breathed in as Jason's voice came across time and space, filling the room. A cloud passed over the moon, and darkness enveloped her like a soft robe.

★ ★ ★

The town of Sparrow had barely finished its first cup of coffee when Miranda hurried down the front steps of the rectory. Her curly chestnut hair was still damp from the shower. She smoothed her black clergy shirt over her rounded figure, tugging it into place. Jeans and high-top sneakers completed her outfit, the casual attire contrasting nicely with her white tab collar.

She glanced at her phone. The ever-punctual Peg Dunbar, secretary at St. Gabriel-by-the-Sea Episcopal Church, would be sitting behind her desk like a captain at the helm of a great ship. Undoubtedly, Peg had already compiled a neat stack of pink memo slips to hand Miranda as she entered the door.

Miranda had suggested that she and Peg sync their Google accounts, and then Peg could enter items directly onto Miranda's calendar and dispense with the paper memos. Without looking up from her keyboard, Peg had said, in her crisp voice, that she had ordered fifteen hundred memo slips from Church Supplies in 1998. She wasn't throwing away the remaining 234 to learn a new computer trick.

Pink memo slips it was, then.

The slips reminded Miranda of order tickets at Famous Bill's Burgers. When Peg handed her one, she almost heard fries sizzling and smelled burgers cooking on the grill. Miranda walked toward downtown Sparrow, thinking about The Pellegrino. Sometimes she really missed being a chef. The camaraderie of the kitchen staff, the exhilaration of the Friday night dinner rush, and the thrill of crafting a new menu. She enjoyed imagining the creation of a beautiful entrée or the presentation of an eye-catching dessert.

Miranda reminisced for a moment about the elegant atmosphere of the front of the house, with its crisp linens, flickering candles, and soothing jazz music, where servers in immaculate white shirts gracefully moved from table to table. In contrast, the back of the house was a frenzied mélange of energy, noise, and organized chaos, where the kitchen manager, who made even Chef Ramsay seem mild-mannered, held court.

Miranda halted in the middle of the sidewalk, breathing in the soft October air. *Stop idealizing it.* The Pellegrino was also late nights, back pain, a balance sheet that never balanced, demanding customers, no time for a personal life. Exhilaration, yes. But also, soul-crushing exhaustion. She turned the corner and headed down Main Street. Billowy white clouds moved across the soft autumn sky. Orange maples lined the street.

Maybe life as a priest wasn't that different from her life as a chef. Parish ministry provided moments of deep fulfillment, if not pure exhilaration: baptizing a new baby, marrying a young couple, sitting with a family as they said goodbye at a hospice bedside. Not the adrenaline rush of a slammed kitchen at dinner hour, but the deep abiding satisfaction of accompanying another person on their life's journey.

She hurried past Sparrow's post office and then stopped to gaze at the new books displayed in the window of the Once Upon a Time Bookstore.

Peg reminded Miranda of a few fearsome kitchen managers she had known. The tall, spare older woman had been the admin at St.

Gabe's for the past forty-three years. A decorous defender of all truth, especially if that truth concerned proper manners or correct grammar. Peg was not one to lose her car keys, miss an appointment, or forget her umbrella on a rainy day. She carried herself with perfect posture, meticulously organized the parish records and files, and made all church decisions *de rigueur*.

And yet, Miranda knew that Peg never refused a kid selling candy bars to raise money for a school trip, worked the soup kitchen in Augusta every third Saturday, and sent Christmas cards with hand-written notes to all the homebound church members. Miranda possessed the good sense to know that without Peg, she would be lost.

She caught her reflection in the window of Asa Bradshaw's hardware store. Mirrored back was a hunched-over, still-young woman with wet hair and a worried scowl. Stopping short, Miranda tugged her tab collar straight and sucked in her stomach while pretending to admire the display of leaf rakes, bags of mulch, and wheelbarrows. She took a long look at herself in the window glass. Lithe and willowy had once described her dream body. But long ago she had accepted that plump and sturdy might be more accurate, or as her aunt had once told her, *big-boned*.

On the other hand, her chestnut hair was thick and wavy, her nose decently cute, and her eyes hazel green. It might be time to give up on lithe and willowy.

"Looking for a rake, are you, Pastor?" Asa Bradshaw said as he stepped out of the hardware store door, interrupting her thoughts. He began to sweep the sidewalk vigorously.

"No, just admiring your display," she replied, smiling at the store proprietor.

"I'd think you would need a rake, living in that little rectory of yours. There's a big oak tree in the front, as I recall." He paused his sweeping and leaned on the broom.

Miranda had lived in a small apartment in the city for so many years that it had never crossed her mind to purchase gardening tools.

"At least St. Gabe's had the good sense to keep their rectory. I don't know what the diocese is thinking—letting Episcopal Churches sell off their clergy housing." He resumed sweeping.

"Thanks. I probably do need a rake."

"Well, come back anytime then. Clergy discount." Asa gave her a nod. The overhead bell jingled as the door shut behind him.

St. Gabriel-by-the-Sea anchored the north end of Main Street, exactly seven blocks from Miranda's rectory. She'd promised herself she'd walk it daily, unless the weather turned truly bad. A little rain was fine, but she'd draw the line at downpours or blizzards. Miranda generally avoided exercise, but with potluck dinners, afternoon teas, and gifts of food from the ever-generous people of St. Gabe's, squeezing into her jeans had begun to require more effort than she liked to exert for a pair of pants. And better to pick up one's exercise regimen than to engage in the tedium of cutting calories and ruining the joy of eating.

She slowed her pace. She needed to work on being more present, more in the moment. She breathed in, counting slowly to five. It was a mindfulness practice she had learned in yoga last week. Opening her eyes, she jumped to miss a dog pile on the sidewalk.

★ ★ ★

Sparrow sat nestled between Juniper Mountain and Silver Point Estuary where, as the townspeople loved to say, the river meets the sea. The entire village could be traversed, end to end, by starting at the south end of Main Street and walking straight north for the distance of five city blocks to where Main Street ended at Brier Road.

On the west side of Main Street, one would pass Loretta's Diner, The Little Black Dress, Asa's Hardware, Reeves Family Insurance, Saint-Gabriel's-by-the-Sea Episcopal Church, an empty lot, and a gravel patch before reaching Brier Road. If you came out the church's front door and crossed Main Street to the east side of things, you would walk up the steps of the Sparrow Public Library. Back on Main Street, you could head south, passing the bank, The Rolling Pin Pastry, the post office, the Once Upon a Time Bookstore, and The Keep Calm and Carry Yarn Shoppe. The end of the street was the best of all: the Malted Milk Bar, open for ice cream in the summer and hot chocolate in the winter.

The journey could be accomplished in about thirty minutes of purposeful walking if one didn't linger too long, gazing in the shop windows. But the citizens of Sparrow always stopped to gaze in the windows. The merchants on Main Street took pride in their window displays. They strove to outdo each other, especially during Christmas and leaf-peeping season.

If you felt like a drive, you might turn left onto Brier, a winding gravel road bordered by long stretches of stonewalls, and head toward Juniper Mountain. In a short time, you would admire green hills dotted with the occasional flock of snowy sheep. The hills soon flattened into open meadows that waved with Queen Anne's lace and buttercups in the summer, goldenrod in the fall. If you headed past Juniper Mountain and kept driving due west, you would eventually run into the White Mountains. Nevertheless, the good citizens of Sparrow hardly ever saw those mountains because they seldom left the town limits.

As the mayor was fond of saying, "We don't need to leave town. Sparrow has it all."

However, although bustling with its enterprise, Sparrow was still something of a forgotten town. It wasn't as popular as Bar Harbor nor as metropolitan as Portland, not as famous as Kennebunkport, nor an easy spin-off of the interstate like Bangor. You didn't even drive through Sparrow on your way to Acadia. All the better, thought the residents of the little town. Who needs the bother of traffic and tourists?

Miranda dropped three overdue books in the outdoor slot at the library, crossed the street against the light, and stood for a moment on the sidewalk looking up at the church, St. Gabriel-by-the-Sea. *A mighty fortress.* The towering edifice brought life to Luther's legendary hymn. During her three years in seminary, she had envisioned herself in a traditional New England church. A white building with a red door, a cross atop a modest steeple. Not a nineteenth-century Gothic Revival with a pitched roof, imposing gables topped with finials, castle-like towers with parapets, and a pointed arch. The church's complicated and expensive maintenance had led more than one building committee to begin and end each meeting with heartfelt prayer. God may be never-failing, but the boiler went out at least once a winter, she'd been told, and the roof leaked all spring.

Miranda gazed up at the stained-glass window above the church doors. Jesus rescuing the lost sheep. Her ordination day flashed in her mind—the Bishop asking, "Will you undertake to be a faithful pastor to all whom you are called to serve?"

Her clear response: "I will, with the help of God."

A breeze carried the scent of salt air mingled with fresh croissants from The Rolling Pin Pastry. Miranda jogged up the church steps, ready to start her day.

CHAPTER FOUR

"Get that beast out of here!" Peg's commanding voice reverberated down the hall.

Miranda broke into a jog, her sneakers squeaking on the freshly polished floor. Peg never raised her voice. She didn't need to. She was imperious even at a whisper.

Children's drawings of Noah's Ark, Daniel in the lion's den, and Jesus the Good Shepherd flashed past as she jogged. The smell of crayons and floor disinfectant mingled with the comforting aroma of freshly brewed coffee. Peg was not a coffee drinker. Chai tea only. At seventy-two, Peg held Sparrow County's First-Place title in the Senior Division Powerwalking category. Too focused on fitness to indulge in coffee herself, she still brewed a fresh pot every morning for her new priest.

Miranda rounded the corner and pushed into the office.

A dog, as tall as a small pony, rested its enormous head atop Peg's desk and drooled on the neatly collated stacks of church pledge cards. Dirt caked the dog's wiry gray coat, and a nest of cockleburs matted its ferociously wagging tail. Long fur tufted over the dog's eyes while longer white hair grew beard-like under its chin, giving him the countenance of a kind old man.

An Irish wolfhound. A neighbor in Cambridge had owned one. Miranda suddenly remembered how the dog would bound up the narrow stairs, shaking the stairwell with its weight and exuberance. It had howled when left alone, barked out the window at passersby on the street below, and had run away a few times.

"Honestly, Lewis. Must you bring it in here?" Peg drew herself up to her height of five feet seven inches and glared at him over rimless half-glasses. Peg stood as if trapped, her back pressed against the window, which looked out to Main Street.

Lewis Walker, Sparrow's dog officer, leaned against the far wall, a long leash wrapped around the length of his arm. Miranda knew that if Lewis couldn't find a home for a dog, he welcomed it into his own home—much to the delight of his three small children, if not his wife.

"It's either here or the Sparrow Animal Shelter, and when I know the owner of a stray, I'm obligated to talk to them first. See if they'll take ownership." Lewis unwrapped the long leash.

"Good morning, Pastor." He gave her an affable look. "Lovely day, isn't it?"

"Gorgeous," she replied, not taking her eyes off the giant dog. The poor thing was thin and filthy.

"Bet you're glad you left Boston," Lewis said.

Everyone congratulated her on her good sense of leaving Boston for Sparrow. At first, Miranda had thought they were being ironic. Then she realized they were dead serious.

"The leaves are about to peak, aren't they?" she replied.

"Oh, no, we have another two weeks, at least. Maybe longer." The autumn leaves were a frequent topic of conversation.

"Good. I plan to hike up to Persimmon's Notch." Persimmon's Notch, just north of Sparrow, sat at the top of a steep climb that ended in a breathtaking view of town and sea.

"Could you two please stop talking about the leaves, as if a dog the size of an elephant wasn't slobbering on my desk blotter?"

As if he understood Peg, the dog raised his massive gray head and lunged forward, plopping two enormous front paws on the desktop. A stack of loose papers went airborne, along with three pencils, a box of markers, and a small pumpkin gifted to Peg by the preschool class.

"Shoo! Begone!" she said. "Immediately!"

Miranda wasn't sure, but it seemed as if the dog smiled at Peg.

Peg leaned across the dog and passed Miranda a pink memo slip. *Porter Cavanaugh, Attorney of Law, Main Street.* Could she stop by at her earliest convenience?

"I believe the old boy likes you, Mrs. Dunbar." Lewis tugged on the leash. "His name's Samson. Fits, doesn't it?" He managed to pull Samson off the desk and all four paws on the floor, taking a day planner and most of the pledge cards with him.

"A wolfhound, right?" Miranda had always wished for a dog, but had imagined a miniature poodle or a Chiweenie.

"Irish wolfhound. Purebred, from what I can tell." Lewis hauled mightily on the leash in a failed attempt to reel in the dog. "Handsome boy, don't you think?"

"Well, big, anyway." Miranda took a step back.

"An Irish wolfhound is the biggest breed out there. Bigger than a Great Dane. And they're smart, too. Hunters in the old days. Wild boar, wolves."

Samson shook his head, flinging saliva and pinging sand against the metal filing cabinets that stood against the wall.

"Got an earache, I'll bet." Lewis frowned. "That's why a dog shakes his head. I wouldn't be surprised, either, living in the rough like he has. Poor guy."

"He has a noxious aroma, Lewis." Peg held a handkerchief to her nose. "Remove him. Please."

Samson turned a gentle gaze on Peg, looking out at her under his shaggy eyebrows.

"He's a good dog, Mrs. Dunbar. Just needs a bit of cleaning up," Lewis said. "And he's still a puppy."

"A puppy?" Miranda gasped.

"Little over a year, I think. Still growing."

They watched as Samson raised his leg to the corner of the copy machine and left a substantial puddle on the tile floor.

"Oh, dear God in heaven." If Peg had been wearing pearls, she would have clutched them. Instead, she clutched a stack of file folders to her chest.

"And housebreaking, perhaps," Lewis added cheerfully.

Peg had always complained that the old floor in her office slanted so severely that a ball could roll across it, out the door, and not stop until it reached the first grade Sunday School room. It seemed she was right. They all watched in a moment of silence as the line of yellow liquid formed a small tributary and headed out the door.

"You know the owner, Lewis?" Miranda asked, tearing her eyes away.

"Well." Lewis looked at Peg, who snorted.

Familiar with her secretary's snort, Miranda knew that sound indicated disapproval. She assumed Lewis had picked up the dog and, for some reason, stopped by the church on his way back to the animal shelter.

People dropped by St. Gabriel's throughout the day for one reason or another. The congregation loved their church, and for them, it was the hub of their community. A noisy preschool occupied the basement, a senior exercise group lifted weights in the choir room, and hardly a day went by that a Scout troop didn't run through the halls.

She glanced from Lewis to Peg. "Whose dog? A church member?"

"In a manner of speaking." Lewis gave her another of his warm smiles.

"Oh, for pity's sake. Tell her." Peg opened a filing cabinet and pulled out a spray bottle of disinfectant and a roll of paper towels.

"Pastor, meet your new dog," Lewis said, and held the leash out to her with a flourish.

"What?" she said. "My dog?"

Before Lewis could reply, Samson flopped down on the tile floor and rolled over on his back, large head flung to one side, tongue flopping out. His vast legs spread open.

"Oh my," Peg murmured.

"You might want to consider getting him fixed," Lewis said. "As soon as possible."

★ ★ ★

Miranda stared across Porter Cavanaugh's cluttered desk. "Carl Quincy left his dog to me?" Miranda sat back. "I just did his funeral."

"Well, according to Mr. Quincy's last will, Samson is yours," Cavanaugh said. "Do you like dogs, Pastor?"

"I love dogs." Her mind raced. "It's just that I live in a small cottage." She had trouble imagining Samson galloping from room to room.

"The old rectory? That's the two-bedroom on Honeysuckle Lane, right? Goes right down to the beach."

"More like a one bedroom with a very spacious crawl space. And yes, it does go down to the beach." Miranda sat back and squinted at him. "Tell me again."

Porter looked down at the papers on his desk. "Carl Abbot bequeathed to you his 110-pound puppy named Samson. A purebred Irish wolfhound. Got him from a breeder in Augusta." He looked up from the document. "Wolfhounds get quite large. My brother-in-law had one. When it stood on its hind legs, it was taller than my sister."

No, the rectory wouldn't work at all. "I don't remember Carl mentioning him?"

"I guess he ran off right after Carl went to Hospice House. Lewis has only just caught him."

They sat for a moment without speaking.

"You could always find a home for him," Porter said. "Or tell the folks at the shelter to just keep him."

"It's more than my small house—I don't think Howard will be okay with it." A dog Samson's size would mistake Howard for a chew toy. Or worse.

"Husband?"

"Hedgehog."

"Ahh." Porter clicked his pen and tossed it onto the desk. "Leave the dog at the shelter then. They'll find a home for him."

"If they can't, will they—?"

"Euthanize him?" Porter was matter of fact. "I believe that's their protocol. After a certain time has passed."

Miranda thought of the dog's sweet old-man look. And how casually he had lifted his leg against the copy machine. "I'll think about it."

"Also, Carl left $5,000 for Samson. I guess to cope with his care and feeding. If you give him to the shelter, I can have the money transferred as a donation."

"I don't know. I mean, if he left that much money for Samson, he must have trusted me to keep him."

Porter gave the slightest glimmer of a smile. "What about Howard?"

"Maybe he'll adjust."

"It's not for me to say, Pastor, but a dog just doesn't seem to be in your future."

★ ★ ★

"You're not keeping it?" Peg asked, handing her a pink memo slip.

"Carl left the dog to me," Miranda replied. "Which means he wanted me to take him." She glanced at the slip. "Linda Darcy?"

"Chair of the deacons. Member of the Thanksgiving Committee."

Miranda read aloud, "Not sure you noticed, but Lucy McClain has missed church for three weeks. I thought you might want to call." She quickly pocketed the memo, hoping Peg hadn't noticed the slight flush in her cheeks. "Did Harry tell you that someone tried to pick the lock on the side door?"

"He did." Peg glanced at her computer screen before looking up. "Didn't look like they got very far, though."

"They dropped a pocket knife."

"All the more reason to remember to lock up at night." Peg shook her head. "They probably weren't going to steal anything as much as they wanted a place to sleep."

"Why do you say that?"

"More people are sleeping homeless these days than the good citizens of Sparrow want to admit. And if you're homeless on a cold night, an old sofa in a warm building is more valuable than anything you could steal."

"Maybe St. Gabe's could step up. Do something about a homeless shelter."

"You'll never convince the Sparrow Town Council."

Miranda mentally added shelter to her list of parish goals. Balancing the hot coffee with practiced ease, she sank into the faded cushions of the Chesterfield chair, which sat like a faded throne across from Peg's desk.

Sam Reeves, the church treasurer, never failed to remark on the chair. "You ought to go on *Antiques Roadshow*. A Chesterfield like that could bring a pretty penny."

Sam owned Reeves Insurance Company and filled his weekdays with claims and clients. But on the weekends, he indulged his love of antiques. He referred to it as *antiquing*, unaware that the transformation of a noun into a verb was an unforgivable sin. At least in Peg's opinion.

Miranda had reluctantly renamed her workshop "Spiritual Journaling" as "Writing Your Spiritual Journal." The new title lacked aplomb but wasn't worth an office grammar skirmish.

"I don't understand why Carl would leave me the dog. I never thought that he even liked me," she said to Peg.

"What do you mean?"

"You know what I mean. There are people at St. Gabe's who don't like me." A new priest, who was both female and outspoken, had made some in the congregation uncomfortable.

Father Geoffreys had shepherded St. Gabe's for three decades before retiring. A kind man, but set in his ways. Over time, he'd grown comfortable letting the vestry handle most decisions.

Now Miranda found herself navigating the remnants of that approach. As she worked to refresh the church and encourage growth, she often encountered resistance—not from individuals so much, but from long-established patterns.

Peg shrugged. "Can't please everyone. I suppose a few folks don't even like me."

Miranda suppressed a smile. Possibly more than *a few*. If her secretary had been born a generation or two later, she would have undoubtedly risen to CEO of Microsoft, Amazon, or JP Morgan.

"Obviously, he liked you more than you thought. He gave you his dog."

"I guess." Miranda took a sip of coffee. "He never acted as if he liked me."

"This is New England. We never act as if we like each other. That doesn't mean we don't."

"I hate to say it," Miranda said slowly, leaning back in the Chesterfield, "but I found it very difficult to like Carl." Throughout her three years at Episcopal seminary, she had imagined that she would unconditionally love every member of her future congregation. Isn't that what a good priest did?

Well, she did love the people of St. Gabe's. In general. But there were a few, maybe more than a few, if she were honest, whom she did not particularly like. A few members who, when she saw them coming down the hall, she had to resist diving into the Sunday School supply closet. She wished that the seminary had offered a class addressing this issue. Perhaps a course titled, Pastoring to the Impossible, 101. Or maybe, Kill Them With Kindness: If Only You Could, Seminar with Thesis.

Miranda watched, mesmerized, as Peg typed, fingers a blur above the keyboard. For a split second, she imagined telling Peg about Tony and the possibility of leaving St. Gabe's. Just thinking about it left her with a sweeping feeling of guilt.

"Well, you might not have liked Carl," Peg said, fingers still flying. The secretary was the only person Miranda had ever known who could carry on a conversation while typing and never miss a beat at either endeavor. "But as I recall, you stayed by his side every day he was in hospice."

"True."

"And last spring, didn't you drive him twice to that doctor's appointment in Portland?"

"I did."

"And didn't you bring him a chocolate croissant from The Rolling Pin that weekend he was in the hospital and called you, spitting mad about the food?"

"Chocolate makes everything better."

"As I always say, no good deed goes unpunished." Peg stopped typing and peered at her. "Which could be why you are now saddled with a huge dog."

"He's a sweet dog."

"Sweet?" Peg slid her chair back. "Are we discussing the same dog? A poodle is sweet. A miniature Corgi is sweet. That dog is huge and out of control." Peg had no room for misbehaving dogs, especially if they were the size of a Guernsey calf.

Miranda watched as Peg stood, did a back extension, then squirted her hands from the ever-present sanitizer on her desk.

"He'll never fit in that house of yours." Peg gave her a sharp look. "And what about Howard?"

"Well. A mouthful of hedgehog would be very uncomfortable. An intelligent dog would only try it once."

"First, I see no convincing evidence that the dog is intelligent. And second, an animal that size could do a lot of damage with a mouthful of hedgehog."

"But if the Sparrow Animal Shelter can't find a home for Samson, they'll euthanize him."

"Oh. Right." Peg looked stricken.

"Apparently, Samson took off. Wolfhounds are known for running away."

"Where were the neighbors?"

"They were the ones who called Lewis, but by then, Samson was on the lam."

"We haven't done well by the dog, that's for sure."

"Do you like dogs?"

"Gracious, no! Especially not when they are unkempt and unruly. But if you adopt a dog, you should be prepared to take care of it. Imagine an old man like Carl getting a puppy."

"I don't think Carl thought of himself as old."

"Not the worst approach to life." Peg stood up and slipped on her cardigan. "But a puppy?"

"Samson's had a hard life already."

Peg peered over her rimless half-glasses at Miranda. Miranda never knew if Peg did that because she was tall or wanted to appear intimidating.

"You don't need that dog on top of everything else."

Miranda didn't even want to ask what Peg meant by "everything else."

"By the way, Adam McClain, Lucy's great-nephew, called for you."

"He did?" Miranda faked a cough. Her words had popped out with way too much enthusiasm. But why would Adam call? The image of the sun on his salt-and-pepper hair and his intense blue eyes came back to her.

"You know him?" Peg gave her a surprised look.

"We've met." Miranda said it casually.

"He said that he had talked to Lucy. Doesn't like the way she sounds. And wondered if you could check on her?"

"On my way." Miranda grabbed her hoodie and headed out the door. She was already thinking about the return phone call after visiting Lucy. *Adam had called her!*

CHAPTER FIVE

Lucy's modest ranch house perched on a rocky bluff, giving a stunning view of the seacoast below. The water spread out in shades of green and blue, calm in some spots and choppy in others. A large cloud drifted overhead, its shadow turning a patch of sea nearly black. Waves crashed against the shore. Silver foam lined the sand. Every year or so, a developer tried to make Lucy an offer she couldn't refuse. She always refused.

Miranda approached the back door, casserole dish in hand—homemade Chicken Alfredo, her heartiest comfort food. Fusilli pasta swam in a rich sauce of butter, cream, and parmesan—a holy trinity for foodies. Not the healthiest, but grieving parishioners rarely craved kale salad. She knocked, then again, harder. A chorus of meows answered from within. Sand grated under her feet on the porch, while unraked leaves carpeted the yard. Three terracotta pots stood sentinel, their occupants reduced to brittle stems jutting from parched soil. She knocked a third time.

When the door opened, Miranda scarcely recognized the older woman. Lucy, usually dressed so fashionably, wore a wrinkled, stained house dress and faded pink slippers. Her lovely silver hair was disheveled, and her usual bright smile, gone.

"Pastor, come in," she said, stepping aside. "Pardon the house. I can't seem to keep up these days."

Miranda went through the door and glanced around. A stack of dirty dishes towered in the sink, and grimy streaks covered the usually spotless floor.

"How are you?" Miranda said. "I was worried about you when you weren't in church."

"I'm fine. Tired."

Miranda eased open the fridge door, a sour odor escaping. She squeezed the casserole between stacks of plastic containers and expired yogurt cups. Jars of homemade jam with peeling labels lined the door. A wilted lettuce head slumped in the crisper. She then settled herself at the kitchen table. "Tell me what's going on?"

Lucy turned away. A fit of coughing shook her body.

Cats mewed, winding between Miranda's legs. The stench of too many cats burned her eyes.

She waited as Lucy caught her breath. Seminary had taught her patience. You don't need to fill silence. Just be present.

"I have the cancer," Lucy finally said. Tears streamed down her face.

"Cancer?" Miranda dug in her pocket. She pulled out a clean tissue and handed it to Lucy. "What kind of cancer?"

"Lung cancer. Like my Edward. He died, you know. The week before our fiftieth wedding anniversary."

"I know." Adam hadn't mentioned anything as serious as cancer the other day on the beach. A pretty big thing to leave out.

"But I don't want to die."

"Of course, you don't." She reached across the table and put her hand on top of Lucy's. The old woman's hand felt thin, papery.

"I want to plant my garden next spring. And enter my pies at the county fair again."

"And you will!" Why did she say that? Miranda had no idea what kind of cancer it was or how fast-moving. She felt an irrational surge of frustration with Adam. "What about Adam? He's looking in on you, right?"

"I haven't told him."

"What? Why?"

Lucy made a face. "He's a good boy, but he doesn't want to take care of an old lady."

"He really cares about you. He came looking for you at the church picnic." She thought of Adam standing on the beach in his impeccable coat and tie, dress shoes slipping in the sand. "You need to tell him."

"I haven't told anyone."

"No one? Is Dr. Hazeltine sending you to Boston?"

Lucy broke into another spasm of coughing, her thin body trembling. She caught her breath. "There's nothing Elizabeth Hazeltine or any doctor in Boston can do for me." Lucy twisted the tissue into a ball and stuffed it into the pocket of her house dress. "I haven't seen a doctor."

"Wait." Miranda sat back, gently lifted a tabby cat off the table, and set it on the floor. "You haven't seen a doctor? Then how do you know you have cancer?"

Lucy leaned her head on her hand and took a raspy breath. "I just know." Her eyes filled with tears again. "With Edward, it started with him wheezing and couldn't breathe. Just like me. And then, by the time he went to the doctor, he had two months to live." She dug out the tissue and dabbed her eyes. "I may not even make it till Christmas, and I've already frozen six pounds of cookie dough."

"You absolutely must make an appointment with Dr. Hazeltine. Immediately. Today."

"And you know what the worst part is, Pastor?"

"Other than the fact that you haven't seen a doctor?"

"This house. I haven't had the energy to do a bit of cleaning and look at it. The boys at Milman's Mortuary will come in here, and they'll see how I've been living, and it'll be the talk of the funeral dinner. But I can't even get up the energy to run the vacuum. I can barely feed the cats."

Miranda stood up from the table. She spotted cat food cans on the kitchen counter. One by one, she opened them, the metal lids made sharp popping sounds and smell of fish filled the air. The cats rushed to the food, resulting in a sudden and welcome silence.

"A bad cough could be anything. Why not go to Dr. Hazeltine and find out?"

"That's what Edward did. Went to the doctor. Next thing you know, he had the cancer."

"The doctor didn't give him the cancer. Cancer." Lucy seemed beyond the ability to make good decisions.

"Thank you for coming to visit, Pastor Miranda. We'll need to talk about my funeral soon."

"You've gotten way ahead of yourself."

"Don't let them sing that awful hymn, "In the Garden." Every old woman has that at her funeral. I can't stand the thought."

"We're not planning your funeral. What if I drive you to Dr. Hazeltine's office right now?"

Lucy stood up slowly, holding the table edge for balance. She looked down at the cats, devouring the cans of food. "What will happen to them?"

"You will take care of them because you are not going to die. How about if I call Adam?" She pulled out her cell phone.

"Goodness, no. Now, please. If you'll see yourself out. I need to lie down."

★ ★ ★

"I don't know what else to do," Miranda said, clinging to Samson's leash. The silver-gray dog Samson lunged forward, yanking Miranda along in his desire to jump up on Peg. Not something Miranda advised. Or could even imagine.

"Lewis told me that the dog shelter won't keep Samson unless I give him up for good." Miranda frowned. "I don't want to, but I'm not sure what else to do." She had Googled hedgehogs and Irish wolfhounds. It wasn't encouraging. Wolfhounds: gentle, loving souls who were also intelligent sighthounds bred to hunt. Bad news for Howard.

Samson plopped down at Peg's feet, suddenly tranquil. But then, when Miranda said his name, he bounced up, gave a gleeful look, and leaped onto the Chesterfield chair. He managed to get most of his sizable body on the chair with his head hanging over one arm.

"Off the chair," Miranda said desperately. She yanked on the leash, exactly as the Dog Whisperer had said not to do it. Samson didn't budge. He was so large he looked about to slide off the chair. Completely relaxed, he sunk into the cushion and gazed at Peg. Then he blinked slowly, closed his eyes, and appeared to sleep.

"Well, he can't stay in my office," Peg said, glaring at the reclining dog over her rimless half glasses.

"I need to leave for the hospital now." Miranda had called Adam and Dr. Hazeltine yesterday, leaving messages. She tried again this morning but got no answer. But before she could head to Lucy's house, her phone had rung with news.

Lucy was in the hospital with a concussion. She'd fallen in her kitchen, tripping over a cat. Jim Combs, the mailman, found her when she didn't answer the door for a package.

Miranda felt a pang of guilt, wishing her calls had connected sooner. Still, she was relieved that Lucy would finally be seen by Dr. Hazeltine. One thing she had learned in the parish: sometimes circumstances took control, despite one's best efforts

"I would shut Samson in my office," she told Peg. "But the shelter workers told me he barks whenever he's left alone. And he has a booming bark."

As if to prove the point, Samson let out a tremendous bark, and catapulted off the chair. He swung around to face the door, a happy smile on his doggy face and his tail wagging like a windshield wiper. She was intrigued by a dog that could drool and grin simultaneously.

"Whoa there," Jim Combs said, stepping in with the mail. "Where'd you get the Shetland pony?" He turned to Miranda. "You know about Lucy McClain, Pastor?"

"I do." She hauled on Samson's leash like she was reeling in a marlin, all to no effect. "Thanks for calling the ambulance."

"Not the first time I've called 9-1-1 while delivering mail. How is she, do you know?" He eyed Samson and took a step back.

"I'm on my way to see her now." Miranda gave Peg a beseeching glance.

"Give me that leash," Peg said, slipping on her cardigan. "I'm taking him for a walk. I'll not have any more defilement of my copy machine."

"Are you sure? He really pulls." She gave Peg a skeptical look.

"I'm a power walker."

"He weighs 110 pounds."

"And I weigh 142." Peg looked at Jim and raised her eyebrows. "Mail?"

He passed a stack of envelopes across the desk.

Samson let out a resounding woof and placed his front paws on Jim's shoulders, licking his face. Jim shoved him down, leaned forward, and scratched the dog's floppy ears. "Aren't you a handsome fellow?"

"I'm looking for a home for him," Miranda said brightly.

"Good luck with that." Jim brushed gray dog hairs from his postal uniform. They listened to his laugh all the way down the hall.

★ ★ ★

Miranda bumped into a young woman as she walked into the ER of the Sparrow Community Hospital. "Oh, sorry! I should never text and walk." Last week she had barely missed crashing into a lamppost on Main Street.

The young woman looked startled. She turned away quickly, her movements jittery. Tattered sneakers, faded sweatpants hung on her small frame. She seemed fragile at first glance, but there was a glimmer of fierce determination in her stance. A hoodie, unzipped, hung loose on her shoulders. Her straight black hair was pulled back in a ponytail. Visible beneath the worn fabric of her clothes was the unmistakable swell of pregnancy.

Miranda watched as the young woman walked toward the nurse's station, her steps uncertain. "The *medico* said to come here. *Sala de emergencias*. Emergency room." Miranda didn't like how the nurse glared at the girl, emanating disapproval.

During seminary, Miranda worked as a chaplain at a community center where Spanish was common. Her high school Spanish came back quickly, helping her connect with the people there. She overheard the words "Dr. Hazeltine" and "community center." Miranda knew that Dr. Hazeltine worked one day a week at a free clinic near Sparrow. The nurse picked up the phone, her eyes never leaving the girl.

In a moment, the doctor swept down the hall. Only the elegant Dr. Elizabeth Hazeltine could make a white lab coat, stethoscope, and name badge look chic. A curly mass of auburn hair shaped her face and gave the effect of being simultaneously tousled and expertly styled.

Miranda glanced at her own outfit. Clergy shirt, worn jeans, and scuffed sneakers. Not exactly fashion-forward. She sighed. Some people just had a knack for looking put-together. She might not be one of them.

A few words with the nurse and a smile to Miranda, and Dr. Hazeltine slipped her arm around the young woman's shoulders, guiding her into an exam room. The nurse stood abruptly and left the desk.

The hospital bed engulfed Lucy, making her appear even more frail than she had seemed the day before. An IV dripped a clear liquid into her right arm, and a gauze bandage swathed her forehead.

"Lucy." Miranda spoke quietly, coming into the room.

Lucy's eyes opened. A smile wreathed her face. "Pastor! Did you hear?"

"Yes, you fell and hit your head. I am so sorry! I should have—"

"Not that." Lucy's eyes were bright. "I don't have the cancer!"

Miranda pulled a chair up to the bed and sat down. "Well, that's good!"

"You know what Dr. Hazeltine thinks my problem is?"

"Other than a concussion?"

"An allergy to cats!"

"No!" Miranda sat back in her chair. *Talk about a Godsend. Now the house could stop smelling like the inside of a litter box.*

"That's why I'm so tired all the time. And coughing. And can't breathe."

"Makes sense."

"Not cancer. Cats!"

"Well, that's terrific."

"I have to find homes for all of them before I can go back to my house." Lucy's smile faded.

"Have you called Adam?"

"I hate to. You know how young people are—always busy. Like you, Pastor."

"Do you have his number?"

"I have it, but—" She gestured weakly at her phone.

Miranda found Adam's name in Lucy's contacts. As the phone began to ring, she handed it back to the older woman.

She slipped out to give Lucy some privacy, although she rather wanted to hear Adam's voice. Miranda stepped into the hallway, thinking about Adam. He lived in Portland and would have to handle Lucy's situation now. Taking care of Lucy and her cat-filled house wouldn't be easy. But that's how family emergencies worked. Someone had to step up. As a pastor, Miranda knew this all too well. Of course, if Adam were in Sparrow taking care of Lucy, they might connect somehow.

Good grief, she thought. What kind of pastor hopes to benefit romantically from the misfortune of an elderly woman? She looked up, her thoughts interrupted by the commanding voice of Dr. Hazeltine.

Back at the nurse's desk, the doctor's usual energy and goodwill were nowhere to be found. As Miranda approached, she heard the doctor's firm voice say, "She is not *illegal*. The term we use here at this hospital is *undocumented person*. And yes, we provide care."

The nurse behind the desk nodded, but her expression was far from pleased. Dr. Hazeltine turned and fell into step with Miranda, her expression serious.

"Is that young woman local?" Miranda asked.

"Local?" Dr. Hazeltine paused. "In a sense. How is Mrs. McClain doing?"

"In good spirits. Cancer-free and all she needs is to find homes for six cats."

★ ★ ★

Later, Miranda stood on the sidewalk in front of the church. No howling, no barking.

She opened the side door and stepped in. Eerily quiet without a dog flying down the hall, knocking her into next week. She walked quickly toward the office. Terrible images flashed through her mind. Samson dragging Peg across Main Street into traffic. Samson knocking Peg onto the pavement and then running away. Miranda broke into a sprint—her second run in two days. She burst through the door, prepared to offer pastoral care or call 9-1-1.

She stopped short. Samson lay on the floor, sprawled next to the Chesterfield chair. His damp coat glistened in the light, no longer matted with dirt and burrs. The coconut scent of dog shampoo filled the room. Samson's eyes were half-closed, content after his bath. His chest rose and fell in slow, deep breaths. His long limbs stretched across the rug from the kindergarten room. His head rested on a neatly folded knitted prayer shawl. Miranda resisted the urge to run her hand through his silky fur. But she didn't want to wake him. He'd earned his rest after the ordeal of getting so clean.

Peg sat in her desk chair with her usual perfect posture, red pencil in hand, editing the monthly newsletter. Samson raised his head and gazed at Miranda. Without moving her eyes from the page, Peg dropped one hand, snapping her fingers once. Samson put his head back down and let out a contented sigh. Miranda stared at Samson, Peg, and then back at Samson.

"How did you do this? It's a miracle."

"When Jesus turned water into wine, that was a miracle. This dog has simply realized his place in the pack. And it turns out, he loves to be bathed."

"Amazing."

"Do you know that you have seven typos in your newsletter article?"

"Only seven?"

"Samson simply knows who the alpha is in the room." She slid the newsletter pages into a folder and handed it to Miranda. "And it isn't you."

CHAPTER SIX

Miranda watched, disbelieving, as Peg walked to her slate-gray Volvo wagon. Stylish, yet utilitarian. Like Peg. Samson followed at her side, his tail up and waving like a conductor's baton. To Miranda's shock, Peg had offered to take Samson home.

A squirrel darted out from under the prayer garden's stone bench, and Samson crouched as if to lunge. A single word from Peg and he sat back on his haunches, quivering but unmoving, his eyes trained on the squirrel. Peg gave a gentle tug to the leash, and they continued to the Volvo wagon. She opened the hatchback and made him wait until she gave the word, and then he leaped in.

"He loves you." Miranda called out from the side door.

"No. He respects me." Peg shut the back of the Volvo wagon and went around to the front driver's side. "Please keep in mind that this arrangement is temporary. The dog stays with me only until you find a family that wants him."

* * *

The screen door of the rectory banged shut behind her. Miranda tossed her hoodie onto the loveseat. Hopping on one foot, she unlaced one high-top sneaker and then the other and then kicked them off.

"Hey Howard. I'm home," she said, padding across the small front room to the Hobbit house.

Usually, he stuck his nose out of the little round door or grunted when she came through the door at night. She listened for a moment but heard only the faint sound of the waves washing onto the pebbly shore. Living in a seaside cottage still felt like a fairytale. Her family had spent two weeks every summer crowded into a beach cabin on Cape Cod. Those summer vacations had been among the happiest of her life. For the other fifty weeks of the year, they lived in a three-bedroom ranch on a busy street in Weston, commuter distance to Boston for her parents. A great neighborhood and a quiet place to grow up—but the rectory, with its five-minute walk down a flagstone path to hermit crabs, driftwood, and seashells, held the captured joy of childhood.

She dug a handful of orange and yellow leaves out of the side pocket of her hoodie and dropped them in front of the silent Hobbit house. Leaves from the maple in the church prayer garden and the contents of Miranda's recycling bin allowed Howard to fulfill his lifelong pursuit of fervent burrowing.

His tiny snout appeared in the round door, followed by the rest of his bristly little body. He blinked at her.

"Sorry to wake you, buddy." For Howard, late afternoon was the middle of his REM sleep. She tossed him an insectivore snack.

She poured a glass of Chardonnay, grabbed a box of Thin Mints, and then settled into the loveseat in front of the fireplace. An open Bible and a stack of commentaries stared up at her from the coffee table. She had yet to write a single word on her next sermon. If she took the job as head chef, there'd be no more scramble to write a weekly sermon. And no more budget-wrangling with the vestry. The review of the annual budget was the topic of that night's vestry meeting, and she had prepared what she hoped was a convincing pitch for purchasing playground equipment.

Miranda took a slow sip of cold Chardonnay. Her mind drifted back to the young woman at the hospital. What did Dr. Hazeltine mean when she said the girl was "local, in a sense"? She crunched through two more Thin Mints and reached for the wine bottle to pour a second glass, but stopped herself. The chimes from the bell tower drifted in through the window. Six o'clock. She needed to be sharp for the church budget meeting. Putting the bottle back in the refrigerator, she ground the beans and filled the coffee maker with cold water. As she waited, she drummed her fingers on the counter. Maybe Peg was right: she did want everything to happen in a hurry.

Miranda took a long sip of hot coffee and polished off another Thin Mint. Peg was right about many things. Was she right that more people were sleeping homeless in Sparrow than its citizens wanted to admit? Miranda thought about the young family living in a camper at the back of the Sparrow bus depot last July. A deacon had alerted her to their presence, but by the time she arrived to see how she could help, they were gone.

Even if the young woman wasn't homeless, she still seemed alone in the world. Miranda shook out another Thin Mint from the sleeve, popped the entire cookie into her mouth, and glanced around the room. During the day, the active grief that had consumed her when Jason died slowly dissipated. The evening brought a hush to the rectory, a stark contrast to her days, filled with the lives of her parishioners—their conversations, laughter, small dramas. When she returned home, the quiet emptiness of the cottage unsettled her. Life with Jason was many things—but never quiet. When he died, she had felt as if her own life had also ended. But almost to her surprise, it had not. The world moved on, and she had moved with it.

Loneliness, however, could strike like a fierce storm. For example, Sunday mornings when the service ended and the church cleared out, she often found herself standing alone in the empty building—everyone off to have lunch with someone else. No one in seminary had told her that the isolation of the small-town pastor—especially when that pastor is a single woman—would be so crushing. Mostly, she missed knowing that someone waited for her at the end of a long day—someone that wasn't a hedgehog. Someone to wake up with on a winter morning. Someone to cook with, eat with, open a bottle of wine with, and light candles with.

Start dating, everyone told her. Get out there. Meet someone. Easier said than done. Especially when the first date conversation began with, "Oh, by the way, I'm a priest." Miranda had made a stab at dating while in seminary but work and studies had monopolized all her time and energy. And now, she lived in an insular community where everyone knew her as the priest at St. Gabe's.

She glanced at the clock—twenty minutes until the Finance meeting. The sleeve of Thin Mints held only crumbs, and her coffee had grown cold.

CHAPTER SEVEN

Heavy footsteps coming down the hall toward the church offices indicated annoyance, more than urgency. Each step was sort of a thump followed by a squeak. Miranda listened. Not high heels. Not boots. She tossed her pen to the desk as her heart sank. Orthopedic shoes. Definitely orthopedic shoes.

Betty Hardacre's arrival shattered the office calm. Peg would have sidelined her, but she was at a dentist's appointment and unable to fulfill her duties as office bouncer.

"Peg taking the day off?" Betty planted herself in the chair in front of Miranda's desk.

"Dentist," Miranda said. "Good to see you, Betty."

Betty could have been a case study for a seminary class on difficult church members. *When Your Parishioner Reminds You of an Old Testament Prophet.* Grade based on your ability not to cry. Betty's dark green dress, right out of the 1950s edition Sears and Roebuck catalog, was tight in the bodice and fell to just below her knees. The same cardigan she wore to the beach picnic was unbuttoned. Miranda noticed that the woman wore pantyhose. No one else in Sparrow wore pantyhose. Not with L.L. Bean and The North Face as Sparrow's primary fashion influencers. Betty's gray hair looked as if it had been curled in tight rows and then teased out, giving it the texture and appearance of a well-used Brillo pad.

"In my day, you didn't miss work for every little thing." Betty glanced around the office as if something had gone missing.

"I'm not sure the dentist qualifies as every little thing, but anyway, how about some coffee? I just made a fresh pot." Miranda rummaged through the cluttered drawer, locating the remote. With a flick, she aimed it at the fireplace. A soft whir preceded the sudden bloom of flames. "We can sit over by the fireplace."

The wind outside had picked up, and the sky was a leaden gray. Perhaps a hot drink by the fire would be just what Betty needed.

Miranda's gaze drifted to the sofa. The cushions seemed oddly squished. The blue and gray prayer shawl—usually draped over the sofa's back, lay on the floor. And the throw pillows were all piled at one end, instead of scattered as she always left them. Maybe Colville had taken a break from his sexton duties last night and had a nap. Well, no harm in the older man stretching out if he felt like it.

"I've no time to just sit around drinking coffee. I've got Delmar at home, and Lord knows he can't be alone for long."

"How is Delmar?" Miranda sat back down. Peg had told her that his dementia had progressed more rapidly than first expected. Miranda's attempts at visiting the older couple had been rebuffed.

"If he'd get with the program, he'd do better." Betty opened a voluminous navy purse with gold clasps. She removed a spiral notebook and pen, then snapped the bag shut, dropping it to the floor with a soft thud.

"What program is that? The Golden Years Club at the Senior Center?" Miranda asked. "I recommended it to another church family, and it proved to be an enormous help."

Betty scowled. "That place is for people without family."

"Dottie Sloane attends every day, I believe. She loves it. It might be a good outlet for Delmar. And give you some time—"

Betty cut her off. "I'm not here to talk about Delmar."

Miranda took a breath and put on her neutral *I'm-listening* face. At least, she hoped that's what her face said. "How can I help?"

"The Thanksgiving Committee needs to get their planning meeting on the church calendar. Peg says it's up to you or Pam Bombard to schedule it, and Pam's dragging her feet. When we made her the chair, I knew she was too busy with those grandkids."

Pam, a recently retired Emergency Room nurse, possessed the same no-nonsense approach to life as Peg. Miranda liked her straightforward style, and the way her face lit up whenever she talked about her grandchildren, her husband, or her beloved quarter horse, Luther. They had already met last week on the Thanksgiving issue.

The Thanksgiving Committee had come under criticism for their usual reenactment of the first Thanksgiving, complete with all the members dressed as Pilgrims with one of the husbands as Squanto. The group hosted a hugely popular Thanksgiving Day meal each year, welcoming both the congregation and anyone in the community who wished to attend. A wonderful chance for fellowship, Miranda thought, and a moment of connection before the hectic season of Advent.

But the mythical portrayal of the Mayflower passengers as hospitable and gracious people was highly insensitive to the harm that the early settlers inflicted on the Indigenous peoples, especially when these colonists were more responsible for displacement and disease than for a meal of thankfulness. Miranda hoped the committee would recognize the Pilgrim reenactment as racially insensitive and stop including it in the all-church Thanksgiving meal. As pastor, she felt determined to guide the congregation toward a more progressive approach. This shift toward social justice needed to begin with the women on the Thanksgiving Committee.

"Okay, let's schedule the meeting," Miranda said. "What works for you?"

"Me? Why do I end up doing everything? Scheduling is Pam's job." Betty fixed an annoyed gaze on Miranda.

Miranda forced a smile as she picked up her phone. "I'm texting Pam now and asking her to call a meeting of the officers. ASAP." Head chef was looking better all the time.

Miranda wanted to present the Pilgrim Problem—as she now called it—to the officers first, without the rest of the committee present. Ramona Duncan seemed like a person who might be open to change. Nothing worried or distracted Ramona—not even the morning that four-year-old Lucas flushed three My Little Pony miniatures down the first-floor toilet before Sunday School.

She took a breath and imagined telling Betty there would be no more Pilgrim costumes. It was racist, she would say. The people of St. Gabe's were better than this. She stiffened her spine and looked Betty in the eye. Tell her now, she said to herself. Then she answered. *No way. Not yet.*

"So you're going to kick the can down the road to Pam?" Betty's mouth was a thin line, and her gray eyes squinted across the desk at Miranda.

"I'm not kicking the can. You just said that Pam should schedule the meeting," Miranda replied in her pastor voice—firm but friendly. "And I agree. Pam's the chair so she schedules the meetings. Let's give her a chance."

Betty sighed, her shoulders drooped. Miranda noticed that the cardigan was missing a button. A husband with dementia would be both exhausting and heartbreaking. The Thanksgiving Committee meeting might be important to Betty for reasons other than simply getting organized and bossing people around. Perhaps it was her lifeline to other women in the church, her opportunity to do something besides care for Delmar.

"Whose decision was it to paint the pastor's office this god-awful color?" Betty twisted in her chair and cast a critical eye at the chocolate brown walls. "Pastor Geoffrey kept it eggshell white. Like a normal person."

"I was going for a look that would be—" Before Miranda could finish her sentence with the word *cozy*, Betty heaved herself to her feet, clutching the giant pocketbook.

"It looks dreary." She stomped across the office, turned, and gave Miranda one last beady glare. "And if I don't hear from Pam soon, I'm calling the meeting myself."

The door shut behind Betty. Miranda sat back and blew her breath out. *When You Don't Like Your Parishioners, and They Don't Like You.* Seniors only, permission from the instructor.

★ ★ ★

Arriving home, Miranda collapsed onto the loveseat, kicking off her sneakers. Betty's warning echoed in her mind as she stared at the ceiling. Would changing the Pilgrim tradition really lead to disaster? But there was no denying it: the church's custom, though well-meaning, was insensitive and racist. It had to stop.

She stood, stretched, and called over to the Hobbit house. "Howard, you awake?" A general scurry was followed by a succession of grunts. She waited for him to emerge from the little front door, snout first. Instead, she heard his tiny snore. Apparently, six o'clock in the evening was too early for any self-respecting hedgehog to get out of bed.

Miranda walked into the kitchen and opened the recipe box on the counter. She didn't need a recipe for something as simple as a French omelet, but she found comfort in her grandmother's recipe cards. Each yellowed card held a favorite recipe from her grandmother or great-aunts, often with little notes at the bottom: "Serve on a cold morning," or "Christmas Day only," or "Nice for company."

She flipped through the cards, wishing for one that said, "Cook this when life is making you crazy." The French omelet card caught her eye. Simple, yet perfect for now. Miranda closed the box, not bothering to read the recipe she'd known since she was a teenager. As she gathered her ingredients, she wondered if ignoring the Pilgrim issue was the best idea after all. Maybe confronting the delicate matters of race and culture could wait until the parish knew her better. Was she just looking for excuses? It would be so easy to take the path of least resistance. As a pastor, that temptation was always there, whispering promises of peace and comfort. But she knew better. If she wanted a church that was really alive, she had to make the hard choices. No shortcuts.

Miranda removed a carton of eggs from the fridge and the blue mixing bowl from the bottom shelf of the cupboard and then scrolled through the playlist on her phone. Lady Gaga. Her cooking music. Cracking three eggs into the blue bowl, she whisked them for a moment, dropped in a generous pinch of salt and pepper, and whisked again. Another pause and she threw in a small handful of fresh herbs: tarragon, chervil, and very thinly sliced chives. She stirred again, satisfied as the bright yellow egg swirled with bits of green. Already she could feel some of her tension drain away.

Maybe all Betty needed was to feel safe. Wasn't that the most basic of all human needs? To feel safe.

Betty was slowly losing her husband to dementia, which meant that her world had turned upside down, with no control. Miranda thought back to the first horrible days with Jason. When they learned his diagnosis, she had despaired and desperately wanted everything to stay the same. Maybe Betty felt as if the church, with all the change of a new pastor, was slipping away as well.

But Miranda refused to dwell on church problems. Instead, she focused on the task at hand: making the perfect French omelet. She pulled out her favorite nonstick pan, knowing that the key to success lay in the quality of the pan. More than the herbs or the grated hard cheese, the pan must be of the best quality. But then so should the cheese. She used only Comte for omelets, since it was savory yet fruity, sweet, and a tiny bit salty. She loved how it burst open the senses in a single bite. But the freshest herbs and the finest aged cheese are useless if the eggs stick to the skillet. As the pan heated through, she sizzled in a tablespoon of butter. Foamy, not brown, she reminded herself.

Lady Gaga finished "Bad Romance" and launched into "Just Dance." How could Miranda be a good pastor to Betty? Help her feel safe? The butter foamed, and she poured in the eggs and herb mixture. She stirred in the center of the pan vigorously but without making scrambled eggs. The green herbs became even brighter in the heat, and the yellow egg reached an almost-ready consistency. Grabbing the cheese grater, she shredded a quick layer of the Comte, then added a pinch of sea salt. She gave the entire pan one more moment to cook without stirring.

Betty wasn't her only worry. What was she to do with Samson—Peg certainly couldn't keep him forever. The burden of Carl Abbot's trust in her weighed heavily. Things just seemed off at the church. She imagined explaining to the vestry what "off" meant. They would suggest she needed a vacation just like they did on the Sunday when she skipped the Lord's Prayer, Communion and went straight to the benediction.

Miranda couldn't put her finger on it. The broken lock. The possibly slept-on sofa. Was there a ghost in the church? Miranda wouldn't be surprised. There was, after all, one living in her own heart: Jason. She grabbed the pan's cool handle, lifting it from the burner. Not a second too soon. With a French omelet, timing was critical, as with most things in life.

The other night, Miranda had returned to the church to pick up a book she needed for her sermon. She slipped her key into the door of the office and froze. She felt like someone was watching her and she spun around, her heart pounding. But the dim hallway was empty. The building silent.

Using a fork, she deftly rolled the omelet into the shape of a cigar and slid it onto a dinner plate. She grated several flakes of Comte cheese on top and sprinkled the omelet with pepper. The hard cheese melted, and the green herbs speckled the eggs.

Bless this food, O Lord, we pray, she said, sitting at the kitchen table. Howard scampered across the tile floor, snorting and grunting. He stopped a few feet from her and looked up, his nose twitching back and forth. She slid her fork through the soft, cheesy egginess.

Things might not be right at the church, but at least she could still make a perfect omelet.

CHAPTER EIGHT

Loretta's Diner bustled with the early breakfast crowd, the fragrant aroma of coffee reviving even the faintest of souls. As Miranda entered, Pam waved from a booth where she sat with Ramona and Betty. Weaving her way through tables in the crowded diner and greeting church members, Miranda caught sight of Betty Hardacre in her brown cardigan, her Brillo pad hair a familiar sight. One look at Betty, and Miranda knew she'd better be on top of her game. *Once more into the breach*, she thought, heading to the window booth and sliding in.

"Good morning, Pastor. Get yourself some coffee because I'm calling this meeting of the Thanksgiving Committee to order," Pam said, her voice business-like. "I've got grandkids waiting for a ride to school."

Miranda filled a red mug—Loretta's signature color—from the table carafe and took a careful sip of the steaming coffee. Miranda fought the urge to lean back and close her eyes. She'd been up since four, lying in bed listening to Howard scurry from room to room. Her mind raced with worries—everything from the scratched-up lock on the church door to the budget mess. And don't forget the great coffee maker debate. Replace the ancient thing or let it continue its quest for sainthood?

"Don't be so formal, Pam," Ramona said, filling her own red mug. "It's Thanksgiving Committee, not mergers and acquisitions between Microsoft and Apple."

"I wish it were," Pam said. "My new MacBook Pro is not living up to expectations."

"I love my iPhone," Ramona chimed in. "Are you an Apple person, Pastor?"

"Microsoft." She took another sip. Loretta's coffee was dark roast and strong, even for Miranda's taste. Much better than one would expect from a small-town diner. And definitely superior to church coffee.

"I have no use for a computer or a fancy phone," Betty barked. "I only bought this phone in case Delmar—well, in case Delmar needs something." Betty's eyes were red and puffy, and her dress was wrinkled. Overall, though, she exuded as much fierceness as ever.

"All right, everyone, focus." Pam tapped a clipboard with her pen. "First things first, let's hear some theme ideas for this year's Thanksgiving Meal."

"Wouldn't the theme be *thanksgiving*?" Ramona proposed.

"It must be around the idea of Thanksgiving. You know, like generosity or gratitude," Pam cleared her throat. "And—as long as we're talking theme, I'd like to float something out there."

Miranda looked up from her coffee. She hadn't expected Pam to jump in so quickly. But this was good.

"You know every year, how the committee members wear Pilgrim costumes?" Pam looked from one woman to the next. "Well, the Pastor here has suggested that we rethink that."

"Excuse me?" Betty's head snapped up. "Rethink what, exactly?"
Ramona blew out a breath. "Here we go."

"Rethink the Pilgrim costumes." Pam's voice was cheerful, but firm.

"Why?" Betty's eyes narrowed.

"Well. Some might say that the Pilgrims were not always the best people to the Native Americans. And to others. And by dressing up as them, we are affirming their—" Pam shot a glance at Miranda. "Affirming their bad behavior."

"Not the best people? Bad behavior? What on earth are you talking about?" Betty looked from Pam to Miranda.

"The Pilgrims didn't treat the Native population very well," Pam said in a more determined voice. "It's as simple as that."

"I beg your pardon," Betty said. "My ancestors came over on the Mayflower. Are you saying that you think they were bad people?"

Ramona checked her phone and leaned over to Miranda. "Usually, her Mayflower ancestors come up in the first five minutes of any conversation. But today—a record three minutes."

"I heard that, Ramona Duncan," Betty said. "I'll have you know: my ancestors are Mary and William Brewster. William signed the Mayflower Compact."

"And here it comes," Ramona said. She leaned back and closed her eyes.

"William was a respected clergyman, and Mary, always his devoted wife. Are you telling me they were not good people?" Betty's eyes flashed. "The Pilgrims founded this country."

"No, they didn't," Ramona said matter-of-factly, sitting up and straightening the collar of her green coveralls. Ramona had embroidered the logo of her plumbing business on the front pocket—Down-the-Drain Plumbers—featuring the silhouette of a Rosie the Riveter-style woman confidently brandishing a pipe wrench.

"The Pilgrims," Ramona said, "were gatecrashers. America wasn't some big empty place just waiting for settlement. It was already settled." She took a sip of coffee. "It's called genocide."

Miranda looked into her coffee cup. Who knew that Ramona would lead the charge?

Betty drew herself up, her already-large bosom expanding to new heights, her face blotchy red. "Genocide!" she spit out. "Genocide?"

"Genocide is the deliberate extermination of an entire group of people," Ramona said in a teacher's voice. She gazed longingly at the door to the kitchen. "Where's our waitress? We need more coffee."

"I know what genocide is." Betty's voice had gone frosty.

"A lot of people think genocide only happens in other countries. Not here in America." Ramona opened a menu. "But it did."

Betty sucked in her breath.

"I wouldn't mind one of those chocolate croissants that Loretta makes." Ramona looked at Miranda. "Did you know she starts baking at three o'clock in the morning?"

Miranda nodded, amazed at Ramona's calm demeanor. Trapped in a booth next to a woman who was about to become a human explosive, Ramona casually perused a breakfast menu. Was it all that experience in the world of plumbing? An image flashed through her mind: a toilet-turned-geyser and Ramona standing there calmly scrolling her text messages.

"Help us out here, Pastor." Pam looked at her beseechingly.

"Yes, well." She pulled her eyes off Ramona, took a breath, and modulated her voice into what she privately called pastor-cheerful. "I think that after we do some research together as a committee—"

Betty cut her off. "Delmar and I have dressed as William and Mary Brewster every Thanksgiving meal for the past twenty-three years. It's tradition. Do you just want to wipe out everything that means something?" Betty's voice broke, but she quickly regained herself.

"Betty, calm down," Pam said. "Let's just consider a more contemporary theme."

"Contemporary! How can the celebration of a historical event be contemporary?"

"Glad you asked," Miranda said. She wasn't sure what to say next, but she launched anyway. "You could say that the Europeans—the Pilgrims—destroyed and claimed the lands of Indigenous people. They enslaved both Indians and African Americans." Miranda looked around the table. Pam and Ramona nodded in agreement while Betty's face went from red to violet. Miranda took a breath and continued. "The settlement did celebrate a Thanksgiving feast, but it wasn't the happy moment of sharing between Pilgrims and Indians."

"Says who?" Betty said in a tight voice. "Squanto brought Indian food, and the Pilgrims taught him how to make—oh, I don't know, Pilgrim food. And they thanked God for the harvest."

Miranda cleared her throat. "And pretty soon after the harvest feast, the Pilgrims enslaved the Wampanoag. So you could say that Thanksgiving celebrates the violence of the Europeans toward Indigenous people."

"In other words, the Pilgrims aren't *politically correct* anymore." Betty spit out the words. "And Delmar and I might as well throw our Pilgrim costumes in the burn barrel with this year's leaves."

"No. Not at all," Pam interjected. "I'm just saying, we've been honoring the Pilgrims every year. Why don't we find a way to honor the Wampanoag people instead?"

Miranda gave her a quick look. Not exactly what they had discussed, but an interesting idea.

"I'm not dressing up like an Indian," Betty thundered.

Miranda glanced around the diner, but no one seemed to have overheard.

"There will be no dressing up like Indians," Pam replied, her voice lowered.

"Indigenous people," Ramona said brightly.

"Excuse me?" Pam asked.

"There will be no dressing up like *Indigenous people*," Ramona said. This time a few heads turned.

"Let's get back to choosing a theme." Pam picked up her clipboard.

"I say we honor the Indigenous peoples. Which means that we ditch the black hats and buckle shoes," Ramona said as if the matter were solved.

"And I say we honor our American traditions and wear the costumes!" Betty retorted.

Pam looked at her phone and then turned to Miranda, eyebrows raised. "Pastor, you have six minutes to fix this."

"I have an idea," she answered. "I'll send out a link to a helpful documentary. Why doesn't everyone watch it, and then we'll meet and discuss what we learned? We'll see where it leads us."

"I am not watching some history program," Betty said. She grabbed the voluminous navy bag and heaved herself out of the booth. "You can forget this rubbish. I'll not put up with any more declamation of our country's past!"

"Defamation," Ramona said, looking over her coffee cup. "Defamation of our country's past. Declamation is a speech."

"You know what I mean." Betty slung her bag over her shoulder, narrowly missing a tray of coffee and egg sandwiches balanced by a nearby waitress. "I'm done. You can organize your own Thanksgiving meal!"

They watched her stomp away, bumping into two tables as she crossed the crowded room. The bell on the door jingled before it slammed.

★ ★ ★

Laughter snapped Miranda out of her daze. She'd left Loretta's in a fog, the Pilgrim talk and Betty's resignation swirling in her head. Somehow, she'd walked all the way down Main Street to the church without noticing.

Peg, Samson, and a young woman stood in the prayer garden. Maple branches stretched above them, a blaze of autumn color. Miranda squinted. Wait. The girl from the hospital?

The girl clutched a stack of paperback books. Samson sat at her feet, eyes full of worship. Same look he gave Peg.

"What's so funny?" Miranda asked, approaching.

"This young woman thinks our Samson looks like a pony," Peg said, smiling. "And that he should be pulling a cart."

"What a great idea—he could take children for rides," Miranda said, turning to Samson. "You could earn your keep, old boy."

"Pastor Miranda McCurdy," Peg said. "Let me introduce Mrs. Alejandra Romero."

"Nice to meet you," Miranda said, taking in Alejandra's appearance. Her dark hair was pulled back in a tight ponytail, and she seemed more at ease than she had in the emergency room. This time, Miranda noticed Alejandra's brown eyes, shining with intelligence. Her warm tan skin glowed in the autumn light, and her features, though soft and youthful, hinted at a determined spirit. "I think I saw you at the hospital the other day," Miranda said.

"*Sí*. I remember." She offered a shy smile, her words careful and deliberate.

"How was the Thanksgiving Committee meeting?" Peg stroked Samson's head.

"Good and bad." Miranda grimaced. "Bad in that we never really made a decision, and good because our committee is a bit more, well, streamlined."

"Betty quit?"

Miranda nodded. "And I have to admit—I'm relieved."

"Don't get ahead of yourself."

"Why?"

"She'll be back."

"Seriously?"

"No doubt about it." Peg glanced at her phone. "It's been delightful talking with you, Alejandra. But I have work to which I must attend." She tugged on Samson's blue leash. "Say goodbye to your new friend, Samson."

"He is beautiful," Alejandra reached out and rubbed his ears. "I miss my dog."

"You have a dog?" Peg jangled her keys in her hand.

"*Sí*. A long time ago. Not now." A shadow flitted across Alejandra's face. "*Mucho gusto conocerte*, Samson. Maybe next time I see you, you have pony cart, yes?"

Peg and Samson walked toward the church, the side door closing behind them.

"I see you like to read." Miranda gestured to the stack of used paperbacks in Alejandra's arms. The girl looked less beleaguered than she had the other day in the Emergency Room. Her hoodie and sweatpants had been washed, but her sneakers were as worn as ever, and still, no socks. And she was every bit as pregnant.

"*Sí*. I would rather read than do almost anything. And I want my daughter to love to read." Her eyes grew soft, and her hand rested on her abdomen. "I read to her now," she said and showed Miranda one of the used books, a worn copy of *Superfudge*.

"I loved *Superfudge* as a kid." Miranda sat on the stone bench in the prayer garden and gestured to Alejandra to join her.

"Judy Blume is excellent. *¿Has leído* Roald Dahl?" She held up *The BFG*.

"Now I'm showing my age. I think I was in college by the time that book came out."

She showed Miranda the rest of her books: dog-eared paperbacks of *Pride and Prejudice*, *The Firm*, *The Shining*, and *Ina May's Guide to Childbirth*.

"Austen, Grisham, Stephen King. I like your style," Miranda said. "You know the baby is a girl?"

"I do," Alejandra replied. "And I am glad. I have four younger sisters in Honduras. So, I know how to raise a girl. Not a boy."

"Your family in Honduras?"

"*Sí*. My husband, Daniel—" Alejandra trailed off, her eyes darting away.

"And you're here—alone? Without Daniel?"

"*Sí*. For now."

The troubled look on the young woman's face told Miranda that she had dug too deep, and she changed the subject. "Did your mother read to you?" Miranda asked in Spanish.

"You speak Spanish?" Alejandra asked, ignoring the question about her mother.

"Some. I took Spanish in high school, and then I did my internship in seminary at a Spanish congregation in Boston. *Tú vives—en* Sparrow?"

Alejandra glanced away. "I'm staying with friends."

"Your English is good. Better than my Spanish."

Alejandra nodded toward the books. "I read much. I listen to—to—audiobooks—when I get them."

"We have some audiobooks in the church library. Although nothing by Stephen King or John Grisham, I'm afraid. Anyway, the church is here for you if you need any help—with the pregnancy, with—anything."

A glimmer of a smile. "*Gracias.*"

"Do the friends that you stay with attend a church?"

Alejandra shook her head.

"We have services every Sunday at ten o'clock," Miranda spoke again in Spanish. At least, she hoped that was what she said. "Stop by if you want," she said, this time in English. "Coffee hour afterward. You know what they say: 'Come for the worship, stay for the coffee.'"

Alejandra looked at her with a questioning expression. Her gaze was direct, a mix of youthful curiosity and uncertainty.

"Just come," Miranda said. "Ten o'clock Sundays. You would be *bienvenido.*"

★ ★ ★

"*Bienvenido* means 'welcome,' right?" Miranda asked. The sounds of Main Street drifted through the window of Peg's office.

"I think so." Peg sat at her desk; the membership roll spread out in front of her. "Alejandra certainly seems nice, but I wonder what her story is." She retrieved a stack of pink memo slips from under the corner of her desk blotter and handed them to Miranda.

"She's staying with friends." Miranda shoved the memos into her hoodie pocket. She poured herself a cup of coffee then stirred in cream. Peg snorted without looking up.

"What? You think she isn't?" She took the coffee over to the Chesterfield chair and slid into its upholstered embrace.

"I hope those friends are prepared to help with a newborn."

"I told her to come by if she needed anything. Maybe she will." She looked over at Samson. He sported a new blue collar and had stretched out on a vast, fluffy dog bed between the bookcase and the copy machine. His barrel chest rose and fell gently. He emitted a quiet, whiffling snore. She looked from the sleeping dog to Peg and back to the dog again. "You're not giving him some sort of sedative, are you?"

"Don't be ridiculous."

Miranda sipped her coffee. "Anyway, this morning's meeting was a bust. Pam broached the topic of ditching the Pilgrim costumes. Not exactly received with wild applause. Betty left in a rage."

"As I said, don't get your hopes up. On the other hand, you never know." Peg drew a heavy line across one of the pages in front of her. "Betty has called the shots for that Thanksgiving meal for the past twenty years. This might be the one thing that could drive her over the edge."

"I don't want to make life harder than it already is for Betty. It's just that dressing as Pilgrims seems incredibly insensitive." Betty's exit from the committee left Miranda with mixed feelings. Moving forward without the Pilgrim reenactment would be easier now. But Betty had enough on her plate with Delmar.

"It's not insensitive. It's racist." Peg looked up from the church membership rolls that she was editing. "Did you know that the Stewardship Committee has Hugh Stevens listed as an active member? He's been buried in the memorial garden for the past six years. Right under the Japanese maple." She shook her head. "And they wonder why his pledge isn't coming in." She paused and looked hard at Miranda. "Sugar coating isn't your style, Pastor. Call it what it is."

Sometimes Peg shocked Miranda with her progressive streak. Other times? Peg could've stepped straight off the *Mayflower*, complete with buckled shoes.

"I don't plan to sugarcoat anything. But I do worry about Betty. I'll give her a call today. Check in on her."

"You might luck out, and she'll go over to the Methodists. They have a Pilgrim reenactment."

"She'd leave St. Gabe's?" That was the problem with the ministry. The very person who needs the church the most does everything they can to make the church not want them.

"Well, she's left three times before."

"Seriously?

"Three times."

"No way. Why?"

"The first time was when the Building Committee replaced the beige carpet in the sanctuary with blue. Then the second time, Father Geoffreys started playing guitar during Evensong." Peg thought for a moment. "Oh, yes, and then when the vestry replaced the old church sign with the new church sign." Peg stood and crossed the room to one of the metal filing cabinets and opened the top drawer.

"What was wrong with the new sign?"

"It was new."

Miranda watched as Peg flipped through several years of old membership files.

Peg pulled one out and slammed shut the drawer. "Father Geoffrey said it was the most pleasant year of his entire career."

Miranda heaved herself out of the Chesterfield chair and refilled her coffee cup. "I should have taken Alejandra to Loretta's. I wonder if she's had breakfast."

"She did seem thin, didn't she? For someone so far along. When I was her age, they told pregnant women to eat as much as they wanted. You would lose it later, the doctors said. What poppycock! I had to take up walking and do Weight Watchers, and it still took two years after my last one was born."

"You look great now."

"I should hope so. Robert is forty-six."

Miranda looked down at Samson. "So why is he sleeping like this?"

"I took him on a sunrise power walk." Peg gave her a triumphant look.

"You didn't?"

"I did. He loved it. And he improved my time."

"I didn't think your time could improve." Last May, Peg had placed third in the Maine Senior Games. She trained with rigorous discipline, leaving her house at precisely six o'clock every morning without fail, except in the dead of winter when she pounded out her miles on the state-of-the-art treadmill she'd set up in her sewing room.

"I've researched how to train a dog to walk on a treadmill. Apparently, some dogs love it. Watched three YouTubes last night, and I think I have the hang of it."

"Treadmill? Samson?"

"Do you have a better suggestion?"

"I just didn't think you were—" Miranda stopped.

"I'll need something for him when it snows. His breed likes the cold—he's a wolfhound, after all, but Maine winters are harsh." She stood and stepped over Samson's tail draped across the floor.

Miranda watched her for a moment, her head cocked. "Are you thinking that you want to keep him, then?"

Peg spun around. "What in the world would give you that idea? I am far too busy to take on the care and feeding of a half-grown puppy." Samson sat up and yawned. "Especially one who is so ill-mannered." Samson lay back down with a thump.

"I was just thinking—"

"Well, stop thinking. I am not a dog person. Never have been."

"Right. We'll keep making inquiries."

"I should hope so." Peg took her cardigan off the back of her chair. "Now, if you will excuse us, Samson has a play date with the Bernese mountain dog on Cherry Street."

CHAPTER NINE

Miranda hated to be late to the church office on a Monday morning, but the air had been so fresh and clear that she had pulled on a fleece vest and strolled along the beach, watching the sun rise over the dark water. She walked farther than she had planned and then had to hurry back to the rectory. Then, still telling herself that she needed to get out the door and to the church, she sat on the front step of the little porch, sipping coffee and listening to the gentle pull of the waves. If she was to live so close to the sea, she needed to develop some restraint about how many hours she spent listening to the gulls, soaking in the sun, and watching the water. Which made her think of Tony's offer.

Would she ever find another home only a stone's throw from sand and surf?

Tony had sent her a link titled "Top Ten Things to Do in Seattle," and Miranda found herself weighing it against her current life. Seattle boasted theater, restaurants, music, art—everything a city could offer, with people her age buzzing about. What, she wondered, was she doing in a small town with a shrinking economy? Serving God, she reminded herself. Building connections with good people. Enjoying the quiet by the sea.

Miranda hurried toward the church, suddenly feeling late. As she approached the parking lot, her gaze was drawn to a white van. It displayed the words "The Pamper Camper" with an illustration of a tail-wagging dog, smiling and covered in soap suds.

"Do you know there's a dog groomer in the parking lot?" Miranda accepted a stack of pink memos from Peg.

"You're not really the detective type, are you, Pastor? I have employed the Pamper Camper for Samson because he needs a medicated bath. More than I can do at home. I cannot spend another night waking up to the sound of the poor thing scratching."

"Oh. Good idea." She crossed in front of Peg's desk, skirted the Chesterfield chair, and went into her pastor's study, and hung her hoodie on a hook by the door. Traipsing through the secretary's office to get to the study always bugged her. The purpose of the adjoining offices was so the secretary could monitor who went in to see the priest. Or, as Peg put it, so that every Tom, Dick, and Harry can't sit in the priest's office and just jabber all day.

The former priest, the sainted Dr. Geoffreys, limited his accessibility to his parish and insisted that no one had stepped into his study until they passed Peg's approval. He had served St. Gabriel for thirty-three years and, by the end, according to some, mumbled his sermons and spent hours on the church Internet scouting out retirement communities in Arizona. But Miranda liked it when people just dropped by to jabber. She had argued with her secretary against this ecclesial bouncer system, but old habits die hard.

Especially with Peg.

She returned to the secretary's office, selected her mug, and filled it with hot, fresh coffee.

"Did you make a pot of coffee here last night?" Peg asked, watching her.

"Last night? No. I was home alone with Howard."

"You spend a lot of your evenings home alone with Howard."

"What can I say? He's a boon companion. Why do you ask about the coffee?"

"I came in today, and coffee had burned in the bottom of the carafe. Like it had been left on half the night."

"You should get a real coffeemaker—a modern one. You know, one produced in the 21st century? They have safety shut offs and other newfangled options."

Peg ignored her. "The office smelled like burnt coffee this morning."

"Maybe it was Colville? He sleeps on my sofa sometimes. Maybe he took a nap, made coffee, and forgot about it."

"Sleeps on your couch?" Peg looked up.

"He works late at night. Probably gets tired."

"He should go home if he's that tired. And anyway, Colville's a tea drinker."

They sat in companionable silence while Peg filed, and Miranda sipped coffee. She found herself thinking about Adam McClain and gave herself a mental shake. Why was he even on her mind? She refocused.

"How did you find a dog-washer who makes house calls?"

"Google. And they're called mobile groomers."

"I wonder what they could do for Howard. He'd probably be insulted that I thought he wasn't up to his own personal grooming needs." She took a sip of coffee. Blue Mountain Roast.

"Other than the scratching, how's it going at night with Samson?"

In response, Peg picked up a yellow legal pad from her desk, pen in hand. "When we find a new home for him, there are some conditions upon which we must insist."

Miranda leaned back, the Chesterfield enveloping her. "Such as?"

"He requires a pillow at night." Peg made a check on the legal pad. "I gave him a pile of blankets to sleep on next to my bed." Peg looked up sharply. "A dog is part of your pack, and so it should sleep in the same room you occupy for sleep. But never on the bed. He whimpered and fussed for an hour. Finally, I gave him a pillow. From the spare bedroom. Settled down immediately." Miranda watched as her secretary made a note on the pad. She looked up at Miranda.

"He snores, you know." For one moment, a glimmer of a smile crossed Peg's face.

"Other requirements?"

"Kibble for now, though I am considering the benefits of a raw diet."

"Sounds reasonable."

"Also, he likes a sock with a knot tied in the end."

Miranda took another sip of coffee and looked at Peg over the cup. "A sock?"

"To hold between his front paws."

"Naturally."

"Gave him one last night. He sat with it on the braided rug all evening. Never moved once through two episodes of *Black Mirror*."

"*Black Mirror*? That's hardcore."

"What do you watch?"

Miranda stumbled, slightly embarrassed at her ecclesiastical taste in television. "Well. I like *Sister Boniface*. And *Grantchester*." She didn't mention that Howard sometimes joined her on the couch. He seemed especially interested in *Midsomer Murders*.

"The poor dog should be glad he's with me."

"Should we hold off on finding a home for him?" Miranda took a sip of coffee and peered over the cup at Peg.

"Whatever for?"

"You know, give him more time in a stable household. He's been living as a stray."

Peg frowned. "Perhaps you have a point. I suppose I could keep him a little longer."

Miranda leaned forward and grabbed a pink memo slip from Peg's desk. *Visit Harmon Holbeck*. She resisted a sigh—some problems in a parish escape even the sincerest efforts of the priest. Harmon Holbeck promised to be one of them.

"I should warn you that The Pamper Camper is pricey," Peg said.

"Not a problem. If anyone deserves a spa day, it's Samson." Miranda leaned back in the chair. Neither of them spoke. Peg was the only person at the church who knew the extent of her financial woes. As sharp-tongued and critical as her secretary could be, she left off any judgment regarding this aspect of Miranda's personal life. Thank goodness for that money Carl had left for Samson's upkeep.

A sweet-smelling Samson burst through the door. His previously matted tail waved with a feathery swish, his gray coat shone with silver highlights, and his bushy eyebrows and straggly little beard were neatly trimmed. He was as fluffed and buffed as any contestant in the winner's circle of the Westminster Dog Show. Miranda wasn't sure, but were his newly clipped nails polished? And did he smell like—oatmeal and honey?

"Oatmeal-honey shampoo with extra-body conditioner," the young woman said with evident pride as she clung to the blue leash. "Took half a bottle. Combed out a pile of dirt and fur. Nails, dewclaws, ears. The deluxe!" She unclipped the leash, and Samson lunged toward Miranda in the Chesterfield chair. Peg snapped her fingers, and he froze mid-catapult, instantly sat, and trained adoring eyes on Peg. She watched as the older woman reached into her cardigan pocket and extracted a small dog treat.

"I've got your invoice right here," the groomer said.

Peg nodded to Miranda. "Give it to the Pastor there. She handles his expense account."

CHAPTER TEN

The members of the Thanksgiving Committee sat in stony silence as Miranda switched on the lights in the Fellowship Hall. "What did you think?" she asked.

The video, *Pilgrims No More*, had ended, and the feeling in the room was chilly. Betty stared, frowning at the blank screen. She had tapped her foot through the entire second half, registering her impatience with the whole thing. Peg had been right. No such luck that Betty would permanently leave the committee.

Donna Mitchell, a devoted member of the Thanksgiving Committee, raised her hand. "You don't have to raise your hand, Donna," Pam said. "Just speak up."

"All right then. I will. With all due respect, Pastor Miranda, you're throwing the baby out with the bathwater here with all this talk about how the Pilgrims were bad people, and we shouldn't celebrate them on November 26th."

Ramona jumped in. "Is that all you took from the video? That the Pilgrims were bad people?"

"That's what I got," Joanne Henry spoke resolutely. According to Peg, Joanne was new to the Thanksgiving Committee but was very dedicated to congregational life. "And I don't care what some people from the History Channel say; the Pilgrims and the Indians worked together as friends."

A drawn-out sigh from Ramona. Always prepared for an impromptu stint of on-call plumbing, Ramona wore her signature green coveralls with the embroidered logo on the front pocket. "It's not from the History Channel. Just because a show is about history doesn't mean it's from the History Channel. And for the record, I'm in favor of ditching the costumes. I've been William Bradford every year for the past seven years now. I'm more than ready to trade my Pilgrim costume for regular clothes." Ramona stirred cream into her coffee and then selected a cannoli from the box in the middle of the table. Miranda had brought a carafe of coffee and a box of cannoli from The Rolling Pin Pastry, a sweet but futile attempt to make watching the video more agreeable.

"You were William Bradford?" Miranda reached for a cannoli.

"I like the men's costumes better. You try wearing a long black dress and then serving Thanksgiving Dinner to two hundred people. You'll be wanting a pair of trousers, too, believe me."

"I understand that the Thanksgiving Committee has dressed as Pilgrims for a long time," Miranda said, deliberately attempting to keep her voice neutral and upbeat. The video had stirred up her own feelings. Seminary had been an immersion in the effects of colonialism on the native people of this country. Colonialism asserted itself today, expressed clearly in the racial inequality in the country and manifested in the rituals of religious life. When she left seminary, she thought social justice would define her ministry.

But after ten months in the parish, she had to admit that social justice took a backseat to almost everything else: demanding pastoral care, endless committee meetings, sermon preparation, budgets, and stewardship. She cast an optimistic glance around the room.

"Can you identify anything valuable about the video?"

Crickets.

"Okay. How do you think an understanding of colonialism could change our Thanksgiving celebration?"

"Maybe we could make a bigger deal out of the Indians. I mean the Indigenous peoples," Edna said. Miranda didn't know Edna very well. She was a widow and, as far as Miranda could tell, very close with Betty.

"Thanks, Edna. Great idea," Pam said. "Tell us more about what you are thinking—how would we make a bigger deal out of Native Americans?"

"Which is it? Native Americans or Indigenous peoples?" Ramona cut in.

"Whatever happened to calling them Indians?" Betty said. "I heard they like to be called Indians."

"Probably better if we don't lump all people into one group," Pam added.

"In other words, Betty, stop referring to them as *they*." Ramona shot her a frustrated look.

"We always have one of the husbands dress up as Squanto," Donna chimed in. "Isn't that honoring the Indians?"

"I was thinking we could have more Squantos," Edna said. "Maybe instead of Pilgrims."

"You can't have multiple Squantos. There was only the one," Betty insisted.

"It's theater, Betty," Donna said. "It's called suspension of disbelief."

Ramona pushed her half-eaten cannoli aside and dropped her head into her arms.

Linda Darcy, a social worker at the public school and a relative newcomer to Sparrow, tossed her knitting needles into the quilted bag at her side.

"Do you people just not get it? Dressing up like the Pilgrims and Squanto is appalling." She glared at the women as if daring anybody to argue. "The first time I came to this dinner, I couldn't believe you still did it. Most New England churches stopped the Pilgrim thing years ago." She looked at her phone. "In the city, anyway."

"Are you calling us a bunch of hicks?" Betty took offense.

"If the Pilgrim hat fits," Linda muttered.

"That's it. I'm done with this nonsense." Betty stood up and slung her huge pocketbook over her shoulder.

"Good Lord," Edna said. "Get a hold of yourself, Betty."

"We have lost all spirit of Thanksgiving and now we're picking at each other. This is not why I have been on the Thanksgiving Committee for all these years." Betty stood defiantly, clutching her oversize purse to her bosom.

Miranda noticed that she didn't make any actual move to leave.

"Betty, sit down. No one's leaving. We're having an open discussion with all opinions welcome," Pam said.

Betty gave a dramatic huff and sat down.

"Would it be so bad to wear regular clothes this year, and not dress as the Pilgrims?" Pam looked imploringly at Betty.

"Everyone looks forward to seeing us in our costumes. People will be disappointed," Joanne said.

"There are lots of people who probably won't even attend if they know we've abandoned our commitment to the Pilgrims," Donna added.

"Oh, for Pete's sake," Ramona said. "Hey everyone, I've got 1970 on the phone. It wants its church back."

"1970 was a good year," Betty said. "That's the year we built the new Sunday School wing."

"And we still used the old prayer book," Edna chimed in.

"Amen to the old prayer book," Donna said, nodding.

Linda packed up her knitting bag, chagrined.

"Pam, as our chair, could you offer some direction?" Miranda gave Pam a beseeching look.

Before she could speak, Shirley Murdock sat up straight in her chair and cleared her throat. Shirley had said nothing so far, and Miranda had wondered where she fell on the Pilgrim issue. She seemed reasonable and, compared to some of the others, progressive.

"I've always liked dressing up and never thought of it as bad," she began. A huff from Betty. "And I am still not convinced it is. But the world isn't what it used to be. Like Ramona says, it's not 1970."

"No one can deny that times are changing," Pam added.

"Which is exactly why we preserve tradition," Betty said.

"I'm not saying get rid of our traditions," Shirley continued. "I'm saying, find a nice, reasonable compromise. Figure out something that would ease us toward being more—modern."

"And how can you be modern about history?" Joanne asked. "History is not modern. It's *history*."

"Thank you, Shirley," Pam said. "I agree about compromise. Let's find a way this year to maintain the tradition that we seem to love so much—and still honor our ancestors."

"Forget compromise," Betty said, turning and looking squarely at Miranda. "I want you to know, Pastor, that you're ruining everything."

Joanne and Donna exchanged glances, and Shirley studied the top of the table.

"You come in here," Betty continued, her voice rising, "and stomp on this church's most sacred traditions."

"Betty, Pastor Miranda isn't stomping on anything. She's—" Pam interjected.

Betty cut her off. "Every year, I look forward to being Mary Brewster and standing next to my Delmar as William Brewster." Although Betty held onto her composure, her voice trembled.

Miranda's heart sank. They all knew about Delmar's diagnosis of dementia. This meant that dressing up as William Brewster was his favorite memory and represented something he could still participate in and enjoy. And who knew how many times he might stand next to Betty as William Brewster. Or stand next to Betty at all.

"We're not saying that you and Delmar won't ever dress as Pilgrims again," Miranda said, making her voice as soothing as she could.

"I thought that's exactly what we were saying." Ramona looked from Pam to Miranda.

"Pastor," Donna said. "You're new here. We get that. But you need to understand that to a New England town like Sparrow, Thanksgiving is a big deal. And it's the whole Pilgrim part of Thanksgiving that people love."

"And the football game," Linda said with a note of sarcasm in her voice.

"Don't forget the Macy's Thanksgiving Day Parade," Ramona chirped, selecting a second cannoli from the box.

"The people here really believe that the first Thanksgiving had pumpkin pies and cranberry sauce," Donna continued.

"Even though flour, butter, eggs, sugar, and cranberries weren't even available to the Pilgrims," Ramona added, spewing a bit of powdered sugar as she spoke.

"People like thinking that the Pilgrims and the Indians were best friends," Donna went on. "And everybody loves the story of how Squanto taught the Pilgrims to plant corn in a little mound of dirt with a fish on top."

"The corn and fish thing never happened," Ramona interrupted. "Did you sleep during the video? Because they talked about that."

"I understand," Miranda said. But she realized that she didn't understand at all. At seminary, they had pounded it into her that she was obligated to nurture church people to drop the shackles of colonialist worldview.

"It's a new direction. That shouldn't be so scary, right?" Pam looked at Miranda, eyebrows raised. "How about if we table a final decision on Pilgrim costumes and start by attempting something easier? Something that doesn't involve costumes. I was thinking—" Pam paused for dramatic effect. "How about the menu? Since we have a professional chef for a pastor—let's focus on food. We could prepare dishes historically accurate to the Indigenous peoples and the early Europeans." Pam looked pleased with herself remembering to say both "Indigenous" and "European."

"How is the food not authentic now? Are you sure the Pilgrims didn't have turkey and pumpkin pie and stuffing and cranberries?" Donna asked.

"I'm at Wikipedia." Ramona held up her phone. "They basically had one thing. Meat. Waterfowl, wild turkey, venison."

"You want us to cook a lot of meat?" Joanne asked.

"Why not?" Pam asked. "A true commitment to historical accuracy."

"What about the 150 people who show up because they want green bean casserole, stuffing, and pumpkin pie?" Joanne said.

"And cranberries still shaped like the can?" Linda said with an eye roll.

"As God intended," Ramona joked.

"Well, we could do a representation of what the Pilgrims really ate. In addition to serving the regular food like we always do," Pam said.

"You mean like a table off to the side with Pilgrim food?" Shirley suggested.

"Exactly," Pam said, glancing at Miranda, her expression apologetic. "Authentic Pilgrim food for people to sample."

Miranda forced a weak smile. A new seminary class came to mind: Lowering Your Expectations 101. On the other hand, baby steps. Maybe a little growth had been accomplished. After all, the women had watched the video, engaged in a spirited discussion, and were making a modicum of change. She would have to take it.

"Watch your emails, everyone. I'll send out a couple of links to let you research. And then at next week's meeting we'll make a plan." She turned to Pam. "Does that work for you, Madam President?" she asked with a genuine smile.

"Works for me," Pam replied. "Next meeting, ladies—bring your Pilgrim recipes."

CHAPTER ELEVEN

Dear Rev. Miranda,

All I can say is that I am glad that my Frank has gone to join our Lord and doesn't know what's happening at his beloved church.

I heard from Betty Hardacre that there would be no more Pilgrims at Thanksgiving! I told her I didn't believe it! I am sure that our Pilgrim forefathers would have liked that we honor them by dressing up! And just how do you expect our schoolchildren to understand their American heritage? How do you expect our church members to understand the spirit of Thanksgiving?

I want you to know that I will not be attending the community meal on Thanksgiving Day put on by the good women of this church. Nor will I be bringing my award-winning elderberry pie to donate.

Sincerely,

Mrs. Joan Connolly,

Cradle Episcopalian

To the Pastor of St.-Gabriel-by-the-Sea:

I hope you know that you've upset a lot of people in this town.

I am not a member of your church, and I never will be. For one thing, I don't believe in God or organized religion or all the nonsense that happens at churches like St. Gabriel. But I do love my country and getting rid of the Pilgrims is against America!

Yours Sincerely,

Ralph Gibbons

Dear Pastor Miranda:

I, for one, applaud your effort to bring about change in this old-fashioned, closed-minded town. Those awful Pilgrims with their cardboard hats and buckle shoes have always offended me. Time to move forward! Good luck in changing a bunch of sticks-in-the-mud who think Eisenhower is still president. And here's hoping you don't lose your position—even though I've heard a lot of people like you.

Signed,

Anonymous

"Did you read any of these?" Miranda waved the letters at Peg. "I honestly had no idea that giving up the Pilgrim costumes would stir up so many people." She waited for a response and then went on. "But that's good, right? To stir people up." She poured a cup of coffee from the carafe, her eyes on her secretary.

Peg slumped at her desk. Peg Dunbar never slouched; she claimed it was the posture of the unproductive.

"Are you okay?" She stood in front of Peg's desk, peering at her.

"I'm fine, thank you." Peg looked up from her screen. "Don't worry about those letters—some people have nothing better to do than complain."

Miranda cocked her head. Peg wasn't typing or filing or making marks on ledgers. She wasn't collating or color-coding or cleaning the supply closet. She was sitting, motionless. Miranda leaned around and peered at the computer screen. Blank.

"Wait till you hear what happened at the Thanksgiving Committee yesterday," she said, watching Peg. "It's possible we made a little progress. At least Betty isn't joining the Methodists." She fell into the Chesterfield chair.

"That's nice." Peg sighed.

Not good. Miranda looked around, "Where's Sampson? Staying home today?"

"No," Peg's voice was suddenly crisp. "I have placed Samson with a family." She stood up, crossed to the filing cabinet, and opened a drawer but just stood staring in.

"What?"

"I placed him with a family." She slammed the drawer shut and returned to her desk.

"What do you mean? What family?"

"To Edison and Laura Doherty. On a trial basis, of course."

"But I thought—" Miranda sat up in the big chair, both feet on the floor, leaning forward.

"You know the Dohertys. Early fifties. Very active. Both children off to college. It turns out they love Irish wolfhounds. They've owned them for years. Right now, they don't have one, and when they saw Sampson at the park last night, they asked if we were still looking for a home for him."

"You gave Samson away?" Miranda stood, staring at Peg.

"They are the perfect family. They understand the breed. They have a big home with a fenced-in backyard, they have the resources and the time to devote to a young dog." Peg grabbed a tissue from the box on her desk. "It was the right thing to do."

"No, it wasn't. Samson is my dog, too, you know. He was my dog. More yours, at least that's how I thought of it. But you can't give him away without talking to me."

"You gave me free rein to find him a home." Peg's face was stricken, eyes filling. "That's what you told me."

"Well, okay. It's what I told you." She fell back into the Chesterfield. "But I didn't think you would do it. You loved him. He loved you." The sight of the empty dog bed next to the copier made her throat go tight.

"I'm a seventy-two-year-old woman. I'm in no shape to own a 110-pound dog that is still growing."

"Don't play the old woman card with me," Miranda snapped. Anger was her default setting when she was trying not to get emotional. "You're in better physical shape than most of us. Anyway, I liked seeing the two of you together. I don't want anyone else to have him. That's all I have to say about it."

"What if he loves it there? A big yard, two people caring for him?"

Miranda didn't trust her voice. She never thought she could be so attached to a dog. But then, a lot of things had changed for her in the past few months. She swallowed hard. "What if he doesn't like it there? How is he going to let us know? Send us an email?" Miranda tried to modulate her voice but couldn't.

"It just seemed—they seemed—I mean, how could I say no?" Peg's voice trailed off.

"What did you say about a trial basis?"

"Mostly for them. I'm planning to visit to see how Samson is doing."

"When?"

"Later this morning."

"Can I go with you?"

"Make it a pastoral visit?" For the first time that morning, Peg gave a flicker of a smile.

"Absolutely."

★ ★ ★

"Oh, thank goodness!" Edison Doherty exclaimed as he hurried down the front steps of their two-story colonial. "Did you find him?"

"Find who?" Peg asked, stepping out of the Volvo wagon and shutting the door behind her.

"Samson. Do you have him?"

"Why would I have Samson?" Miranda vaulted out of the passenger side.

Edison, always in a suit and tie, looked as though he had been hiking through the woods, his trousers tucked into old green Wellingtons, his shirttail out.

Before he could answer, Laura Doherty appeared around the corner of the garage. "Peg! Please tell me he ran home to you."

"What happened?" Peg came to the point.

"I'm so sorry. But we got up this morning, and he was gone. We have a dog door from the kitchen to the backyard." Laura's voice was frantic. "It's just the right size for a wolfhound, and the backyard is entirely fenced in. It's completely secure. So we thought if he had to go out during the night he could go out through the dog door and come back in. All our other dogs did it that way. And we practiced with Samson before we went to bed, and he seemed fine going out the dog door and coming back in."

Miranda glanced at the Doherty house, a three-story colonial white with blue shutters, the front yard perfectly landscaped. She could see the corner of the chain-link fence that enclosed the back. Everything about the home and property said dog perfect.

"He dug his way out," Edison said. "There's a huge hole at the far end of the yard, and gray wiry fur caught on the fence. I can't believe he squeezed under, but he did."

"It must have taken him half the night," Laura added. "I can't believe we didn't hear him."

"We've been searching since five o'clock this morning." Edison said, his voice anxious.

No one spoke for a long moment. What Peg said next, Miranda would never forget. She would never forget that Peg Dunbar, who could be as abrupt and harsh as one could imagine, met this moment of loss with grace and charity.

"This is not your fault," she said. "Not in the least. Samson lived on his own for months, running wild. Living under porches, in sheds. Scavenging. It's what he is used to."

"We should've anticipated that he might dig out," Laura said, her voice breaking.

"I wouldn't have," Peg told her. "I would have thought the backyard was secure, too."

Edison's face, although still painfully distraught, relaxed the slightest bit. "We're just sick about it. You have to know that."

"Have you called Lewis at the shelter?"

"We've called in everybody but the cavalry." Laura and Edison looked at each other. "We should have called you right away," Edison said. "I'm so sorry that we didn't. But to be honest, I couldn't bring myself to tell you that we'd lost him. It was so obvious to us how much you love Samson. We felt honored that you entrusted him to us."

"We'll find him," Laura said. "I know we will."

"If only I'd had him chipped. All he has is a collar with his name. Not even an address." Peg's voice was heavy with regret.

Miranda's heart broke for her. On the short drive back to the church, they leaned out the windows by turns shouting Samson's name. When Peg drove into the parking lot, she turned off the ignition and sat without moving.

"What are you thinking?" Miranda asked finally, using her warmest pastor voice.

"I'm thinking that I was the one person he trusted, and I gave him away."

CHAPTER TWELVE

When they returned from the Dohertys' house, Peg called the Sparrow Dog Shelter. Lewis promised an all-out search and rescue.

"But don't you worry," he added. "I'm betting the old boy shows up at St. Gabe's tonight in time for dinner."

Miranda wished she shared his optimism. With the long stretches of rocky beach and thickly wooded areas around Sparrow, finding Samson felt akin to the proverbial needle in a haystack.

"Are you certain you don't want to drive around town and look for him?"

Peg was already stationed behind her computer and nimbly typing. "I'm creating a flyer to put up around town," Peg said, not moving her eyes from her screen. "I'll use his photo and list my cell number."

"I'll help you when I get back." She could keep an eye out for Samson and finally visit Harmon Holbeck. "We'll find him," she told Peg from the doorway. "I know we will."

* * *

The old sea captain's house rose against the cerulean sky. It was a fortress of peeling paint with more than a few broken shingles, and every window was a dark rectangle. However, the house still conveyed a certain dignity and elegance. A solid hedge of wild blackberry bushes blocked most of the wide front porch, and a dense thicket of scraggly pines bordered the lane.

Miranda listened for a moment to the rhythmic crash of the waves on the shore just beyond the house. She couldn't see it, but she knew that a vast rock formation jutted out into the water, marking what the townspeople called Holbeck's Point. The day held the warmth of early October air, a salty breeze blowing off the water, seagulls calling overhead. She shaded her eyes as she peered upward.

Atop the house was a rectangular platform bounded by a low railing with a rounded cupola in the center—a widow's walk. She envisioned the nineteenth-century wife of a sea captain pacing the walk, ocean wind whipping her long skirts as she gazed out to sea, waiting for her husband's ship to appear on the horizon. Would he return, or was she to be widowed?

Miranda imagined herself on that rooftop perch, watching for Jason to return. After he died, she'd had her own version of watching for him. A kind of hovering anticipation, always waiting, like a widow gazing at the sea. The hope stuck there, giving her the constant feeling that he was just about to burst through their apartment door laughing, calling out her name. Once, on a street in Cambridge, she was sure she had seen him—his loping walk, sandy hair, favorite green sweater. She had followed down the sidewalk, finally turning around and returning home, more lost and alone than ever.

She wondered if a woman in this house had been widowed. Had she ever returned to the rooftop walk to watch and wait long after she knew her husband had been lost at sea? Miranda shook the image from her mind and continued down the lane to the old house.

She crossed the wide front porch, splintery boards creaking, and lifted the heavy brass knocker on the oaken door, banging it down three times. She waited. Nothing but the sound of seagulls and waves. She tried again.

The porch wrapped around the house and, on the eastern side, faced the sea. Empty of chairs or tables, there was nothing to indicate that leisure time was enjoyed, that anyone sat and gazed at the water.

Nothing to suggest that anyone lived in the house at all. A pile of rotting lumber lay on the wide floorboards and an old dresser missing its drawers sat at one end. A pile of yellowed newspapers was jumbled in front of the door as if the paperboy had faithfully delivered them and finally given up. Sand had drifted up over the steps. The double doors, which she imagined were once majestic and welcoming, were now covered in old plywood, weathered, and the nails rusty. Harmon must have shut out the world a long time ago.

"What do you want?" a voice bellowed from above.

She backed up a few feet looking straight up at the house, the sun in her eyes. "Hello?" she called out.

"I said, what do you want?"

A tall, gaunt man stood on the widow's walk. Long gray hair lifted in the breeze, a rugged fisherman's sweater, and old khakis. He waved his cane in the air and yelled, "I said, *what do you want?*"

"I'm Miranda McCurdy. The priest at St. Gabriel's."

"I know who you are. My inquiry remains the same."

"I was hoping we might visit."

"I no longer attend your church, in case you haven't noticed, so I do not know why you have presumed to come here and shout at me on my own property."

Miranda resisted pointing out that she had knocked politely, not shouted at all.

"Please leave. And take that filthy dog with you."

Her heart leaped. "Dog?" She almost shouted again.

"That mangy gray dog. Looks like a wolf. Get it off my property."

Her heart soared. "You've seen Samson! When? When did you see him? And where exactly?"

"Next time I alert the dog officer." She heard a rasping door open that she assumed was the opening to the cupola, and then the sound as it scraped shut.

Harmon was gone.

★ ★ ★

"Samson!" Peg scanned the bushes opposite Harmon's house and then put two fingers in her mouth and let out a whistle to rival the Burlington-Northern coming into the depot.

"I wish Harmon had at least given me more information. Like exactly where and when he saw him," Miranda said.

"Oh, not Harmon," Peg replied bitterly. "Samson!" She walked a few paces toward the tree line behind the house. "He's perfectly agreeable when he needs help from you. But you can forget it if you need help from him."

Miranda wondered what happened to Peg's earlier assessment of Harmon—he's a poor soul who needs to be left alone. She also wondered where she learned to whistle like that. "If Samson made it all the way here, he's covered a lot of territory overnight," she said.

"The dog's an athlete," Peg replied, letting out another ear-splitting whistle. "If you travel as the crow flies, the Dohertys are only about a mile north. I've power walked farther than that with him. He could do a mile without slowing down."

Miranda liked the hope she heard in Peg's voice.

Miranda ran up the porch steps and banged the knocker on the heavy door. "Harmon needs to tell us exactly when and where he saw Samson."

"He can see half the county from that widow's walk. According to Harry Hopkins, that's where he spends his days, rain or shine. He even storm-watches."

"Or he could at least tell us which way Samson was headed." She banged on the door another time, but still no response from within. She pounded again before giving up. They walked to the far end of Harmon's property, whistling and calling for Samson.

"Has Harmon always owned this house?" Miranda looked back at the rambling old structure.

"The house has been in the Holbeck family for generations. But once Harmon made his fortune as an artist, he purchased all the land surrounding it. He owns everything, even part of the beach."

"He lives as a recluse?"

"Not entirely. I see him at the farmers market on occasion. Or the library. As you know, he's stopped coming to church."

"Why?"

"Fell out with the vestry a few years ago. A budget fight over fixing the steeple. He stormed out and never returned. But he keeps up his pledge, which I find admirable."

They continued down to the water and walked along the outcropping of rock at Holbeck's Point. The tide was out. Pockets of saltwater, shells, and seaweed bundles marked the sandy stretch.

"Harmon was an artistic prodigy," Peg told her. "Or so they said. He went off to Rhode Island School of Design in Providence right out of high school, but after a few months, he moved back home. I never knew why. Harmon, Sr. converted an old greenhouse on the property into an art studio for his son."

"What kind of art?"

"Oil painting. Then just as he began to gain some notoriety and success—" Peg twisted around and gazed up at the top of the Holbeck house. "There was an incident. A long time ago now. Anyway, now he stands up there on the widow's walk."

She turned back and gazed out to the horizon. "I've heard that the more dangerous the storm, the more likely it is that Harmon will be up there. The fire chief has begged him not to."

"Some people put themselves in harm's way as a form of tempting fate." She looked at Peg's profile as they headed up the embankment to the Volvo. "What was the incident?"

Peg shook her head. "Another time."

They walked around Harmon's house to the drive where Peg had parked. "At least we know Samson headed south from the Doherty.

Toward town, and not the highway." Peg stood with one hand on the door handle of the Volvo. They paused, reluctant to abandon the search.

"I wonder if he will make his way to your house?" Miranda finally said. Peg lived on the edge of town in a Cape Anne she had remodeled herself.

"My back porch was the site of his last meal, so maybe." A shadow crossed her face. "I can't believe I gave him away. I just can't."

"The Dohertys were the perfect family! You thought you were giving him a better life."

Peg's eyes filled. "If we find him."

Miranda interrupted her. "*When* we find him."

"Right." Peg plucked a tissue out of the sleeve of her cardigan and blew her nose. "When we find him—I would like to keep him. As my dog. I don't want Laura and Edison to feel bad—as if I don't trust them. It's just that—" The always steady and sensible Peg broke off, unable to speak.

"He's yours! I'll explain to the Dohertys. Legally, he's mine, which means I can give him to whomever I want. And I am officially, right now, giving him to you. As I should have done from the start."

"And you're absolutely sure that you are fine with that?" Peg dabbed at her eyes with a tissue.

"Entirely sure. Beyond sure. You and Samson were meant to be together." Miranda resisted hugging Peg. The older woman was not a hugger. "Now, all we have to do is find him."

On the drive back to the church, they discussed how to proceed. Miranda thought Samson was attempting to find his way back to Peg, and Peg was sure he was hopelessly lost. They pulled into the church parking lot. The afternoon shadows had grown long and the air chilly. She jumped out of the Volvo.

Peg had planned to drive down Main Street in case any merchants had seen him.

"Don't forget that you need to return that call to the Sparrow Lion's Club," Peg said to her through the lowered front window of the Volvo. "No doubt they think they can dump the whole Gifts for Children Drive on you. You're new here, and so every group in the county wants to hit you up to lead their committees and do all the work they can't get anyone else to do. You tell them no; you have enough church work hanging over you."

Miranda found comfort in the fact that her secretary had returned to giving orders. "I think Gifts for Children is a great program."

They stayed silent a moment, Peg behind the wheel staring straight ahead and Miranda watching her through the open window.

"Do you want to pray?" Miranda asked, standing at the open driver's side window.

"Right here in the parking lot?"

"Why not?" She didn't clasp hands with Peg as she might have with most parishioners, but she rested her hand on Peg's arm and closed her eyes. "Loving God," she began in a clear voice, "who watches over all creatures, bring Samson back home safely. Give him what he needs to find his way, let him suffer no ill effects from his separation from those who love him, and let him meet only with kindness. We thank you, O God, for your mercy and love and for your son who went after the one lost lamb, leaving the other ninety-nine behind. Amen."

"Amen," Peg echoed quietly. She pressed the ignition button of the Volvo. "And don't forget to take a good look at that budget proposal spreadsheet. I put it on your desk. Sam Reeves has allocated far too much money to youth ministry. In my day, youth raised their own money. Bake sales, car washes, yard clean-up." She checked her mirrors. "And would you please text June Watson on the Altar Guild. Arrangements of colorful autumn leaves on the altar are lovely, but enough is enough."

"Got it. No gifts for children, no money to youth, too many beautiful leaves. Anything else?" "Don't be cheeky." Peg paused, holding Miranda in her gaze. "And Pastor. Thank you."

CHAPTER THIRTEEN

Miranda watched as the taillights of Peg's Volvo disappeared around the corner. The morning had begun bright and clear, but now gray clouds covered the sun. It was as if the whole world had gone from crisp and sunny October to dismal November, all in one day.

A sleek, silver Lexus wheeled into the church parking lot and stopped in front of the sign, *Reserved for Church Administrator*. It was right next to Miranda's spot with its sign, *Pastor Only. Thou Shalt Not Park Here*. The sports car made her 2009 Honda Accord look more rust bucket than ever. The Lexus screeched to a halt, its engine still humming. In one fluid motion, the driver threw the gear into park and flung open the door. Adam McClain emerged, stepped onto the pavement and slammed the door shut with a resounding thud, as if to punctuate his arrival.

"I was hoping to find you here, Pastor McCurdy," he said, frowning.

"In the parking lot?" she replied.

The wind ruffled Adam's hair. Not so much product this time, she thought. Today's suit was dark blue, corporate, professional. Not the usual Sparrow, Maine attire: a haphazard mix of hiking gear and gardening clothes.

"I meant, at the church." He folded his arms across his chest, unfolded them again, and then shoved both hands in his pockets. "It's about Aunt Lucy."

"Is she all right?" Miranda found herself switching from checking out the ticked-off hot guy to concerned pastor. "I visited her the other day. Is she back home?"

"They're releasing her sometime tomorrow. Which is good. Well, staying a little longer would have been better." He seemed momentarily thrown off his game, as if he had rolled in with one agenda and was handed another. "It isn't that." He shot her a dark look. "That's not what I want to talk about."

"Okay?" Miranda didn't move toward him.

"When going over my aunt's finances, I noticed that she makes a substantial gift to this church. A weekly gift. I don't know if you are aware of that."

"Of course I'm aware of Lucy's generosity to St. Gabe's."

He cleared his throat. "Oh. Right."

She waited. Adam stood there. Six feet of annoyed cute. His eyes were even more startlingly blue in the blue suit. "Did you have something you wanted to say?"

"I'm wondering what you do to get an old woman on a fixed income to write a check of that size every week to your church?"

"What I do?" Miranda felt a rush of adrenaline.

"And, in addition to the weekly check, she makes another considerable donation at Thanksgiving for something called The Harvest Fund. A little suspicious if you ask me."

Suspicious? Miranda's palms broke out in a sweat. A sure sign of pastoral fury. How Lucy McClain spent her money was up to Lucy.

"Let's get a couple of things straight, Mr. McClain." She drew herself up to her full height of five feet, three inches. "First, I do not discuss a church member's contribution with anyone but the church member herself."

"That's convenient."

Her hackles, if that's what you call the hair on the back of your neck, rose. "I believe the word is *confidential*." She wasn't about to be intimidated by a Lexus-driving city boy. Even if he did border on devastatingly handsome.

"You smell like cinnamon," she said, startled.

"No, I don't."

She breathed in again. "And cardamon."

"I definitely do not smell like cardamon." A hint of amusement flickered across his face. All threat was gone.

"Yes, you do," she replied, breathing in deeply. "You smell like cinnamon and cardamom. Like I'm in a bakery." She gazed into his eyes. "I'm having a full-on olfactory memory just standing next to you."

He cocked his head, his eyes meeting hers. "What's your memory?"

"If you must know, the first time my parents took me to Mike's Pastry in Boston's North End."

"Home of the Cannoli?"

"You know Mike's?"

"School of Architecture at Boston University. Mike's Pastry was my Saturday morning go-to before heading to the library."

"Boston University, School of Theology. I stopped at Mike's before a day at the library."

"We could have been there at the same time."

"Standing in line."

"Because that's what you do at Mike's." Despite herself, she laughed. "I've stood in line once, on the sidewalk, in January."

"You could have been that woman who finally made it to the counter, and then couldn't decide what she wanted."

"That woman?" Her eyes narrowed. "I knew exactly what I wanted from Mike's before I even left my apartment."

"Sorry. Let me guess." He gazed at her thoughtfully for a moment. "Chocolate covered cannoli?"

"Nope."

"Espresso cannoli?"

She shook her head.

"Caramel cannoli?"

"Seriously? Caramel? Who gets a caramel cannoli?"

"What, then?"

"Mike's original."

He shook his head. "You just don't seem like the plain-cannoli-kind-of-girl."

"What can I say? I'm a purist."

He held her in his blue eyes for a moment. She was the first to break away. "And what was your favorite at Mike's?" She was dismayed to hear her voice croak.

"No favorite. I was that guy who couldn't decide until they got to the counter."

"I knew it." The clouds overhead cleared for a moment. A breeze ruffled his dark hair. "About Lucy's church donation. You seemed worried earlier."

"Maybe we could continue this conversation someplace other than the church parking lot. Not that I don't love the ambiance."

"Sure. And you can tell me why you smell like Mike's Pastry."

"How about a coffee, then? At that diner down the street? Lorinda's or Lucinda's or something?"

"Loretta's." She picked up the canvas bag filled with all the confirmation workbooks.

"Let me take that—looks heavy."

For one second, Miranda was going to protest. The switch from grumpy old man to chivalrous thirty-something cute guy had been abrupt. On the other hand, the bag was giving her a neck cramp.

"Thanks," she said, swinging it in his direction.

"Good God, what do you have in here?" He grunted as he flung it over his shoulder. "A dead body? A piano? The tenor section of the church choir?"

★ ★ ★

She led Adam to the back booth, where he thumped the bag onto the floor.

"Sorry," she said. "I'll carry it back."

"No way. I would feel guilty if I let a woman carry such a heavy bag while I walked beside her."

"Really?" She slid into the booth.

"What?" he said, his voice defensive. "Does that make me sexist?"

"No." She thought for a moment. "It's just that when you live alone, like I do, you get used to doing everything for yourself. And so, it's unexpected when you don't have to, that's all."

"Oh. I guess that's true. I don't date much so I—not that I think this is a date. Oh my God. I mean, I was only referring to—"

She decided to save him. "I know what you meant. I'm good."

Loretta appeared at the end of the booth, tapping her pen on her notepad.

"What happened to all of your wait staff?" Miranda asked. Loretta didn't usually wait tables in the middle of the afternoon.

"Don't ask," she said. "What'll you have?"

"I heard the Pastor likes carbs that are sweet," Adam replied. "How about two donuts with coffee?"

Loretta gave him a skeptical look. "The Pastor doesn't eat donuts."

Adam looked at Miranda with his eyebrows raised. "Okay. I don't see cannoli on the menu." He turned to Loretta. "So what does she like?"

"Pie. Crepes. Scones." Loretta tapped her order pad again.

"All right then," he said. "What kind of pie do you have today?"

"No pie. I have a nice rhubarb tart, though. Made it with the rhubarb that I put up last summer."

"Isn't a tart the same as a pie?" Adam asked.

Loretta sighed.

"A tart is like a pie." Miranda cut in. "A tart lacks the pastry top."

"So a tart is a pie, but without the top?"

"Exactly."

"You know a lot about food," Adam said. "Do you like to cook?"

Loretta snorted and shook her head. "Two rhubarb tarts, two coffees." She walked away.

"I was head chef at a restaurant in Boston—before I was ordained."

"Are you kidding me? What restaurant?"

"The Pellegrino in the Back Bay."

"Oh my God. I love that place." He sat back, stunned. "And you were the head chef?"

She nodded.

"Wait a minute." Red blotches began on his neck and moved up. "Why didn't you tell me at the beach the other day when I was telling you how to cook chicken?"

She grinned. "I guess I just wanted to see how long you'd go on."

"I can't believe I explained how to grill chicken to the head chef from The Pellegrino."

"I think what you did is better called 'mansplained.'"

"I totally apologize." He grimaced.

"No need for an apology. Proper meat temperature is critical." She laughed. His discomfort was reassuring. You had to be a good person to feel uncomfortable and to apologize.

"I still can't believe you didn't stop me. Or Ramona. I thought she was laughing and rolling her eyes a lot. At least I didn't tell her when to use a plunger and when to use a snake."

"Do you know when to use a plunger and when to use a snake?"

"I do actually. And if you'd like, I can mansplain it to you later."

Loretta slid a cup of coffee in front of each of them, followed by two plates generously piled with crumbling, luscious rhubarb tart. She waited while Miranda cut off a piece and lifted it to her mouth.

"Umm—" Miranda said, chewing and swallowing. "Perfect. Extra butter in the crust?"

Loretta nodded.

"Generous with the sugar?"

"Double."

"That's why the rhubarb is so good—tangy-sweet." Miranda examined the crust. "No soggy bottom? Hard to achieve with rhubarb."

"Sprinkled a little almond flour on top of the dough, right before I baked it," Loretta said. "Soaks up your juices." Loretta walked away.

Tart first, then coffee—they moved in unison.

"And you left the position of head chef at Pellegrino's to become a priest? Why?" Adam put his cup down and picked up his fork again.

"Long story. It'll take more than coffee and a rhubarb tart to tell."

"Fair enough. But I'd like to hear it someday."

She liked it that Adam wanted to know her past. Chef to pastor—few asked. He had an intense way of paying attention, of concentrating on the other person.

"I'll definitely need wine and something that involves a lot of melted cheese."

"That can be arranged. Wine and melted cheese happen to be my specialty." He loaded his fork with rhubarb tart. "Were you a baker also? Or does a chef always do both? Sorry to sound so ignorant."

"I'm not a baker—by any means. But after so many years in the restaurant business, you learn a lot. And you appreciate good food of any sort—pastry to pasta. I like Loretta's because it's a first-rate restaurant dressed up like a small-town diner. And it's nice to have someone to talk shop with."

They dug into their rhubarb tarts.

"You never told me why you smell like cinnamon and cardamon."

"Oh, right." Adam finished the last bite on his plate and wiped his mouth with a paper napkin. "Well, I feel ridiculous saying it now—since I'm sitting in the presence of a real chef. But I love to bake. And cook. And chop vegetables. And read recipe books. The old-fashioned kind, not the digital kind. This afternoon I went over to Aunt Lucy's and prepped some dishes for her so she could just pull them out of the fridge. Her favorites: macaroni and cheese, ham balls, cheeseburger pie." He gave a slight grimace. "My aunt thinks that it's not food if it isn't full of carbs. I added a big bowl of fresh greens, but I have little hope. The last thing I baked, thus my fragrance, was a giant batch of cinnamon and cardamon snickerdoodles. Her first choice to have with tea."

"That's nice of you."

He sipped his coffee. "Well, snickerdoodles are mostly sugar and butter."

"You know what Julia Child said? If you are worried about too much butter in your diet, substitute with cream."

They both laughed.

"How'd you get into cooking?" she asked, watching him.

"Easy-Bake Oven. When I was nine."

"I had an Easy-Bake Oven! I loved it. Those things were awesome."

Adam shot her his adorable smile. "I know, right? To this day, when I smell slightly uncooked chocolate cake batter, I'm back in the kitchen of my parents' house, waiting for the little timer to ding."

"Did you know Betty Crocker designed the Easy-Bake Oven to get kids interested in baking with packaged mixes? They thought it would create a generation of adults who would buy their products."

"Well, it worked. I love a good cake mix." He drained his coffee cup just as Loretta came by.

"That might have been the best rhubarb tart I've ever tasted," Adam told her. "It was precisely how I like rhubarb."

Loretta topped off his coffee and walked away.

She grinned. "I don't think she believes you."

"Well, the truth is, rhubarb might not be my favorite fruit."

"It's not a fruit. Vegetable."

"No. Are you sure?"

"Quite."

"Interesting. What about tomatoes?"

"Fruit. Don't tell Ronald Reagan."

"Green beans?"

"Also, fruit."

"Corn?"

"A fruit and a grain."

"Impressive." They both sat in companionable silence for a moment, sipping their coffee.

Finally, Adam spoke. "My mother was the one who always looked out for Aunt Lucy. But when my parents moved to Portugal—their retirement dream home—she told me that I needed to step up. I'm the only one in the family nearby. Honestly, I didn't think it would amount to much. I've never taken care of anyone before. Or anything, really."

"Not even a dog or a cat?"

"Not even a geranium." He took a sip of coffee. "It's just me alone, in my apartment in Portland. Are you—?" He looked at her over his coffee cup.

"Alone?"

"Well, yes." Adam cocked his head. "I was just wondering—"

"Well, there's Howard."

"Oh. Right." He put his coffee cup down. "Sorry. Aunt Lucy made a point to let me know you weren't married or with anyone. But of course, she wouldn't know everything about your personal life. Have you and Howard been together long?"

"A year. We're taking things slowly." She wished she could keep her face from erupting into a goofy smile, but she couldn't. Playing things cool with a guy was not her strong suit. "He's a hedgehog." She was interested that Adam looked a tiny bit relieved.

"I'd like to meet Howard someday. If that isn't too forward?"

"Please, Adam. You're smothering me." His smiling face fell slightly, making Miranda quickly add, "*Kidding!* Howard would love to meet you, but only if you arrive after dark. He's nocturnal. He'll be cranky if you wake him during the day."

She gazed across the table and felt her fingertips tingle. Miranda had two kinds of anxiety that could make her fingertips tingle. She called them nervous-nervous and nervous-happy. Nervous-nervous meant she was about to step into the pulpit on Easter morning. High-stakes preaching was a reason for the nervous-nervous response. Major fingertip-tingle.

But she was nervous-happy when something wonderful was about to happen, and she didn't know if she was ready for it. Or maybe it was something she always thought she wanted, but now that it was imminent, she got nervous. Nervous-happy. Like when she realized Jason was about to kiss her for the first time. Or now. When she sat across from Adam McClain with his I-smell-like-a-bakery cuteness. She wished she could sit on her hands and stop the tingling. Instead, she gazed into her coffee and smiled.

"What?" he said.

She had to think fast. Explaining her nervous-happy fingertip tingle was not exactly on the sophisticated side of things. "I was just imagining you in an apron covered with flour or dabs of chocolate or smudges of cake batter. It doesn't seem like you. You're so, so—tidy."

"Tidy! Wow. That's manly. I haven't been called tidy since the third grade. I got points from Mrs. Bradley for being tidy, as I recall."

"When I cook, I'm pretty messy. I can't see you being messy."

"You're right, picture this. A spotless apron, ironed. Immaculate oven mitts. A perfectly organized kitchen. And in the background, Sinatra singing "Fly Me to the Moon." And that's me, cooking."

"Sinatra is your cooking music?"

"What's yours?"

"Beyoncé, Lady Gaga, Taylor Swift."

"Well, then you win for coolest. I win for tidy."

She laughed. "We'll have to cook together and see what happens."

"You're on." They sat in silence again, sipping coffee. She liked it that he could be silent. Some people seemed to feel the need to fill every space with talking.

"Well," he said finally. "To finish what I was saying about Aunt Lucy. I assumed that taking care of her would be pretty minimal—she's always been so healthy and active. Then suddenly she's in the hospital, the house has to be cleaned out, five cats need homes, and, well, here I am. In Sparrow, Maine, going through an old lady's checkbook hoping for the best."

"That's a lot."

"All this summer, I kept thinking that I needed to come up from Portland to visit, but I never did. Until I got the call from her in the hospital. Believe me, the guilt was staggering."

"I understand guilt. But you're here now."

"True. And I did fumigate that house of felines."

"Not a small task."

"And I found homes for all of them."

"Amazing."

"Even Mr. Snuggles."

"What was wrong with Mr. Snuggles?"

"Asthmatic, diabetic, has attitude."

"Wow."

"I'm serious when I say that I want to meet Howard."

Miranda forced herself not to grab him by the sleeve of his expensive suit coat and drag him back to the rectory. Instead, she smiled as casually as possible and watched as Adam opened his wallet and tossed several bills on the table.

"He likes purple cabbage and fresh snails."

"I'm all out of fresh snails, but I've got lots of purple cabbage. Come on." Adam slid out of the booth. "Let me slip into my orthopedic back brace, and I'll haul that bag of yours to the church."

CHAPTER FOURTEEN

Miranda had already enjoyed a delightful cup of coffee sitting on the front stoop of the rectory as the sun rose. She sat in the Chesterfield chair now, coffee mug in hand.

"He found homes for every one of Lucy's cats," Miranda told Peg. She had given a rundown of yesterday's conversation with Adam, leaving out how his eyes were the color of an October sky, and that he was planning on meeting Howard. "And fumigated the entire house."

"Goodness," Peg replied. "He's a saint." She shut the file drawer and sat behind her computer screen. "I thought I'd spend my lunch driving south of town looking for Samson."

"I'll go with you," Miranda said, eager to do anything that might lead to finding Samson. "Why south?"

"Just a feeling. If he left the Doherty's and ended up at Harmon's, then he's headed south." Peg gave her an inquisitive look. "How old is Adam?"

"No idea, why?"

"He must be about your age?"

"I would guess, probably."

"Is he single?"

"Hmmm—I think so." She felt her face grow hot and she took a long sip of coffee.

Peg resumed her typing.

Miranda cleared her throat and said in her most business-like tone, "I'm glad Adam is more comfortable with Lucy's gift to the church."

"Are you nervous about church money?" Peg asked.

"I'm worried about the pledges. They're barely trickling in." Miranda had spent the evening reviewing the proposed budget for the upcoming year and the latest pledge sheets. Of all the things she didn't learn in seminary, church finance was the most worrisome.

"Nonsense. The pledges are fine. Right up to par with other years."

"You're kidding?" She stared at Peg across her coffee cup. "It's always like this?"

"Like what?"

"Like forty percent in the red. We'll never close a gap like that by the end of the fiscal year." She watched as Peg stood and walked over to the copy machine.

"Don't forget the Harvest Fund."

"The Thanksgiving collection?"

"After the meal, the kitchen ladies—dressed as Pilgrims, by the way—take up a collection. They walk around with big black hats turned upside down."

"They use the Pilgrim hats to collect the money?"

"They do."

"And enough is collected to balance the budget?" Miranda had thought the Thanksgiving collection covered the costs of the meal. No one had told her it was an actual fundraiser.

"The Harvest Fund tides us over every year. You'll see. Nothing to worry about." Peg pushed the button on the copy machine and watched as it spit out pages. "Of course, that means that we need a big turn-out for the meal."

"You don't think—"

"You think people might boycott? Is it definite they won't be wearing the Pilgrim costumes?"

"Still undecided."

"It's not that I disagree with you. I don't like the costumes, either, but you know how church people dislike change. And they express their dislike with their checkbooks."

"So if the Thanksgiving meal has a low attendance—"

"Let's not jump to conclusions," Peg said, dropping the stack of copies on the desk. She strode across the hall to the supply cabinet, returning with a fresh packet of paper and a box of pens.

Miranda watched as Peg refilled the copier trays. "That machine's on its last legs. How do you keep it running?"

"Lots of patience and a spot on the prayer list." Peg began to collate the papers on her desk. Miranda started to respond, but the sound of the door drew their attention. Harry stepped in, his salt-and-pepper hair slightly disheveled.

"Any news on the dog?" he asked, glancing between them.

"Not yet, Harry," Peg replied

"I've been keeping an eye out. We'll find him." He turned to Miranda. "Have you got a moment, Pastor?"

"Of course," she said, gesturing toward her office.

"No, I won't take up your time. We can talk right here. I just wanted you to know that it looks like someone pushed a window open into the basement. No damage to the window or anything, but it was open. I saw it when I drove by this morning taking Margery to school."

Every morning Harry drove his wife of thirty-seven years, to Sparrow Middle School, where she taught math. On their way to there, they often stopped at Loretta's for coffee and pastry.

"Someone gained entrance?" She thought of the aroma of freshly brewed coffee late the other night. "But why break-in? It is so easy to slip into a church. The doors are unlocked almost every evening with AA, Boy Scouts, committee meetings."

"Well, I don't know if anyone came in through the window or not. And I don't know how long the window has been like that. It just happened to catch my eye."

"Which window?" Peg asked.

"Basement. The one that goes directly into the electrical closet. You can barely see it under the rhododendron. It could have happened weeks ago or just last night. Who knows?"

"Should we report it? Or just fix it?" Miranda asked.

"I've already done both," Harry replied. "Now about that proposed budget. Margery and I both think we need to allocate more money to youth. Give it some thought."

CHAPTER FIFTEEN

Dazzling October sunshine poured through the window of Miranda's bedroom that Saturday morning. The clear air and blue sky were so enticing that she was drawn almost straight from slumbering in bed to strolling on the rock-strewn beach. She followed her early morning walk with a leisurely cup of coffee on her front stoop, listening to the waves. Finally, when contemplating a return to bed, she headed to the church. The only thing that could force her to work now would be to sit at her desk in her office with no distractions. She grabbed her phone and keys and dropped a few insectivore pellets in front of the Hobbit house door in case Howard awakened hungry.

She set off at a leisurely pace for the church.

* * *

Finally. A pink memo slip from Peg that wasn't a reminder of a task she needed to accomplish, or worse, something she had forgotten. "If you come in to work on your sermon, there's a plate of cookies in the kitchen for you—leftover from the Saturday morning Diaconate meeting.

Miranda shrugged off her hoodie. It was nice to have a secretary who thought of everything. Even cookies. She realized she had never baked or cooked anything for Peg. Could that be true? She would rectify that oversight as soon as she had a free evening. She tossed the memo on her desktop.

Starting a sermon was like climbing a mountain. You stood at the bottom and stared up, wondering how you would ever reach the top. But then, one step at a time, you could do it. Although some sermons moved forward more quickly than others. She often felt torn between the need to be entertaining and bringing a meaningful message that reflected the scripture for that Sunday. She sighed. She would start the sermon, make some serious progress, and then—and only then—would she reward herself with a cookie. But first, a pot of coffee. While the coffee perked, she checked the tiny office fridge for cream. None. She headed down to the kitchen, and there they were: six maple leaf-shaped cookies frosted with orange frosting and arranged in a circle on a paper plate. She ignored them. Not until she accomplished something. Not until she at least started the sermon.

Back in the office, coffee mug in hand, Miranda read aloud—using her pulpit voice—the lectionary text for the week: the Story of the Ten Bridesmaids.

Then shall the kingdom of heaven be likened unto ten bridesmaids... And while they went out, the bridegroom came; and they that were ready went in with him to the marriage: and the door was shut. Afterward came also the other bridesmaids, saying, Lord, Lord, open to us. But he answered and said, Verily I say unto you, I know you not.

Finally, she thought, taking a sip of the hot coffee, a parable that holds the promise of good preaching. Would she miss the deep dive into scripture that sermon preparation required, if she went to Seattle? No more researching a favorite topic, struggling with the Greek or the Hebrew, wresting a coherent, meaningful theme from a parable or verse, and shaping it into a compelling message relatable to even the most disinterested parishioner.

She paced the length of her office, pondering the scripture and trying to think of a title. A good title meant she was on to a good theme. "Always a Bridesmaid, Never a Bride" might work. She sat behind her desk and wrote as fast as she could, completely stream of consciousness for several inspired pages. She read it over, making corrections.

"Not bad," she thought. "I deserve a cookie."

But the maple leaf cookies had vanished. No frosted maple leaves, no crumbs, not even an empty plate. Had Miranda absentmindedly put them in the fridge? She had once placed her Bible in the microwave and her coffee cup in the bookcase. She peered into the fridge: three juice boxes, a deluxe package of communion wafers, and an unopened bottle of sacramental wine. The church kitchen crew were meticulous and relentless cleaners, especially after the legendary baked bean incident of '05, as the story was told to her, a container of three-bean salad had turned slowly into a science project.

Miranda closed the fridge door and wandered into the Fellowship Hall.

"Hello?" she called out, her voice echoing in the empty room. Who would help themselves to an entire plate of cookies? Sure, one or two, but all of them?

"Hello?" she called out again and waited. Nothing but the old boiler kicking on and the light hum of traffic on Main Street.

She returned to her office and called Harry. Harry Hopkins was the best senior warden a priest could hope for. He was sensible, compassionate, and a person of faith. As a bonus, he also had a sense of humor, like the frosting on the cake, or in this case, the cookie.

"I know this is probably ridiculous," she said when he answered the phone. "But a plate of cookies disappeared from the kitchen." She had to give Harry credit. He took her seriously, as if she had said the steeple had been set on fire and the knitting ladies kidnapped.

"I'll be right there," he told her. "Stay in your office. In fact, close the door and lock it from the inside."

"Really?" she asked, feeling foolish. "Is the average cookie thief armed and dangerous?"

"Do it. I'm on my way," he replied.

When Harry arrived, they walked through the entire building, checking doors and windows. From basement to bell tower, nothing seemed out of place.

"What about the Boy Scouts?" Harry asked. "Any of them in the church this morning?"

"I haven't heard a sound," Miranda said. "And it's hard to miss the Scouts. I'm positive the church was empty when I got here, and I locked the door behind me."

"How much time passed between seeing the cookies and realizing that they were gone?"

"An hour. Maybe a little longer."

"I don't like it, Pastor," Harry said, shaking his head. "I don't like it at all. A pushed open window, missing cookies."

"I don't suppose missing cookies is a reason to raise the alarm," Miranda pointed out. "We can hardly call the Sparrow police chief and report the theft of six orange-frosted cookies shaped like maple leaves." Miranda noticed that Harry didn't even smile.

"Let's go down to the kitchen, and you show me exactly where you saw the cookies," Harry suggested.

They walked to the kitchen, and Miranda pointed to the table. "They were right here. On the table." A paper plate with six orange-frosted cookies shaped like maple leaves sat in the middle of the table.

"They honestly were here earlier. I mean, they were here and then they weren't."

"And now they are," Harry noted, picking up a cookie and taking a bite. "Linda Darcy's. Did you know she makes these with real maple syrup?" He chewed thoughtfully for a moment.

"You couldn't have missed them?" He gave her a warm look. "The second time around? I can be very absent-minded myself. I go out to the garage to do one thing, do another, and completely forget why I was there in the first place."

"No," Miranda said, her face growing hot. "These cookies were not here earlier. Like I said, they were, and then—and then—they weren't."

The words sounded implausible even to her own ears. A chill ran down her spine. If the cookies had disappeared and then reappeared, it meant someone was in the church.

It meant that Miranda hadn't been alone.

CHAPTER SIXTEEN

The members of the Thanksgiving Committee stared silently at the small duck. Shimmering teal feathers, a black beak, and webbed feet. It lay on the stainless-steel table in the church kitchen like a corpse waiting for its autopsy. The response of the women ranged from mildly disturbed to openly horrified—all except Ramona. Dressed in her plumber's coveralls and Red Sox ball cap, she exuded a matter-of-fact attitude, as if she were evaluating a leaky pipe.

"It's so wild-looking," Joanne said softly.

"Noble," Linda added.

The duck's head gleamed with a deep-sea green, and the intricately feathered brown wings had an intense blue patch on either side.

The bell in the clock tower chimed three times, and the boiler kicked on.

"Everyone, if I could have your attention, please." Pam spoke without moving her eyes from the duck. "Maybe we could get started."

"Are we sure this little duck is an authentic Pilgrim dish?" Betty sounded skeptical.

"You'd know it was if you'd read the article Pastor Miranda sent around," Ramona said.

"For your information, I did read that article." Betty glared at Ramona and crossed her arms. "I don't want to cook *just* meat. Especially meat that comes with feathers and feet."

"Not just any meat—waterfowl," Donna said. "According to the article, the Pilgrims ate mostly waterfowl."

"This is definitely waterfowl." Edna grimaced.

"Where did this example of—of—native waterfowl come from?" Miranda looked at Ramona questioningly.

"My brother, Billy," Ramona said. "Duck season opened last week."

"I see." Miranda fought the urge to begin the prayers of the dead. "So does your brother eat the birds he kills?"

"Goodness, no. For Billy, it's just target practice."

Edna turned away, fanning herself with a dish towel.

"Look how blue the spots on his wings are," Shirley added, her voice almost a whisper.

"How do you know it's a he?" Donna asked.

"It's a male," Ramona said. "That's why its markings are so bright and colorful."

"I've never plucked a bird in my life." Betty frowned. "I remember my mother talking about having to pluck a chicken, but I've never done it. I've never seen anyone do it."

"It's not that hard," Ramona said. "I Googled it."

"*Why* are we doing this again?" Joanne feigned ignorance.

"We're doing it," Pam's voice was strained, "because we want to lend an air of authenticity to our program this year."

"We're doing it because Pastor Miranda says we can't wear our Pilgrim costumes," Betty said.

Pam shot Betty a glance. "Okay, Ramona. If you're the expert, tell us what to do."

Ramona shoved her hands in the pockets of her coveralls and leaned over the bird. "The first thing you do, is you boil a big pot of water. And then you dip the duck in the boiling water, but not for too long, or it starts to cook. Then as soon as you pull it up out of the boiling water, you dunk it in ice."

"Whatever for?" Betty asked.

"Makes it easier to get the feathers out," Ramona said.

"Right here in the church kitchen?" Betty asked.

"You got a better idea?" Ramona parried.

"Yeah. The Sparrow Meat Market." No one even smiled.

"Come on, everyone," Linda said. "We've made it this far." Miranda had to admire her fearlessness. "The little guy sacrificed himself so we could be authentic. The least we can do is follow through."

"Won't it make for an awful mess?" Joanne said, not looking up.

"It was messy back in the days of the Pilgrims," Linda said. "Thanksgiving was not this sanitized affair where everybody just showed up with a covered dish."

"And a bunch of Tupperware containers for taking home leftovers," Ramona chimed in.

"With a store-bought turkey where all you have to do is remember to take that package of giblets out of the inside," Edna added.

"I like the ones with the pop-up timer," Donna said.

"We need to stay focused," Pam cut in. "Ramona?"

"It's basically a seven-step process," Ramona continued. "Dunk it in boiling water, then in ice. Pluck. When all the feathers are out, you hang it upside down and gut it. Whatever you do, don't cut into the glands, or it'll give off this horrible smell. But you want to get the glands out. Nobody wants to eat glands."

Miranda nodded, remembering when she'd prepared button quail at The Pellegrino. Those tiny birds were barely bigger than a large egg. Tricky.

"Is that it?" Pam asked.

"Nope. Then you cut off the feet and the head and do something with the organs—I forget what."

"Save the liver," Miranda said. "It's delicious—and expensive."

"And then you're done, right?" Pam kept her eyes on the dead bird.

"Almost. Then you wash it. Rinse it down with warm water. Then you're done. Well, then you're ready to roast it in the oven." Ramona looked triumphant.

Everyone turned at the sound of a cupboard door opening. They watched as Joanne lifted a stockpot off the top shelf. No one spoke as she placed it in the sink and turned on the tap.

"Well, we need to get the water boiling, don't we?" she said. "If we want to be authentic to the Pilgrims?"

★ ★ ★

The duck roast did not go well. At first, the women rallied to the task of preparing the bird for the oven. But two hours of messy, tedious work just about did them all in. Removing the feathers was endless. Cutting off its feet was brutal—although the heavy kitchen shears helped—but when Joanne nicked a gland with a paring knife, they all rushed out the side door to stand in the parking lot gulping air. Miranda considered calling a halt.

However, to everyone's credit, they had soldiered on. Finally, the little bird, thinner and sadder than anyone could have imagined, was ready for the roasting pan. The women slid it into the oven and then collapsed into chairs in the Fellowship Hall. Their spirits rose as a delicious aroma filled the room.

Unfortunately, roasted wild duck smells far better than it tastes. Miranda had forgotten how greasy wild ducks could be. As oil seeped into the pan, she tried to cheer everyone up.

"The fat's not all bad," Miranda said. "We can use it for cooking later." But seeing their faces as more grease leaked from the duck, she knew they weren't buying it.

Linda had declared that she could hear her left ventricle slamming shut.

They all had a taste. Words like *tough*, *greasy*, and *gamey* were muttered. Edna dramatically spit hers into the sink, flipping on the garbage disposal and running the tap. When they finally tossed the bird's remains into the trash, Pam opened a bottle of communion wine and filled paper cups from the Sunday School supply closet. Miranda knocked hers back like a shot and held it up for a refill. Authentic Pilgrim food had been permanently removed from the Thanksgiving menu.

★ ★ ★

Miranda poured a glass of Chardonnay and carried it to the front stoop of the rectory.

Streaks of pink and gold flamed in the early evening sky. Miranda sat on the top step and tugged her purple fleece jacket close against the cool sea breeze. A row of sugar maples lined the opposite side of the sandy lane, and she luxuriated in the drama of the brilliant orange leaves. Just beyond the maples, a rocky embankment led down to the beach. Smoke plumed out of her neighbor's chimney, and she breathed in the scent of a wood fire. An evening with this kind of chill made her wonder how cold a Maine winter might be. She had arrived in Sparrow in late March, a chill, damp month in coastal New England.

Colville had left a basket of red and yellow apples on the bench in the mudroom, and she planned on baking some sort of apple extravaganza to take to Peg. Peg didn't eat many sweets, but she needed cheering up, and to Miranda, cheering up meant something with butter, sugar, and heavy cream.

She went inside, poured more wine, and returned to the stoop. This was when she really missed Jason. He would have helped her figure out the Seattle dilemma. He had been a part of her life as a chef, but never her life as a pastor. It was nothing they had ever shared. Which meant that Miranda-the-Pastor was a life lived entirely without him. Was that why she was even considering going back to the restaurant world? So that she could reclaim Jason?

The shadows grew longer. She and Jason often went up to the roof of their Cambridge apartment building and watched the sunset, the lights slowly blinking on across the city. They talked about their day, shared a bottle of wine. She wiped her teary eyes with the sleeve of her hoodie.

Jason hated it when she did that. She could almost hear his voice. "You know, I can get you a tissue."

She was surprised that his face came so clearly to her tonight. Lately, she found that she couldn't conjure him up. His smile, his sandy eyebrows and green eyes, the way his hair fell over his forehead as he leaned over the potter's wheel in his studio. Gone. As if he had moved away.

In truth, she had moved away, and he had stayed. Although her life had changed in huge and dramatic ways since she had seen him last, Jason was frozen in time. She pictured him the last time they were together. He lay still, his breathing raspy, the various machines in the room blinking and beeping. She felt again the darkness and despair of those last hours. The hospice nurse coming in and out. The attending doctor. Father Mike, the hospital chaplain who had stood beside her the entire time, her anchor in a tossing sea.

She slipped her phone out of her hoodie pocket and clicked on the archived voicemail.

★ ★ ★

Miranda stood in the cozy kitchen of her small cottage and breathed in the familiar scents of home cooking: the comforting aroma of that morning's freshly baked bread, last night's pot of simmering tomato sauce, lingering scents of basil, oregano, and rosemary. Throughout her life, each kitchen she had called her own had been a sanctuary of sorts. Whether it was in an apartment or a house, the kitchen was where she found comfort, peace and inspiration. The simple act of cooking and baking brought her a sense of emotional balance where she could shake off some of her stress. And find at least a little sense of serenity.

The warm yellow walls, the framed print of the cover from Thomas Keller's *The French Laundry Cookbook*, and copper pots and pans hanging from the ceiling gave the small space a cheerful appeal. A small round table held a vase of purple chrysanthemums, given to her by the deacons the day before in church. The deep, rich hues of the flowers seemed to come alive in the early evening light, their petals unfurling in a riot of violet hues.

The deacons couldn't have known it, but at her wedding, she had carried purple chrysanthemums. Were the flowers a reminder of the beauty of new beginnings, or a reminder of what she had lost? She gave herself a shake. Enough already.

"Hey Google," she commanded. "Play Beyoncé." She needed to reboot her brain and move back into the present.

As the pulsing beat of "Single Ladies" boomed through the kitchen, Miranda slipped off her fleece jacket and donned her favorite apron—the one she had worn on her last night at The Pellegrino. With a soft sigh, she opened her grandmother's treasured tin box of recipes. No more sweet apple dishes. Peg needed something substantial and satisfying—a dish that only a former professional chef at a prestigious Boston restaurant could master.

Her eyes fell on the recipe for *Timballo di maccheroni*, a hearty baked pasta dish made with spaghetti-like maccheroni, and a medley of vegetables that Peg would like: eggplant, mushrooms, peppers, and tomatoes. Normally, her grandmother would include seafood in the dish, but Peg was a committed ovo-vegetarian. *Timballo*, though a bit complicated to create, was still the epitome of comfort food—exactly what Peg needed.

Since Harmon's sighting from the widow's walk, Samson had vanished without a trace. Not a good sign, considering how large and gregarious Samson was. Miranda dreaded the day they heard the terrible news from Lewis or, worse, from the highway department. Samson knew nothing about oncoming traffic. She took a deep breath, focusing on the task at hand, determined to lose herself in the creation of a sumptuous dish. Cooking was how she worked out her demons.

With a new sense of purpose, Miranda plucked the recipe card for *Timballo di maccheroni* from her grandmother's tin box and took a quick inventory of her pantry. The list of ingredients was extensive, but each was pretty basic, and basic ingredients, she had long ago learned, were the cornerstone of good cooking: macaroni pasta, Béchamel sauce, tomato sauce, mozzarella cheese, Parmesan cheese, olive oil, and breadcrumbs for topping. She then glanced into the fridge: one lone eggplant, two red peppers, three medium-sized tomatoes, and a container of sliced mushrooms. Everything she needed.

Her earlier melancholy lifted as she chopped, diced, and measured. Food and cooking, she thought, would make a great sermon.

The Last Supper Seen from the Perspective of the Cook
Manna from Heaven or Was it Pasta?
Loaves and Fishes: Main Course or Just the Appetizer? Lots of potential there.

Miranda filled a pot with water and placed it on the stove for the pasta. She then heated some olive oil in a pan and, as soon as it began to sizzle and pop, she added diced onions and garlic. She stirred, breathing in the fragrant aroma, until they were translucent. The image of a roasted duck floating in its own oil briefly crossed her mind.

"Google, play Taylor Swift!" Miranda let the upbeat lyrics of "End Game" drive out the last of her grief. She turned up the volume and sang along as the aroma of onions, basil, and oregano filled the kitchen. She had always loved to sing, but after her first Sunday at St. Gabe's, she noticed the deacons surreptitiously cutting her microphone whenever a hymn began. So she sang in her kitchen, if nowhere else.

The water boiled over with a foaming hiss, and she grabbed the pot, slid it to another burner, and poured in the *maccheroni*. She had doubled the recipe so she could take one casserole to Peg and keep another for herself.

Howard, awakened by the rising moon, appeared in the kitchen doorway, his snout twitching.

"Good evening, Howard. Or should I say, good morning?" Miranda opened the fridge again and removed a container of chopped purple cabbage. She tossed a handful onto the tile floor under the round kitchen table. "Your breakfast."

When the pasta was a minute past *al dente*, she drained it, reserving a little starchy water. Then she tossed diced eggplant, peppers, and tomatoes into the pan with the pasta, and while everything simmered, she grated mozzarella cheese into a bowl and mixed in a handful of breadcrumbs.

Tired of Taylor Swift, she told Google to play Justin Timberlake's "Can't Stop the Feeling!" Jason's favorite song. Whenever he heard it coming from the kitchen, he would grab a wooden spoon for a microphone and sing, doing all sorts of ridiculous dance moves around her. Unlike Miranda, Jason had a rich voice that found the note and beat without effort. She grabbed a clean dishtowel and wiped her eyes again.

She added the *maccheroni* to the vegetable mixture and stirred until all the pasta was coated, then spooned it into a greased baking dish. She topped each casserole with breadcrumbs, put them in the oven, and set the timer for fifty minutes. She had once ruined a *Cotolette alla Parmigiana* and filled the kitchen with black smoke by picking up a volume of John MacQuarrie's *Principles of Christian Theology*. Four chapters and sixty-seven minutes later, the smoke alarms had blasted throughout the apartment.

★ ★ ★

"You didn't need to bring a casserole to cheer me up. I am perfectly fine."

"I know you are," Miranda said as she sat back into the Chesterfield chair, careful not to spill her mug of coffee. "But a little comfort food is good."

She watched Peg open a package of brown card stock from the supply closet. "What are you doing?"

"The Scoutmaster called; he's running late. I'm pitching in to get the craft ready for the Webelos meeting. For some reason, they need ten brown oak leaves for every Scout."

"How many Scouts?"

"Seventeen."

"That's a lot of oak leaves. Want some help?"

"You have bigger fish to fry." Peg opened her desk drawer and pulled out a folder labeled *Stewardship*. "Have you looked over the pledge card ideas yet?" She handed the folder to Miranda. "The stewardship chair wants an answer so they can be printed today."

"Look them over? Why?"

"Six different designs. They want to know which one you like."

"How designed can a pledge card be?"

"You'd be surprised."

Miranda dropped the folder in her lap. "Did Harry tell you about the disappearing cookies?" She recounted the story as her secretary traced oak leaf patterns onto the card stock.

Peg looked up. "Hmm—mysterious cookie shenanigans, an open window, and an attempt to pick a lock with a pocket knife."

"Remember how the other day we thought Colville had slept on my sofa and left the coffee pot on?"

Peg nodded, turning her focus back on oak leaves.

"I asked him about it. Turns out he wasn't even in the building that night. He had gone on a fishing trip with his son."

"They probably returned the cookies when they heard you." Peg picked up the card stock page and began to cut out the leaves.

"Who?"

"Whoever is living in the building." Peg leaned back, brown card stock in one hand, scissors in the other, and glanced at the calendar on the wall next to her desk. "They've been here for two weeks at least."

The women sat in silence, staring at each other. Finally, Miranda spoke. "They could be here right now."

"Could be."

"You're awfully casual about all this." She would have expected Peg to organize a search party. Peg had protested when the Men's Group held a meeting on Tuesday instead of their scheduled Monday. She had banned the knitting ladies from the Youth Room after they left empty teacups on the ping-pong table.

Peg shrugged. "I volunteer at the homeless shelter in Portland. You'd be surprised how many people are without safe and secure housing. When I was a girl, people had family. Working full-time meant you could afford a decent place to live, food on the table, healthcare, a pension, even. But things have changed. And not for the better."

"So you're okay with someone living in the building?"

"Of course not. It's just that homelessness is complicated. It's not as simple as going to a shelter."

"I agree."

"The members of your vestry won't agree. I can tell you that right now."

"So what should I do? Find the homeless person and throw them out?" Miranda heard her voice get tight. "Not on my watch."

"Good heavens. Don't get so dramatic. Whoever they are, they'll move along before you know it. People who experience chronic homelessness know how to find temporary shelter and then disappear before they're discovered."

"We're a church. We should do something."

"You can't change the world."

"Are you sure?" Miranda gazed at Peg over her coffee cup. "Isn't that why I became a priest? To change the world?"

"And I thought it was for the money and prestige." Peg gave her a glimmer of a smile. "Decide on those pledge cards so I can get them printed. And don't forget your clergy meeting at the hospital."

CHAPTER SEVENTEEN

Miranda dug her phone out of her pocket. Five o'clock. She had searched for her car in the hospital parking lot for an embarrassing ten minutes, then remembered she had walked to the clergy meeting. The plan had been to make good on her goal of getting more exercise, but now the thought of walking all the way home was just annoying. She zipped her hoodie against the damp breeze and, head down, started down the walk-in front of the hospital. Suddenly, something heavy slammed into her. She reeled sideways into the decorative shrubbery planted at the edge of the parking lot.

"Oh my gosh." A man's voice said from above. A thicket of leafy branches blocked her sight. "I am so sorry. Give me your hand. Here." A strong arm pulled her up. "My apologies, I'm trying to get to—Oh. Pastor Miranda!"

"Adam." Miranda picked a bit of leaf from the corner of her mouth. "Nice to see you again."

"I doubt that, since I just knocked you over!" He looked her over, his blue eyes concerned as she plucked several spiky green leaves out of her hair. "Are you sure you're okay?"

"I'm fine. Really."

Adam looked flawless, as always. Sleek business suit, perfectly knotted tie pulling together the collar points of a crisp white shirt. How could she have worn her oldest hoodie and white cross-trainers? At least her black clergy shirt and collar were wrinkle-free for once, though the patina of mulch and yew leaves might have ruined that.

"Where are you going in such a hurry?" She spat out the final leaf.

"Aunt Lucy. I'm sorry, but if you're okay, I've got to go—emergency surgery." He turned and ran in loping strides toward the hospital's main entrance.

"What happened?" she shouted after him. Miranda followed him inside. If Lucy was having emergency surgery, she needed her priest.

Miranda skidded to a stop at the nurse's station in time to overhear Dr. Hazeltine say to Adam, "Mrs. McClain was admitted two hours ago with an emergency appendectomy. She did very well and has just been brought into recovery."

"Appendectomy?" Adam took a deep breath and ran his long fingers through his wavy hair. "And she's in recovery now? I mean, she's elderly and I—" Adam's voice caught.

Miranda realized he couldn't speak.

Dr. Hazeltine put a hand on Adam's arm. "Mrs. McClain has been my patient for twenty years. I just checked on her, and I couldn't be happier with her condition."

"Yes. All right then." Adam leaned against the nurse's station. "It's just that no one could reach me, and so I only just got the message, and I was in Portland. I came as quickly as I could."

"Would you like to see her?" Without waiting for an answer, the doctor turned on the heel of her black Italian shoes and walked down the hall. "Come with me."

A blue hospital blanket engulfed Lucy as she slept deeply. A machine beeped at the head of the bed, and an IV was attached to her thin arm. Miranda wished she had one of the prayer shawls she usually gave to parishioners in the hospital. She would bring one tomorrow.

Adam caught his breath.

Miranda saw as he gently rested his hand on top of Lucy's hand, covering it entirely. "Oh, Aunt Lucy," he said quietly. "I'm sorry I wasn't here for you today."

Lucy's eyelids fluttered, but she slept on.

"You were at work," Miranda said softly. "In Portland. You couldn't have known she would need an emergency appendectomy."

Adam straightened the hospital blanket and brushed his fingertips over Lucy's forehead. "She called me this morning to say she was having stomach pains," he said, his voice tight. "I was walking into a meeting. I told her that she was probably fine and to lie down and that I would call later." He turned to Miranda, his blue eyes clouded with emotion.

"But I didn't call her. In fact, I forgot about her until I checked my messages. By then, she was already in surgery."

Miranda didn't reply for a moment. When she did, she chose her words with care.

"An elderly person in need can be exhausting—emotionally and physically. And even though you're not Lucy's daily caretaker—as I recall, your mother said you were to 'check in on her'—things are falling on you. Big things. From cats to snickerdoodles to medical emergencies."

Adam removed a handkerchief—pressed and folded—out of his pocket.

The man uses an actual handkerchief. Miranda usually kept a tissue balled up in her jeans pocket. Or a piece of toilet paper.

He pressed the folded handkerchief against each eye and cleared his throat.

She gave him a moment. "For example," she continued, "Lucy called you this morning about the stomach pains. I don't think it is such a terrible thing that you forgot to call her back later in the day. As a pastor, I've done worse, believe me."

"That's generous of you. Are you always this nice?"

She laughed quietly. "I try to be."

He slid the handkerchief back into his pocket. "Where were you going earlier? Before I knocked you into the shrubbery?" He smiled, his blue eyes gazing into hers.

To Miranda's surprise, she felt an unfamiliar flicker of longing. She swallowed hard and cleared her throat. "I was about to walk home."

"Walk? You don't drive?"

"I'm trying to get more exercise."

"Couldn't you just go to the gym?"

"I'm not really the gym type."

"There's a gym type?"

"Yes, and it's not me." She didn't add that she couldn't afford a gym membership.

"Are you determined to walk home? Or may I offer you a ride? I owe you." He reached over and removed a piece of mulch from her hair.

"Sure. But first, I want to say a prayer for Lucy."

"Can you include me in that prayer? I need some help with all this."

CHAPTER EIGHTEEN

"A strawberry box," Adam said, standing in front of the rectory. "With a slate roof. Fascinating."

"Excuse me?"

"A strawberry box house. An architectural style from right after World War II. Lots of them constructed in this part of the country." She thought she must not have looked appropriately impressed because he added, "And Canada."

"I thought it was a Cape."

"Ah, rookie mistake." He pointed to the bottom of the front wall. "This style uses a square foundation—instead of the usual rectangular. It's named after the boxes that once held strawberries."

"How cool."

"And yours has a slate roof which was a little unusual. But slate was a common material in the mid-century." He paused and appeared to be deep in thought. "I think there were two slate quarries in Maine at one time."

"Really?' Miranda looked with new appreciation at the blue squares covering the roof.

"I'd love to take a look at your house. I mean, if you feel like inviting me in. And, of course, it would be my big chance to meet Howard."

Inside, she took his overcoat and gestured. "Take a look!"

"Sweet," Adam said. He wandered into the bedroom and then the kitchen, removing his suit coat and loosening his tie. Miranda was glad she had straightened up before leaving that morning. All underwear was tossed into the hamper instead of scattered across the bedroom floor.

"This house would be far too small for anyone in today's world, but for the World War II generation, it was not just adequate. It was a luxury," Adam commented.

"It's perfect for me. And it's been well cared for by the church. Congregations often neglect their rectories."

Adam tapped a beam. "They don't make houses like this anymore."

She had never seen him in his shirt sleeves. Undeniably a good look. "Speaking of houses, I need to let Howard out." Adam followed her to Howard's Hobbit house and tiny fenced yard. "Howard, wake up. It's nighttime."

"That's something you don't hear often," Adam remarked, peering into the little pen. "Wake up, it's nighttime."

"The joys of a nocturnal pet." She opened the gate to the tiny fence so Howard could scamper around the rectory. "He probably won't come out until we walk away."

"Where did you get a Hobbit house?"

"His previous owner was a big Tolkien fan, and apparently, keeping your hedgehog in a Hobbit house is a thing."

"Cute. I feel bad I didn't bring the customary purple cabbage or fresh snail."

They watched as Howard inched out of the door, snout twitching. He blinked and looked up at Miranda as if to say, "Well? Is this all?"

She walked over to her desk in the corner and pulled out the blue recycling bin from underneath. She dumped the half-full container on its side, and a week's worth of paper cascaded out. Howard immediately scurried over and disappeared, emitting a series of snuffling grunts and snorts.

"A pile of loose paper?" Adam said. "That makes him happy?"

"Hedgehog heaven."

"Good to know."

Their eyes met and she felt a rush of adrenaline, which made her feel as if she needed to say something brilliant, clever, or amazingly witty. But for the life of her, she couldn't think of a thing. Instead, she trailed behind Adam as he walked into the kitchen. He rapped his knuckles midway up one of the walls.

"Solid as a rock. And look at those crossbeams," he laughed. "Sorry, I'm kind of a geek when it comes to old architecture. Have you ever been inside the button factory in Sparrow?"

"I thought it was abandoned?" She had been intrigued by the tall, nineteenth-century brick structure at the south end of town. "A magnificent old building."

"You like old buildings, then?"

"Of course. You can't be a pastor in New England and not like old buildings, since so many of our churches are antiques. And that includes their plumbing and electricity." It wasn't just old church buildings that she liked, but old manuscripts, ancient liturgy, and historic hymns. She had a rich appreciation for the things of previous generations. "I'm a pastor. All pastors look back with appreciation and yet forward with hope."

"Great way to put it." Adam's eyes met hers again. "Old buildings are what I do for a living. I'm an architectural historian."

Miranda pulled out a kitchen chair and sat down at the table. "Really? I knew you said you went to architecture school, but I didn't realize what that meant exactly."

"I do mostly preservation," he said, walking across to the mudroom. "I research and seek to understand an old building—like the button factory—and then repurpose it, if possible."

"Are you repurposing the button factory?"

"Trying to. Would you like to see it sometime? I could give you a tour," he offered, his gaze shifting to the side yard.

He looked back at her, a hint of surprise in his eyes. "Really? You'd be interested?"

She laughed. "Really. Of course."

Adam smiled, seeming pleased. "Great. We could go next week if you're free."

"Sure." Calm down, she told herself as he admired the double-glazed windows in the mudroom. A tour of an old building isn't exactly a romantic date. Though with those eyes, he could make a sewage plant tour exciting.

★ ★ ★

Adam tilted the dish of *Timballo di maccheroni* toward Miranda. "There's a small portion left," he said. "It's yours if you want it. Speak now or forever lose the pasta."

"I don't want it."

"You're lying. You know you want it."

She did want it. "Let's split it."

"Fine, but we have to split it the way my mother always made my brother and me split things. One of us cuts it in half, and the other chooses their piece."

"Brilliant. All right. You cut. I choose." She watched as he drove the spoon down the middle of the piece. "And I graciously select the smaller piece," she said.

"Ah, I knew your generosity would win out. My brother would not have been so kind."

She waited while he slid the piece of the *Timballo* onto her plate and then stabbed a corner with her fork. "You and your brother are twins, right?"

"Aaron is seven minutes younger than I. Lives in Des Moines with a lovely wife and three daughters."

"Do you see him often?"

"Not like I should. Christmas, weddings. And I hate to say it, funerals."

"Any sisters?"

"One. Older. She lives in Connecticut. I always tell people that she's the one with the Mercedes, swimming pool, and—" Adam's eyes flashed at her over his wine glass.

"Room for a pony!"

They laughed together. "Hyacinth Bucket in *Keeping Up Appearances*."

"You like Hyacinth?" He took a sip of wine.

"Of course. I love British comedies."

"Me, too. What's your favorite?"

"Um," Miranda thought for a moment. "It's a tossup between *Derry Girls* and *Ghosts*."

"Both admirably funny. Guess what my favorite is? And I'm not just saying this either. You know, because of present company."

Miranda scraped a bit of melted cheese stuck to the bottom of the baking dish and popped it into her mouth. "*Rev?*"

"Not even close."

"I give up."

"*The Vicar of Dibley.*"

"Ha! I do love Dawn French." She watched Adam refill their wine glasses. They had been sitting in the kitchen talking for almost two hours. When had she enjoyed sitting and talking with a man her age for two hours? Not since Jason.

"How about you? Siblings?" Adam asked.

"Nope. No siblings."

"An only child?"

"Afraid so."

"That was my dream life, you know. All the attention, all the time."

"It had its drawbacks."

"I suppose."

They sat quietly for a moment, hearing Howard scurry across the bedroom floor. The clock in the hall chimed nine times.

"If you don't mind my asking," Adam said. "Aunt Lucy mentioned that you were once married but now you're not. Are you divorced?"

"My husband passed away," Miranda said evenly. "Five years ago."

Adam held her gaze, his blue eyes warm. "I'm sorry."

"Thanks." She waited for Adam to ask how her husband died. It was the box people felt required to tick off.

"Is that why you became a priest?"

Okay. Points for Adam. "His death had a lot to do with it."

He leaned back, the antique wooden chair creaking. "Tell me. If you want to."

"Well, let's see. I grew up in the Episcopal Church. Sunday School, church camp, Confirmation. But then, when I went to college, I left it all behind."

"Left the church behind or left God behind?"

"Good distinction. The church, mostly. I suppose I always kept my belief in God. But not in any active sense." She pushed her hair back behind her ears and twirled the wine in her glass. "When Jason, my husband, was first diagnosed with ALS—"

"ALS?" Adam's eyebrows shot up. "Brutal."

"Yes." She looked out the kitchen window for a moment and then turned back to Adam. "I took a leave of absence from the restaurant to stay at home with him full-time." She cleared her throat and gulped some wine. "And I am glad I did. He died sooner than—than I thought he would. He got a chest cold, which you don't want if you have ALS. I admitted him to the hospital right away. And I was entirely certain that I would be bringing him back home. But he went into respiratory failure. And well, that was the end."

They both sat, unspeaking. Miranda was grateful for the stillness. Most people felt the need to fill in the silence, but Adam simply waited.

"I sat in the room next to him long after he was gone. The doctor took forever to arrive and sign the death certificate." She stared into her wine glass. She didn't usually go into detail about the night Jason died. Sitting at his side in the darkened hospital room, listening to his breathing grow slower and more labored, longer and longer moments between each breath, until the moment when there was only silence.

"I waited on the doctor. A nurse came in and shut everything off. You know, all the machines he was hooked up to. Removed tubes. I hadn't seen Jason without something blinking or beeping for so long that the emptiness was—desolate. I sat alone in the dark, just light from the hall. Then I felt a presence beside me. I turned and saw someone sitting there. For a moment, I thought it was an angel. She smiled.

"In a way, maybe it was. It was Father Mike Newcomer, the hospital chaplain. He stayed next to me while the doctor came in and declared the time of death, and then he stayed until the funeral home finally came and took Jason." She stopped and took another sip of wine.

"Then he sat with me in the hospital lobby waiting for my parents who drove up from the Cape." She paused, remembering. "And that whole time, we barely spoke. But I found so much strength in his—presence." She turned and looked into Adam's eyes.

"When it was over—the arrangements, the funeral—I tried to return to my old job. At Pellegrino's. But it wasn't for me anymore." She leaned back in her chair. "I applied to seminary, and the rest is history."

"Just like that? You went from head chef at Pellegrino's to seminary?"

"Well, not entirely just like that. But that was the start."

"You're amazing." Adam lifted his glass.

"Not really." They clinked glasses, and she smiled. "You don't know how much I muddle through."

"You survived a devastating experience and emerged from it wanting to help people."

"Not to sound horribly sentimental, but I followed my heart. My broken heart, to be honest. And to be even more honest—helping people was the only thing that helped me."

"Again, amazing." This time he said it quietly. "And now you're here. In Sparrow."

She nodded.

"I'm glad you're here." His voice quiet, serious.

She breathed in for a moment. "Me, too."

He picked up the wine bottle and refilled their glasses. "Do you miss The Pellegrino and all that came with it?"

"I sometimes do. Mostly when I cook. "I can't help comparing my life as a priest in Sparrow to a chef in Boston. Or, you know—anywhere."

"So how does it all look? When you hold it up to being a priest in Sparrow?"

She hesitated, wondering if she should tell him about Tony's offer and her dilemma. She decided not to. She liked being the only one who knew she could stay or leave. If Tony's offer ever got out to the church members, all ecclesiastical chaos would break loose.

"Sometimes," she admitted. "But being a head chef isn't just cooking; it's a lot of other stuff that's not so much fun: hiring, training, state regulations, budgets."

"So it's a job?"

"It can be."

"Not all glamorous like being an architectural historian?"

She laughed. "No. Not glamorous like that." Their eyes met and she held his gaze for a long moment.

"It's late." He stood quickly. "I should call the hospital and check on Aunt Lucy."

"Of course," Miranda nodded. "I'll clean up here."

Adam stepped outside to make the call, his voice a low murmur through the window. Miranda busied herself stacking the dishes and wiping down the table, trying not to eavesdrop. When he returned a few minutes later, his expression was hard to read.

"Everything okay?" she asked, pausing with a stack of plates in her hands.

Adam ran a hand through his hair, his brow furrowed. "Yes and no. Aunt Lucy's stable. But they want to run more tests tomorrow."

"I will check in on her first thing tomorrow."

"Thanks. And thanks for dinner. It was nice. Talking and everything."

"It was nice." The intensity of her desire for Adam to stay caught her off guard and made her feel a bit uneasy. It had been a while since she had felt such a strong connection to someone. Adam was charming, funny, smart, handsome. Everything she had loved about Jason—only different. She realized she had been longing for the company of a man like Adam. She also knew that men like Adam were hard to find. And suddenly, she didn't want him to leave her.

"Let me help clean up before I go." He grabbed the empty serving bowl from the table with one hand and scooped up the empty wine glasses with the other.

"Oh, no. It's hardly anything." Miranda felt a pang of disappointment. She didn't want the evening to end. What she really wanted was to feel his arms around her.

"Well, then," Adam said, setting the dish and glasses on the counter by the sink. He turned back to Miranda, his eyes meeting hers.

He reached for her hands, his touch gentle but sure. Miranda's heart raced, her palms suddenly warm against his.

"Thanks for the *Timballo*. And the wine. And the conversation."

He leaned in slightly. Miranda's breath caught. Her gaze flicked to his lips, then back to his eyes. A familiar mix of excitement and nerves fluttered in her stomach, urging her to step closer.

She hesitated. Should she lean in, too? Or was she misreading the moment? "Thanks for coming to my strawberry box house." Did she really just say that? *Thanks for coming to my strawberry box house? What a complete dork.*

Adam laughed and dropped her hands. "I love your strawberry box house. This sounds like the world's worst pick-up line ever, but I really would like to come back and look at your rim joists."

Miranda laughed out loud, her awkwardness dissipating.

He turned and called into the front room. "Howard? Very nice to meet you. Next time I promise to bring purple cabbage and fresh snails." He turned back to Miranda. "Is he snubbing me or is he always like this?"

"He's snubbing you."

"My fault. My mother told me always bring a hostess gift."

She walked him to the stoop, listening for a moment to the waves breaking onto the beach.

"Give me a call," she said, trying to sound casual but not disinterested. But also, not too interested. But interested enough. *Oh, give it up.*

"I will," Adam whispered as he leaned in closer to her. She could feel the heat radiating from his body, causing her fingertips to tingle wildly. But before she could fully indulge in the moment, lift her lips to his, he pulled away. Still, he hesitated, holding her in his gaze. Then he turned and hurried down the steps and to his car. "Thanks for dinner," he called back.

The quiet purr of the silver Lexus was the only sound on Honeysuckle Lane as she watched the taillights disappear. *Thanks for coming to my strawberry box house.* She shook her head. Was it any wonder that she hadn't been kissed in five years?

CHAPTER NINETEEN

A square of yellow light from the basement window cast a feeble glow on the rhododendron bush. She must have left the lights on in the Youth Room. Miranda shoved her car back into park and disengaged the seatbelt. All she wanted was to go home and collapse on the couch with a glass of wine. It had been three days since her pasta dinner at the rectory with Adam, and her phone had stayed silent.

Texting him first seemed needy. Maybe a joke about coming to look at her rim joists? Wasn't relaxed how you did things these days? Feign complete disinterest in the other person? At least, that's what she had read on a romance blog. Which was about as close as she would ever get to figuring out the dating scene.

Jason and Miranda had married in their early twenties, so at forty-two, her dating savvy was embarrassingly limited. Of course, she and Adam—rim joists aside—were not dating. Not anything close to it.

She sat for a minute in the dark parking lot, staring at the light burning in the Youth Room window. The Youth Room, the meeting site of tonight's confirmation class, was a mildewy space with a smell of pizza and sneakers. Bean bag chairs arranged in a circle on the floor, a slouchy sofa pushed against the wall, thick blue carpet from the '90s, and a giant poster of Laughing Jesus taped to the cinder block walls. The Youth Room was in the basement at the end of a long, shadowy hall. Maybe the light could just stay on.

Miranda opened her car door and slid out, zipping her hoodie against the chill. She walked across the dim parking lot and opened the door to the empty, shadowy building. How could a building be so warm and cheerful during the day but so creepy at night? The heavy side door closed behind her with a bang that echoed in the cavernous vestibule. She thought about the conversation with Peg. Was someone living at the church? There hadn't been any further evidence for a while. No more pushed-in windows, missing cookies, or burnt coffee pots.

She fumbled for the light switch and started down the wooden stairs that led to the Youth Room, each footfall producing an echoey creak. She startled as the old boiler kicked on.

At the bottom of the stairs, she flipped another switch. The single bulb provided barely enough illumination to see to the end of the hallway. She would tell Colville to replace it with an LED bulb pronto. A line of light shone under the bottom of the Youth Room door. Obviously, she remembered to shut the door but not to turn off the light. She paused, her heart pounding. There was no reason to get so spooked.

Just as she grabbed the door handle, there was a click, and the light from under the door went out.

Someone was in there.

Miranda froze. She couldn't turn and run down the hall and up the stairs as much as she wanted to. That would mean turning her back to the door and to whoever stood behind it. But throwing open the door, and charging in, was equally terrifying.

"Pastor, is that you?" Colville Dubey's gruff voice called out. An arc of bright light from his flashlight illuminated the dark hall. "Good heavens," he said, coming up to her. "What are you doing down here?"

"Someone is in the Youth Room," she whispered.

"Is that so?" Colville said loudly. "Who?"

"I don't know," she replied in a stage whisper. "The light was on, and now it's out."

He grabbed the door handle. "Hello, there," Colville called out in a cheerful voice. He shoved the door open and, reaching inside, flipped on the light.

In front of the picture of the Laughing Jesus stood Alejandra Romero.

★ ★ ★

Harry arrived at the church looking as if he had been asleep for at least an hour before Miranda called him.

"Harry Hopkins," she said, standing as he came into her office. "Meet Alejandra Romero."

"Pleased to meet you, Mrs. Romero." Harry gave a concerned smile, glancing from Miranda to Alejandra. "No, no. Don't stand up. You look, well—very—" He turned to Miranda.

"*Embarazada*," Alejandra said, one hand resting on her abdomen. Her eyes were tired and her long black hair was pulled back in a sleek braid that fell halfway down her back. She wore a simple white cotton blouse, a small tear on the sleeve, denim jeans with holes at the knees and frayed hemlines. Her clothes were clean but had seen better days. Miranda noticed that she wore the same pair of sneakers, scuffed and worn.

"Pregnant," Miranda translated. "Probably close to full term."

All she had told Harry on the phone was that the cookie thief was at the church, and she wanted him to meet her.

"Her?" Harry had said.

"Her," Miranda replied.

She didn't mention that they had already spent the past two hours sitting in her office, eating leftover chocolate cake from the Sunday School Committee meeting and sipping on steaming cups of coffee. Alejandra told Miranda her whole story. Or at least a lot of it.

When Miranda heard what Alejandra wanted, she reached for the phone and called Harry. "And anyway," she had said to Harry on the phone, "Colville's here. He's upstairs, vacuuming the sanctuary."

Harry slipped off his jacket and sank into one of the wing chairs. "I wouldn't mind a slice of that cake, if you don't mind," he said with a glance at the coffee table strewn with empty plates and coffee cups.

"Coming right up," she said. You had to love a senior warden who would eat cake at midnight with the person who had been hiding in his church.

As Harry tucked into his chocolate cake, she gave Alejandra an encouraging look.

"I have been living here in the *iglesia*, *Señor*," Alejandra began. "In the church."

Harry swallowed a mouthful of cake and dabbed his mouth with a paper napkin. "I figured that much out, Mrs. Romero." He glanced at Miranda.

"I thank you for your *generosidad*," Alejandra said.

"Yes, our generosity. Of course, but Mrs. Romero, people can't live in the church." Harry's voice was gentle, yet resolute. "It's not meant for that. There are building issues. Insurance. Fire hazard. Why don't you let me give you a ride to the shelter in Portland?"

At the word "shelter," Alejandra paled. She lurched forward to stand. Nine months pregnant made jumping to one's feet impossible. She fell back and began to talk rapidly in Spanish.

Miranda interrupted. "He isn't sending you away. No one is. Tell the whole story. He'll listen. *Escuchará*."

"Listen to what?" Harry said.

"What she really wants."

"Which is?" He gave her an open look.

"Sanctuary."

Harry's eyes went wide. "Sanctuary?"

"Yes."

"You don't mean where people live in a church when they're illegal? To keep from being deported?" His eyes shot to Alejandra and back again to Miranda.

"Alejandra is an asylum seeker. She is not illegal. Not really, anyway." Miranda could hear the defensiveness in her voice. This wasn't how she had wanted this conversation to go.

Alejandra reached into her sweater pocket and withdrew a crumpled envelope. She handed it to Harry, who removed the letter and read silently.

"Good grief, this is complicated," he muttered and continued reading. "It says here that your asylum application was denied, but your case is being referred to Immigration Court. And you can't be deported while you're waiting for Immigration Court." He looked up. "So why hide out in the church?"

A look of frustration crossed Alejandra's face. *"Embarazada y deportada."* She blew out her breath. *"Embarazada y deportada."*

Harry looked at Miranda. "What?"

"Pregnant and deported. Pregnant women are automatically deported now."

"That's not true." He handed the letter back to Alejandra. "And what do you mean 'now'?"

A tight knot formed in Miranda's stomach. A familiar feeling these past few years. "It's the policy put in place by the last administration. No more babies born on United States soil to take up taxpayers' money."

"Oh, come on." Harry's voice was as edgy as she had ever heard from her senior warden.

"You don't believe me?" Miranda leaned forward, her eyes not leaving Harry's.

"No, I don't." His face had turned red.

"You and I must watch different news stations."

"Let's not go there, Pastor." Now, more than an edge.

"Go where, exactly? Like it or not, pregnant and deported is a thing. A woman about to give birth is unlikely to win in Immigration Court. And a woman alone? Forget it."

Miranda took a breath. Calm down, she told herself. Professional at all costs. This was the closest she had come to politics with church members. But why did welcoming a refugee—certainly a biblical imperative—have to be political?

Harry threw his head back and stared at the ceiling. Then, finally, he sat up and looked up at Miranda. "They're not going to deport a pregnant girl."

"Oh yeah? Children in cages?" Miranda felt herself losing her tiny grip on calm. "Or do you not believe that?"

"No. I don't, as a matter of fact. That was all the media."

"I have colleagues who have been to the border. Episcopal priests. They saw it with their own eyes."

Harry and Miranda glowered at each other across the demolished remains of the chocolate cake. Alejandra had slumped back on the couch, her eyes closed.

Harry stood up and walked to the window behind Miranda's desk. He stared out. "This is a mess, Pastor."

"I know you don't want to talk politics, but there is a reason it's a mess." Miranda knew she shouldn't be so sharp with Harry, but she hadn't realized that he was so—. She interrupted her own thoughts. They were on a slippery slope. Her only concern right now was Alejandra.

"Will you support offering her sanctuary in the church?"

"What does that even mean?" Harry looked at her incredulously. "She can't just live here forever."

"She doesn't want to live here forever. We would help her. Start by getting her an immigration lawyer, for one thing. Churches do this. They become places of sanctuary and help people like Alejandra." She felt her frustration mount.

"Get her a lawyer? Who's paying for that?"

"Fundraisers, crowdsourcing. I don't know. But what's your plan?" She glanced at Alejandra, who was looking increasingly uncomfortable with the rising tension. Miranda turned to her with a forced smile. "*Momentito, por favor.*" We'll be right back.

Alejandra nodded.

"*Discúlpenos.*" Excuse us.

Mirando and Harry stepped out into the hallway, closing the door behind them.

"You have no idea the hornet's nest you're kicking," Harry snapped. "No idea. You thought that Pilgrim thing of yours caused problems? That'll be a walk in the park compared to this."

"My *Pilgrim thing*?" She thought Harry had supported her efforts to bring the Pilgrim costumes to an end. Well, she had assumed he supported her. If she didn't have the support of the senior warden, then what did she have?

Harry's face softened. "You're right about those ridiculous costumes. But why do you have to change everything all at once?"

"I didn't ask her to seek us out. To find us and ask for sanctuary."

Harry blew out his breath. "What do you want me to do?"

"Can you call an emergency meeting of the vestry?"

"And divide the vestry like Moses and the Red Sea?"

"It's their decision, though, right?"

"I don't know. Harboring illegals isn't exactly spelled out in the church by-laws."

"Offering sanctuary isn't *harboring illegals.*"

"Sounds like it is to me."

"She's about to give birth, Harry." Miranda had been running on nervous energy for the past two hours, but she suddenly felt as tired and frayed as Alejandra looked. They stood in silence for a long moment.

"I think the vestry will do the right thing." Miranda finally said, infusing her voice with as much certainty as she could muster.

Harry grunted. He stood and slipped on his jacket. "She'll stay here for now?"

"I'll set her up here in the Youth Room. There's a couch. A bathroom down the hall."

"She'll need more than a couch and a bathroom."

"I know. But people will help out. You know, bring food, donate bedding, clothes."

Harry grunted. "When's that baby due?"

"Not sure."

"Why do you want to do this?"

"Because we're the church. And if we don't step up, what good are we?"

★ ★ ★

Peg froze at her keyboard. "Alejandra Romero? In the Youth Room? So that whole time we were chatting out in the prayer garden, she was living in the church?"

Miranda sank into the plush Chesterfield chair, the weight of exhaustion from a sleepless night settling heavily on her shoulders. Even a steaming cup of Jamaican Blue Dark Roast wouldn't chase away her fatigue. "You don't seem very surprised."

Peg shrugged. "Nothing surprises me these days."

"She's from Honduras and is at risk of being deported. She wants sanctuary from St. Gabe's."

Peg's eyebrows went up. "Sanctuary? Here?"

Miranda nodded over her coffee cup.

"Why us?"

"Probably because we were easy to break into. Open window and all. She's sleeping in the Youth Room."

"So we'll be like those churches on the news?"

Miranda leaned back and closed her eyes. "Exactly."

"And you want the church to do this? Stick its neck out for a girl no one knows?"

"I do. Mary gave birth in a borrowed stable." Miranda sat up, careful not to slosh her coffee out of the cup. She glared at her secretary. Exhausted, yet ready for a fight. "Offering hospitality is biblical. It's the whole message of the Gospel. And anyway, Alejandra's nine months pregnant." She fell back on the chair again. "She needs us."

The two women sat in silence for a moment, listening as the bell in the clocktower chimed nine times.

"If we give her sanctuary—officially, instead of her just hiding out here—she can't leave the building, right?" Peg asked.

"As soon as she steps outside the door, she risks being picked up by the Department of Immigration."

"And you are certain that they won't just come through the door and arrest her?"

"Technically, they can. But historically, ICE leaves churches alone." Miranda had spent half the night watching YouTube videos that explained immigration and the sanctuary movement. "People seek safety in a church so they can pursue their case legally. You know, instead of getting deported."

"Is that what she is doing now? Pursuing her case legally? From the couch in the Youth Room?"

"I'd say being nine months pregnant is probably her biggest concern at the moment."

The piercing noise of a smoke alarm filled the room. Peg jumped up. "Downstairs?" she said.

Miranda catapulted from the upholstered chair, this time spilling her coffee.

With hearts pounding and adrenaline pumping, they rushed into the hallway.

"Kitchen!" Peg shouted above the blaring alarm.

They sprinted down the stairs, their feet pounding against the tile floor. As they burst into the kitchen, Alejandra stood at the sink, her hand gripping a smoking skillet with a faded potholder. She was trying to stop the alarm by running water over the pan. She turned to face them with a look of panic.

"*Lo siento, lo siento*!" A stream of Spanish followed.

Peg grabbed the skillet while Miranda flipped off the stove burner and turned on the overhead fan.

Alejandra stood staring at them. Unzipped halfway, her faded Patriot's hoodie revealed a wrinkled and soiled T-shirt with the words "Portland Lobster" in faded letters. Her sweatpants looked a bit better than the shirt, but now the sole of one of her scuffed sneakers had broken away from the toe. Miranda realized that she would have to ask around for anyone who wore Alejandra's shoe size. The refrigerator would need to be stocked. Toiletries donated. Bedding, pillows, a change of clothes. Her mind raced.

"*Lo siento*. I wanted *comida*—food." Alejandra's thin cheeks were pink with shame.

"Why don't you sit down, and I'll see what I can make for you?" Peg said, turning to Alejandra pleasantly. "Do you like scrambled eggs? I think I can find a few eggs left from the Men's Breakfast last Friday. Maybe the Pastor here will pour you a glass of juice."

They sat across from Alejandra soon after, watching her finish a second plate of eggs.

"How old are you?" Peg asked.

"*Tengo diecinueve años*," Alejandra answered. "I am nineteen." Her long black hair was pulled back in a tight braid, and her eyes were red as though she had been crying.

Miranda thought she looked vulnerable and fierce at the same time.

"You're young to be so far from home." Peg exchanged a glance with Miranda.

Alejandra leaned back in her chair, her eyes filled with tears.

Miranda reached over and took Alejandra's hand. She was surprised at how small and cold it was. "Here." She grabbed several paper napkins and handed them to her. Alejandra wiped her eyes.

"Let's not get ahead of ourselves," Peg said as she refilled Alejandra's juice glass. "You need a good night's sleep and a few days of decent food." She paused. "And then, we will go from there."

Miranda noticed that Peg had said *we*.

CHAPTER TWENTY

Miranda awoke to a loud pounding on the rectory's front door and Peg's voice calling her name. Miranda jolted awake. Alejandra's face flashed in her mind, along with the image of a burning church. Alejandra had made a solemn vow to stay away from the kitchen stove. As Miranda stumbled out of bed, she braced herself, half-expecting to find Peg and the Sparrow fire chief waiting on her porch.

"Coming!" she yelled, crossing the front room in her bathrobe, and flinging open the door. Her secretary stood under the dome of the porch light, dressed in workout clothes and holding a flashlight.

"I heard from Lewis," Peg blurted out, her voice tight with concern. "Some campers at the State Park reported a gray wolf nosing around their campground. The ranger thought it sounded more like a big dog, especially since the gray wolf isn't exactly native to Sparrow State Park. The ranger called Lewis, and Lewis called me."

"Samson's been mistaken for a wolf before," Miranda said. Hope began to flicker. "I'll be ready in a minute." She dashed back into her bedroom and threw on whatever clothes lay on the floor by her bed. *Oh please, God,* she prayed fervently. *Let it be Samson.* She grabbed her old sneakers and ran out to the Volvo.

"They told the ranger that he took off into the woods," Peg said. Miranda grabbed the dashboard as Peg threw the Volvo into gear and peeled out of Honeysuckle Lane.

The Volvo skidded to a stop in front of the brown wooden sign, *Sparrow State Forest—Ranger Station.*

Peg leaned out the Volvo's window and let loose with an ear-splitting whistle while Miranda jumped out and shouted, "Samson!" She waited and then yelled his name again. Silence.

A lone blue pick-up truck with a Vermont license plate sat at the far end of the parking lot. Streaks of pink had appeared at the edge of the horizon as the morning sun peeked over the tree line. She would have found the quiet woods and crisp air any other day peaceful and refreshing. But this morning, it felt ominous. Zipping her hoodie, she wished she had grabbed a warm hat before heading out.

"Looking for that big dog?" A voice called out. Three college-age kids—two girls and a boy—emerged from the woods. Rumpled and bleary, they lugged backpacks and camping gear and headed toward the pickup.

A dense wall of trees surrounded the parking lot on three sides. Miranda peered at a map of the trails taped behind a plexiglass panel. The Northern Loop Trail wound for several miles into the forest before it circled back again. But then, who was to say Samson would stay on the trail? Irish wolfhounds were bred to hunt, which meant that Samson would take off into the dense woods at the first interesting scent.

Peg whistled again. "Samson!"

"I still say it was a wolf," one of the girls said, her hair pulled back in a blonde ponytail. She dragged her backpack along the ground. All three laughed.

Sheer anger rippled through Miranda. These woods went on for miles. A dog lost in Sparrow State Park might never be seen again.

"Sorry, but this isn't funny," she said in her most authoritative pulpit voice. Or at least as authoritative as she could muster at six in the morning without coffee.

"Oh, sorry. It's just that Kayla here," the boy said, glancing over to one of the girls, "is, like, totally afraid of wolves. And when—" He paused and looked sheepish.

"And when *what*?" Peg said crisply.

Kayla dropped the strap on the backpack. "When I screamed, he ran off," she said. She pulled off the scrunchy that held her ponytail and shook out her long hair. "It's not my fault your dog looks like a wolf."

"Forget it." Miranda grabbed Peg's arm and pulled her toward the trailhead. They headed into the woods, Miranda nearly jogging to keep up with Peg. She shouted again and Peg whistled. Maybe he wasn't so far in that he couldn't hear them calling.

"You shouldn't let him run loose," the girl yelled behind them. "Fence your yard."

★ ★ ★

Loretta's Diner bustled with a noisy breakfast crowd, and the familiar sound comforted Miranda. She hoped it might offer the same to Peg. The search for Samson along the Northern Loop Trail had led to nothing but three deer ticks and a new appreciation for Peg's athleticism. Miranda wondered if she should also take up power walking. They had hiked about two miles down the trail, shouting and whistling, before turning back. By the time they reached the Volvo, Peg had fallen silent.

Now Miranda peered over her menu at Peg. "We'll find him. I know we will."

Peg shook her head. "No. He's gone. That's all there is to it. I have to face facts."

"He is not," she said in a fierce voice. "I refuse to accept it. We will find him if it's the last thing we do." Nonetheless, she dabbed at her own eyes with a paper napkin.

"Sometimes in life, you simply have to accept defeat." Peg took a sip of tea.

"Defeat? Are you kidding me?" Peg was her rock. Miranda couldn't let her give up like this. "Just because he's in the woods doesn't mean he won't find his way out. Aren't wolfhounds considered super-smart dogs? They're hunters."

"Well, there is no question that Samson is a very smart dog."

"Exactly."

"I just don't know if he is smart enough to rescue himself."

"But maybe he is! He survived for months on his own before Lewis caught him."

"If he finds the trail, he might head down it. You know, toward the trailhead and the parking lot. And with the foot traffic on that trail this time of year, leaf-peepers and all." Peg appeared thoughtful. "He would undoubtedly be drawn to people's voices. You know how social he is."

A small light glimmered in her eyes. "I'll call the ranger when we get back to the church and see if he'll keep an eye out. Maybe make signs to put on a few trees down the trail." Peg put her menu down and locked eyes with her. "Once more into the breach, Pastor."

"Once more into the breach. But first, breakfast."

CHAPTER TWENTY-ONE

The view from the balcony made Miranda catch her breath. And cling to the railing.

"*¿Sabes la altitud?*" Alejandra asked Harry.

"She wants to know how high up we are?" Miranda wasn't sure that she wanted to know. She wasn't great with heights.

The climb to the top of the belfry to show Alejandra the eighteenth-century Revere bell had begun with a simple church tour. Harry loved the history of St. Gabe's, and he decided that if Alejandra was going to call the church home, at least while waiting on the upcoming vestry meeting, she needed to understand its history. Miranda was amazed at Harry's change of heart and attitude. She wondered if his progressive wife, Margery, had something to do with it. Or maybe Harry was just a good person and, given time to think it through, had realized that the church should help Alejandra. Whatever it was, she was relieved to have him on her side.

Miranda hated it when someone she really liked and respected, such as Harry, supported things she opposed, like closing the borders.

At first, they had stood inside the ringing chamber where the rope hung from the ceiling. With Harry's help, Alejandra pulled the rope, and they listened as the heavy Revere bell tolled above them. Miranda couldn't believe Alejandra wanted to climb up to the belfry, especially with a baby due any day now. But when Alejandra saw that little door to the steep steps, there was no talking her out of it. Miranda watched, a bit worried, as Alejandra tackled those narrow wooden stairs. She took it slow, stopping now and then to breathe, but she kept going. Miranda had to hand it to her, Alejandra made it to the top.

The wind whistled between the louvers, narrow horizontal boards that enclosed the tower. Harry had just explained that they were installed to help spread the sound. They stood on the wooden platform. The floor seemed solid, she thought, looking down. But old. The original planks were from 1877. Miranda looked back up and out the tiny east-facing window. The stores and people walking along Main Street looked like figures out of a dollhouse. She raised her eyes and took in the spectacular view of the Atlantic.

"We're about one hundred and twenty feet up," Harry said, and Miranda translated. Alejandra grinned. Miranda realized it might have been the first time she had ever seen the young woman so happy. Alejandra rested one hand on the bell and the other on her large stomach, the wind whipping her hair.

"How much does the bell weigh?" Alejandra directed her question to Harry.

"A thousand pounds, give or take," Harry said. "They put this bell up here in 1877. No idea how they did things back then. Didn't exactly have a Demag Crawler Crane."

"Right," Miranda said, nodding as if she knew what a Demag Crawler Crane was.

"You should know that Paul Revere didn't make this bell himself. But there's a good chance that his grandson did. The Revere Foundry had a long life after Paul Revere was gone," Harry informed them.

They stood silently for a moment, gazing out at the incredible view.

"Come over to this window, Mrs. Romero," Harry said as he squinched past Miranda in the small space—most of the room in the belfry was occupied by the bell—and made room for Alejandra to look east at the ocean. Miranda made her way over to the west-facing window. Rolling hills swept outward, undulating with red, orange, and burgundy trees. She should climb up to the belfry every time she needed sermon inspiration.

"*Unquiet are its graves; But peaceful sleep is ever there, Beneath the dark blue waves,*" Harry recited. "Nathaniel Hawthorne. One of my favorites."

"Pastor Miranda," Alejandra said, "a poem about the sea?"

Harry looked at Miranda skeptically. "Do you have a favorite poem about the sea? They didn't make your generation memorize poetry like they did mine. Which is too bad if you ask me."

"Hey, don't underestimate my generation," Miranda replied. "Let me think. Okay, how's this: 'The Lord maketh heaven, and earth and sea,'" she recited. "'And all that therein is. Which keepeth truth forever.'" She paused. "Psalm 146, verse 6. I think, anyway. It might be Psalm 6, verse 146."

Suddenly, Alejandra let out a deep moan and clutched her stomach. She bent her knees, and Harry quickly stepped behind her and lowered her to the floor. He shot a frantic glance at Miranda. "If she goes into labor up here in the belfry, Margery will murder me for bringing her up here."

Miranda grabbed both of Alejandra's hands. She was surprised at the strength that radiated from them. "What's going on, Alejandra? Are you okay?" Miranda said in halting Spanish.

Alejandra pressed each side of her abdomen. "It hurts. *Creo que es la bebé.*" She moaned again.

"Oh Lord," Harry said. "Even I know the word *bebé*. We've got to get her downstairs. I cannot believe I let you talk me into coming up here, Pastor."

He frowned at her over the top of Alejandra's head.

"Me? You were the one who wanted to show her the bell."

Alejandra cut them short. "Help me," she said, struggling to her feet.

They squeezed around the massive bell and inched over to the door. Once through the door, Harry went backward down the steep, narrow stairs guiding Alejandra along step by step. Miranda, behind her, had one hand on Alejandra's shoulder, the other gripping the stair rail.

Once they got down out of the belfry stairwell, moving was more manageable. Harry and Miranda each took a side, escorting Alejandra to Miranda's office.

As Alejandra sank into the loveseat, Harry said, "I'll get my car and bring it around to the side door."

Miranda unfolded a prayer shawl and settled it over Alejandra's legs. "You want to kick your sneakers off?" she asked, untying the shoelaces without waiting for an answer. "Why get your car?" she said, turning to Harry.

"To take her to the hospital. Why else?"

She felt a rush of frustration. "Do you want her to finish labor with deportation officials standing on either side?"

"I thought hospitals were safe like churches."

"They used to be. But not now. Not for the past two years." She and Harry locked eyes.

A groan from Alejandra.

"I'm calling Margery," Harry said. "She'll know what to do." He tapped the screen of his cell phone, raising his eyes to give Miranda a piercing look. "And no one mentions that we were in the belfry."

★ ★ ★

"Braxton-Hick's contractions," Margery said. "False labor."

Miranda quickly translated to Alejandra. The young mother's head fell back on the pillow.

"I can't believe you don't remember," Margery said to her husband. She turned to Miranda. "I had false labor with Michael James, our oldest. It isn't quite like labor, but at this point of a pregnancy," Margery smiled at Alejandra while Miranda translated, "it sure feels like it."

"*No trabajo de parto.*" Miranda said.

"That's right. *No trabajo de parto.*" Margery repeated. "Tell her that false labor is like warm-up exercises for the uterus. It means things are getting ready."

Miranda translated haltingly to Alejandra, not at all sure what word she actually used for uterus. Alejandra nodded and bit her lower lip.

"When is your due date?" Margery's gaze shifted to Alejandra. "Dr. Hazeltine told me three to four weeks from now," Alejandra said.

Harry let out a low whistle. "The vestry doesn't even meet till the end of the month. So, you're saying the baby could get here before then?"

"That's right," Margery stood. "Should make for an interesting meeting. And for goodness' sake, stop hovering. She's not having a baby today. Well, probably not, anyway."

Harry gave Margery a skeptical look. "Now, who's not remembering?"

"Remembering what?" Miranda looked from one to the other.

"Well." Margery gazed into Harry's eyes. "Our Sammy was nine days early."

CHAPTER TWENTY-TWO

"Take a look at that grip bar, Pastor Miranda," Lucy McClain said, beaming.

Miranda stood with her back pressed against the pink shower wall in the pinkest bathroom she had ever seen. Pink toilet, pink sink, pink window shade. Even the grip bar was pink. Did grip bars come in all colors? She hadn't spent much time thinking about grip bars. She didn't feel like thinking about them now—she was too preoccupied with tonight's vestry meeting.

Harry had moved up the date for the meeting. He wanted the vestry to decide about Alejandra before she went into labor for real.

"A perfect grip bar," Miranda agreed.

"Grab ahold and see how sturdy it is," Lucy said.

Miranda grabbed. "Very sturdy."

"I said to Adam I was worried that I might fall in the shower, and when I came home from the hospital, there it was." Lucy's face was wreathed in smiles. "Come look at this."

Miranda followed Lucy down the short hall and into her kitchen. No stench of cats or stacks of dirty dishes. She smiled, imagining Adam in an apron and up to his elbows in dish suds. She pushed his image out of her mind. He had not called her after their dinner at the rectory.

"A bluebird nesting box," Lucy said triumphantly, peering out the kitchen window. "I've always wanted one. I love bluebirds. Do you like bluebirds, Pastor?"

"I do."

"I told Adam that a nesting box on that old fence would be perfect, and you know what? He bought one from Asa at the hardware and put it up. When I saw it, I said all I needed now were the bluebirds." She put a hand to her heart. "And you know what he said?"

Miranda shook her head.

"He said, 'Aunt Lucy, if I could buy you a flock of bluebirds, I would.'"

"He's very good to you, isn't he?"

"I should say he is. Not many young men would be so attentive to an elderly great-aunt." Lucy poured tea into delicate porcelain cups. "I do miss my cats, though." Her voice trembled.

"I'm sorry about that," Miranda said. "Losing a pet's like losing a friend." Lucy dabbed her eyes with a tissue. "They went to good homes, though. And it's wonderful to be able to breathe again."

"Well, oxygen is important." Both women laughed.

"Dr. Hazeltine said I could go back to Silver Sneakers yoga at the church."

"Great news."

Lucy leaned in. "Pastor, can you keep a secret?"

"Of course."

"You can't tell Adam I told you this."

"Oh?" Miranda's mind raced. "Anything you tell me is confidential." She felt a little guilty playing the priest-confidentiality card, but she wanted to know.

"It's just that I thought Adam might be sweet on you."

"Really?" she said, dismayed that her voice came out as a high-pitched squeak.

"But he's not."

"What? Oh. Well." Miranda laughed in a way she hoped was nonchalant.

"I told him you're smart and pretty and he would do well to set his cap for you. But he said you're not his type."

"You did?" Miranda set her cup down slowly.

Lucy stood up and went to a cupboard next to her refrigerator. "You like sweet things, don't you, Pastor?"

For a split second, Miranda thought she meant Adam. Then she realized the older woman meant cookies. "Yes, I do. I do like sweet things. Sweets, I mean."

"Adam says you're a hearty eater for a girl." Lucy brought a bag of Fig Newtons to the table.

"He said I'm—what?"

"A hearty eater. And I told him that that would be a welcome relief. Most girls these days starve themselves. Very unhealthy. And why would anyone want to be that thin?"

She had traveled the emotional rollercoaster in the past few minutes from hope to embarrassment to disappointment. Now the roller coaster had glided to a stop on indignation. She hadn't eaten so much that night at the rectory. Or was he remembering the rhubarb tart? And wasn't he eating along with her? Just like a man. He can enjoy a good meal, but a woman can't?

"I've told him he's too picky." Lucy shook several fig bars out of the bag and onto a plate.

Clearly, she fell below Adam's standards. Rather than speak, Miranda gulped her tea.

"More tea?"

She nodded.

"For as long as I've known him, Adam has always liked the flashy types." Lucy held the plate of cookies to Miranda.

She started to take a Fig Newton and then hesitated. Hearty eater, indeed.

"I thought he had outgrown that nonsense and would want to settle down. With someone like you."

"A not-flashy-type?"

"Exactly."

Oh, what the heck. She took two cookies off the plate.

CHAPTER TWENTY-THREE

Miranda waited in her office until she was sure the last car had driven out of the parking lot, then made her way out of the quiet building. The vestry meeting had dispersed an hour ago, but the heated conversations had continued in the church parking lot. Every priest knew that parking lot conversation following a vestry meeting was a sign of trouble. It meant that issues had gone unresolved and opinions unheard.

Though the question of sanctuary had been left unresolved, she couldn't imagine whose voice had gone unheard. As the vestry members parried angrily back and forth, the tension rose until Harry looked as though he was ready to throw the whole lot of them out the nearest stained-glass window.

Walking down the hall from her office, she heard laughter coming from the Youth Room. Margery had told Miranda that she and Pam were setting up Alejandra with an old DVD player and watching *Zootopia* together. She thought she could smell popcorn. On any other evening, Miranda would have happily joined them. But she couldn't look Alejandra in the eye.

Miranda and Harry agreed they would meet tomorrow morning and tell her that the vestry had not reached a final decision. Nine months pregnant, the girl's fate hung in limbo because twelve church members had been divided down the middle and were not brave enough to do the right thing.

Miranda shoved against the heavy outside door and felt both satisfaction and embarrassment at the bang when it hit the church wall.

Slamming doors was a little immature, but she didn't care. Her disappointment in the vestry members left her wanting to yell at someone, cry, or both. At one point during the heated meeting, she had accused the dissenting members of reading a different Bible than she did. A few looked sheepish, and a few others stared back stonily.

She locked the church door and gazed up at the night sky. A luminous moon had risen above the tall steeple. Below, the whispering maple canopied the prayer garden and stone bench. Usually, a moment such as this would inspire a prayer of thanksgiving for simply being alive in this place. Not tonight.

She jerked open the door of the old Honda and slid in, yanked the shoulder strap down, and buckled it. She rested her forehead on the steering wheel. The vitriol of a few members of the vestry had left her shaken. They had not seemed to understand that hospitality was a biblical imperative. Hospitality was the mandate of the Gospel. Good churches welcome all people. So what did all this tell her about her own church? Was she shepherding a congregation perfectly comfortable deporting a pregnant woman back to the country where her life was in danger? What kind of church does that?

Her church, apparently. At least, her vestry.

She drove slowly under the streetlamps toward Honeysuckle Lane. Nine o'clock on a Tuesday night, and Sparrow had rolled up its sidewalks—although The Speckled Sparrow, the town's only pub, was making a fair trade. Miranda looked wistfully at its warmly lit windows. Not that she wanted a drink so much; it was the camaraderie with others for which she longed. In seminary, she and her friends had frequented a favorite pub just off-campus. Laughter-filled conversations from theology to politics to romance had transpired around the scarred wooden tables.

A wave of loneliness swept through her. Miranda had not really made any friends in Sparrow. Not real friends—not women her age. The women in Sparrow talked about children and husbands, in-laws, and the latest changes at the school. She couldn't relate to any of that. And there was Adam. She had thought—oh well, obviously she wasn't his type. That ship had sailed. Time to move on.

She pulled the car over to the side of the street and, grabbing her phone, she scrolled to Tony's number in her contacts. She hesitated only a moment before leaving a brief message. "Hey. Call me tomorrow."

She tossed the phone onto the passenger seat and drove home.

★ ★ ★

"Bad idea," Harry said. "I won't do it."

"Why not?" Miranda fell into the love seat in her office and, picking up the remote, clicked on the fire. The day was brisk. Definitely autumn in New England. She gestured to the wing-back chair, but Harry silently walked over to the window and stared out at Main Street.

The bell in the clock tower chimed nine times. Less than an hour until Tony said he would call. She hated that she was so unsure about her future. Every time she decided to take him up on his offer, she would be drawn back into life in Sparrow. How could she leave it all? But if she did leave it all and walk away, she would be set free. A tempting thought.

She had one more card to play. And if it worked, she would stay. And if she played her final card, and lost, then she would pack up for Seattle. Miranda would ask Harry to call a meeting specifically to explore the church's identity. Who were they as a church? She'd invite guest speakers, including someone from immigration resources. Alejandra would be there, sharing her story. The congregation needed to see a face and hear a voice.

"I refuse to invite the congregation to go ten rounds with each other. It's bad enough we have the vestry dissolving."

"Dissolving? What are you talking about?"

Harry fell into the wingback chair across from her. "Since last night's meeting, two have threatened to resign if we don't give the girl sanctuary, and two have threatened to resign if we do. And it's not just the vestry, either. The Christian Education Committee wants to know how we are going to address the issue of Safe Church. The youth leader wants her room back. The Words of Life book group is now reading some manifesto on immigration, and my wife asked me why my vestry is stuck in the dark ages."

"It's taking us out of our comfort zone. That's good."

He leaned forward. "Look. Pastor. I have nothing but respect for you. When you first came here, I'll admit, I wasn't sure. My sister's church hired a female priest, and it didn't work out. But Margery told me to stop being such an old curmudgeon and join the twenty-first century. So I did, and I'm glad I did. You're the best thing that's ever happened to this church. You really are."

"Thank you." Miranda hated herself for the fact that tears pushed against her eyes. She blinked them away. She was more exhausted than she had thought.

"It's just that—" Harry hesitated.

"What?"

"That you have no idea the negative effect something this divisive can have on the congregation."

"Of course I know that! You think I'm not worried about the church dividing?" An edge of anger rose in her voice. "But we don't know that's what will happen. Not for sure, anyway."

"Is it worth the risk?" Harry gave a hard look.

"Yes. It is absolutely worth the risk. It might energize us. Point us in the direction of true mission, radical hospitality, genuine compassion." Why were church people so afraid of any risk? Christ's followers should be at the forefront of change, not cowering from it. Harry stared at the fire, silent.

Miranda took a deep breath, her shoulders rising and falling slowly. When she finally spoke, her voice was low and measured, each word carefully chosen. "What's your biggest fear? As senior warden?"

He turned his eyes back on her. She noticed how tired he looked. "St. Gabe's has always been a happy church—not always bickering like some churches. This immigration thing will set us at each other's throats."

"Do you really think that?" Would refusing to grow and change make a difference? Would being a *happy* church mean remaining ignorant?

"You know how this whole country has been these past couple of years." Harry blew his breath out. "The polarization, the anger. I have a brother who hasn't spoken to me since he found out who I voted for."

Miranda nodded. She still wondered what kind of ballot Harry had cast. She wasn't sure she wanted to know.

"What if the same thing happens to St. Gabe's?" Now he was glaring at her. "This congregation may have been in Sparrow since 1874. But let's face it, financially, we're holding on by a shoestring. Better than a lot of churches, but still, a shoestring. We're aging. The youth are our future, and where are they?"

"Young people don't go to church because churches are all talk, no action. We're seen as irrelevant," Miranda said. "But offering sanctuary? That's relevant. That's Christianity with some backbone."

"Fine. I'll make the call." Harry's voice was tight. "A Congregational meeting then. But I want it on record: I'm against this whole thing. Totally against it."

Miranda felt a wave of frustration mixed with disappointment. If she didn't have Harry, then who did she have?

"But listen to me." Harry locked eyes with her.

"I'm listening."

"If we go before the congregation—you know, at Congregational Meeting—then you and I go as a united front. Personally, I don't agree with you. But if this is what you want—what you think is the right thing—then I'll stand with you."

This time her tears spilled over. If Harry noticed, he didn't mention it.

"No one is going to say I didn't support my priest." He looked fierce as he stood and shrugged on his coat.

Miranda couldn't trust herself to speak.

"And anyway, if I didn't support you on this one, there'd be no living with Margery."

As Harry closed the door behind him, her phone buzzed.

A text from Tony. *I knew you would come to your senses.*

He had added an emoji of six smiley faces in chef's hats winking at her. It suddenly hit her that she would be working directly for him. Okay, that was sobering. She had enjoyed working for his mother at The Pellegrino. Mrs. Barici had been tough but fair, and although she expected her staff to work hard, she worked twice as hard herself. Tony would be different. She knew that. His work ethic was less first-generation-immigrant and more entitled-Millennial.

She tapped her phone screen and waited as the phone rang, imagining Tony at the gym, where he spent most mornings. When he answered, she could hear the pounding beat of workout music in the background and the thump and clank of weight machines.

"Randa!" he said, answering the phone.

"Miranda," she said. "Remember? Never Randa."

"Right. How are things in Mayberry?"

"They're good. Listen, I need more time to decide. About the job. Until the week after Thanksgiving." Miranda swallowed hard, her throat constricting. The weight of indecision pressed down on her shoulders. How could she walk away from everyone? Everything? She needed time—just until after Thanksgiving. Then, perhaps, the path would be clearer. She'd ensure Alejandra found sanctuary somewhere, tell Peg about Tony and the chef's job. Guilt washed over her in a relentless wave.

"You're joking, right?"

"Nope." By Thanksgiving she would know.

"Seriously? A week after Thanksgiving? That's when I want you in Seattle."

"I'll give you a rock-solid answer. I promise."

"Fine. But not a minute more. I need you on board. And if I can't have you, there are plenty of other chefs out there who will jump at the chance."

CHAPTER TWENTY-FOUR

"Here you go," Kensleigh said, sliding two plates of hot pancakes onto the table along with a platter of sausage links.

The pancakes were exactly as Miranda liked. A mound of butter melting in the center with little rivulets running to the edges and dripping down the sides. She poured maple syrup over the stack and then watched Peg scrape off the butter and dribble a teaspoon of syrup in the center of her short stack.

"Ever since I reduced my carb intake," Peg said, sliding into the window booth at Loretta's. "I've been dreaming about pancakes."

"And sausage?" Miranda asked. "What happened to ovo-vegetarian?"

"If I am going to break my training diet with pancakes, I might as well go whole hog. No pun intended."

Miranda leaned back and breathed deeply. When Harry left her office an hour earlier, she had felt buoyed by his affirmation of support. She was determined to sustain that good feeling at all costs. "What are you training for?"

"The Wobble Gobble on Thanksgiving Day," Peg replied. "I hope to improve on last year's time."

Miranda slid a pancake onto her plate. "Do you think I eat too much?"

"Eat too much? What brought that on?"

"Nothing. Just thinking."

Peg shrugged. "Eat what you want. Now tell me about the vestry meeting last night. Harry looked pale as a ghost this morning. You know how he hates conflict."

"He may hate it, but he's not afraid of it. There's a difference."

"True enough." Peg stirred sugar into her Chai tea.

Miranda filled her in on the highlights of the meeting. "I'd say that the worst part was that church members—people who I have always really liked—got ugly."

"What do you mean? Ugly?"

"Well, Martin Cahlin threatened to report Alejandra to the police for trespass."

Peg snorted. "Marty Cahlin. I've known him since Mrs. Conrad's first-grade class at Sparrow Elementary. He was a bully then and he still is. Ignore him."

"He wasn't the only one. Norma Menkes wants to change all the locks on the doors and Ed Compton suggested we charge rent. As if Alejandra had a stash of money somewhere and she was holding out on us." She took another sip of coffee. "It's hard to hear good people say horrible things. You know, support beliefs and policies that are simply unchristian."

"It's happening everywhere. Intelligent people making fools of themselves."

They sat in silence.

"All the more reason for pancakes," Miranda said finally.

"And sausage," Peg added.

"I think part of the problem last night was that no one on the vestry had the facts about immigration or the border or asylum seekers. And Alejandra wasn't there to speak about her personal experience. People need to meet her. Hear her story."

Peg looked at her sharply. "And you're sure that you want to do this?"

"What are you saying? It's not like I can back out now." An irrational disappointment swept through her. Not even Peg was on her side. "I thought you supported sanctuary for Alejandra?"

"I certainly do support it. However, there are few church members who will not go down without a fight."

"Well, I can fight, too," Miranda said. She took a sip of coffee. "Although, I prefer to persuade."

"Some people think a priest shouldn't rock the boat."

"Yeah, and to those people, I say that Jesus was a big boat rocker. What would you have me do? Pack her a lunch and send her on her way?"

"Of course not. But I did some research, and becoming a sanctuary church is—complicated. It's noble, sure, but it's also a major commitment."

"Well, I won't argue that."

"No. I mean a serious commitment. We'll need volunteers around the clock, every day. There's the cost of food, utilities, maybe even medical care. Legal risks if things go south."

The warmth of Harry's affirmation faded, replaced by a creeping chill.

"It's both a worthy cause and a potential nightmare for our resources and unity." Peg took a sip of her tea.

The door to the diner jingled.

"Oh dear," Peg whispered, looking up. "It's Betty Hardacre."

They both smiled congenially as the older woman barreled up to the booth.

"Good morning, Betty," Miranda chirped, amazed at how cheerful she could sound. "How are you today?"

"How am I today?" Betty spit out the words. Her face was red and blotchy, and her hair more Brillo pad coiffure than ever. Miranda noticed that she was now missing two buttons from her brown cardigan. "How would anyone be when they find out that their church is hiding an illegal alien in the basement?"

"Youth Room," Peg said.

"Excuse me?" Betty snapped.

"We're hiding her in the Youth Room."

"It has a couch," Miranda added.

"If you two want to play dumb, go ahead. But it won't be so funny when the FBI raids St. Gabe's."

"ICE," Peg said. "We'll be raided by ICE." She scraped more syrup off the top of her pancakes.

"Alejandra is not illegal," Miranda said, adding a generous dribble of syrup to her pancake. *Hearty eater. You bet.* "She has documents. And she's not hiding exactly—well, it's complicated. But no laws are being broken."

Peg gave her a subtle glance. She needed to talk with the immigration people. Was Alejandra breaking the law by not responding to the Immigration letter? The letter sounded like Alejandra had two choices: Apply for an appeal or return to Honduras. Sleeping in the Youth Room of an Episcopal church was not listed as another option.

"If she's not an illegal, then why does she have to hide out in St. Gabe's?" Betty crossed her arms over her chest.

"She's not safe," Miranda answered, forcing her voice to stay calm. "She could be deported at any time."

"So she parks herself on our doorstep? On our dime?"

"Think of it this way, Betty," Peg jumped in. "Alejandra is like a present-day Pilgrim. But, instead of being welcomed by native peoples, she is being welcomed by all of us at St. Gabriel-by-the-Sea."

"The Pilgrims," Betty hissed, "were God-fearing Christians seeking religious freedom. Not some Mexican girl who got herself knocked up and now wants welfare and food stamps."

"Can I find you a table, Mrs. Hardacre?" Loretta appeared at Betty's side, one hand on her hip and, in the other hand, a coffeepot. Loretta's friendly smile didn't reach her eyes.

With a huff, Betty turned and stomped across the room. They watched as she flung open the door and stepped into the morning sunlight of Main Street.

Loretta topped off Miranda's coffee. "Enjoying that sausage today, Mrs. Dunbar? Last I heard, you were a vegan."

"Ovo-vegetarian."

"Which means?"

"Plant-based but with eggs."

"And the sausage?"

"Some days just call for sausage," Peg said. "And today is one of those days."

CHAPTER TWENTY-FIVE

"Of course, Lewis," Peg said. "Thank you. I understand." She put the phone down, picked up a red pencil, and drew a heavy line across the middle of the worship bulletin. "Are you aware you have the wrong Old Testament text for this Sunday?" Without looking up, she continued reading, red pencil poised.

"I'm mixing things up a bit," Miranda said. "What did Lewis have to say?" Lately, Peg had stopped mentioning Samson. Miranda wasn't ready to give up yet and didn't want Peg throwing in the towel either.

"Do you want me to do an insert about All-Hallows-Eve?"

"Sure. What did Lewis want?"

"I called him. About Samson." Peg's voice caught but only for a second.

"And?"

Peg stood up and moved to the copier, her back to Miranda. "Nothing. No one has seen him."

"Don't worry, he's bound to show up sooner or later." Peg fitted a stack of paper into the bottom drawer of the copier. "You haven't forgotten Confirmation this evening, have you?" Peg said, turning around.

"Forget it? When our topic is Sacraments: An Overview, Part Two?"

Peg gave her the smallest of smiles. "How did Part One go?"

"You don't want to know."

An hour into prepping for Confirmation class, Miranda came up for air at the sound of Peg's voice. Peg worked the front office like a bouncer, standing guard and vetting each person who wanted to see the pastor. Today, she used her firmest church secretary's voice.

Peg knocked and then opened the door and slipped in, shutting it behind her. "My apologies but—you have visitors. And although I explained that making an appointment was customary—" Peg stood to her full height. "They were unrelenting."

"Who is it?"

"Sylvia Clacken and Mike Loeffler from the Pastor-Staff Relations Committee."

"Oh. Why?" In the Episcopal church, the six-member committee, known as the PSRC, dealt with any problems between the pastor and the congregation, especially anything to do with congregational conflict. She knew that Sylvia was the recently appointed chairperson of the committee. "They're not on my calendar, right?"

"No. This is a surprise visit."

Miranda dropped her voice. "Alejandra?"

"And maybe the Pilgrims."

★ ★ ★

"As you know, Pastor." Sylvia settled into the loveseat next to Mike and across from Miranda in one of the wing-back chairs. Sylvia's perfume wafted across the room. Miranda knew that Sylvia owned a real estate agency with an office on Elm Street and was very successful. At least that was the church gossip.

Sylvia was immaculately put together. Perfect white teeth, stylishly bobbed hair, flawless skin, red nail polish. Miranda shoved her hair behind her ears and smoothed the front of her clergy shirt. She really needed to buy an iron.

"Our committee is tasked with overseeing the Pastor." Sylvia opened a thin leather notebook and clicked her pen.

Mike tugged at his collar. He was the information technology guy at the community college, and though she hated to say it, he looked the part. Awkward gait, ill-fitting khaki pants, a blue tie with a brown stain. On the other hand, Miranda reminded herself if it weren't for Mike's expertise, the church would still be without a website or any social media presence. He gave Miranda an apologetic smile.

"Let me correct you. Overseeing the pastor is not the job of the PSRC. At all." A prickle of heat crawled up Miranda's neck. She forced herself to take a centering breath.

"All right then—*helping* the pastor." Sylvia glanced down at her notebook. She read aloud, "Helping the pastor to interpret her role and ministries."

"We're here on a friendly visit," Mike added quickly.

"What other kind of visit would there be?" Miranda looked from one to the other.

"It's just that we thought—it would help you if you knew what we've been hearing," Sylvia said.

"Hearing?"

"About things happening here at the church."

"Are you here with the knowledge of the entire committee? Or on your own?"

"The whole committee," Mike said.

"Are you telling me that PSRC had a meeting?" Now she really needed to breathe. "I thought church policy was that PSRC only met with the pastor present. No secret meetings." No significant church meeting was supposed to occur without the pastor's presence or, at the very least, an invitation extended to them. This exclusion was a deliberate violation of long-standing protocol and trust.

"It wasn't secret. Not at all." Sylvia exchanged a glance with Mike. "More like spontaneous. Just some of us talking."

"Here's the deal, Pastor," Mike said, leaning forward. "You're upsetting a whole lot of people, and we just think that you need to tone it down."

"Upsetting who, exactly? And tone what down?'

"Doesn't matter who," he said. "Believe us when we tell you, there are people who are not happy."

"Give me names. Without substantial sources of information, this is hearsay. Worse yet, gossip." She fixed Sylvia with what she hoped was a kind but firm gaze—a gaze that hid her growing anxiety. Were people in the congregation turning against her? Pulling back the support they had given so generously?

Sylvia crossed her legs at the ankle and gave her linen skirt a slight tug. "We aren't telling names."

"But you need to." Miranda forced herself to speak in her most neutral voice. "If there are truly people in the congregation who are upset—and I don't even know why they are upset or what *upset* means exactly—then it is imperative that I discuss it face to face with them. Not just assume that their concerns are being brought accurately by you."

"I know my wife doesn't like what's going on, that's for sure." Mike leaned back in his chair, frowning.

"Then Joanie should come and see me." A knot of anxiety tightened in Miranda's stomach.

Mike exhaled loudly—part snort and part laugh. "She's not going to come and see you." He leaned back on the loveseat and glanced out the window.

"Why not?"

"That's what this committee is for," Sylvia cut in, her voice more edgy than before. "To let you know how people feel."

"Actually, that is not the purpose of the PSRC." Miranda sat back and tried to look confident, not defensive. She was stunned that the PSRC had met without her present. Such a meeting was against the policy of the church. Spontaneous or not. Did Harry know about the meeting? "Why don't you tell me what the problem is—" Miranda paused, choosing her words carefully. "As you see it."

"This girl living in the church. Lots of people are upset about that."

"I understand. But the vestry will determine if she stays. Not me."

"Yeah, well," Mike said.

"Yeah, well—what?" Miranda leaned forward.

"Well, the problem with the vestry is, some of the members really like you."

"How is that a problem?"

"They're going to support you, no matter what."

Miranda looked from one to the other. "Tell me," she said, "what do the two of you think about offering sanctuary to Alejandra?"

"This isn't about us." Sylvia's voice had gone from edgy to frosty. "We just thought that you would want to know that people are coming to us and saying—" She looked at Mike.

"—that you've gone too far this time," he finished Sylvia's sentence.

"This time?" Miranda's head started to roar.

"Well, you've ruined Thanksgiving, and that's a time-honored tradition here. Lots of people aren't even coming to the meal now." Mike shifted in his seat, not quite meeting Miranda's gaze.

"Do me a favor," she said. "Please stop saying lots of people. If you had to count, is that five individuals? Ten? Fifty? A hundred?" Miranda sat back and waited for an answer.

"It's too much change all at once," Mike ignored her question. "We're going to lose members."

"We already have lost members." Sylvia cut in.

"Name one." Miranda waited.

Mike grimaced, and Sylvia straightened her spine. "Betty Hardacre, for one."

"Anyone else?"

"You don't care about Betty?" Sylvia's voice rose, indignation coloring every syllable. "She's been a member of this church for almost forty years."

So much for a friendly meeting. "Of course I care about Betty. But face it: Betty has left before."

A quiet smirk from Mike.

"We're not here to argue." Sylvia closed her notebook. "We just thought you'd want to know what was going on in your own church."

Sylvia stood, and Mike pushed himself off the couch with a slight grunt.

At the door, Sylvia stopped, her hand on the doorknob. She turned back to her. "Don't say we didn't warn you, Pastor."

CHAPTER TWENTY-SIX

Pam and Ramona, there to strategize for the congregational meeting, sat at the small kitchen table as Miranda cooked. The October sun filtered through the mullioned windows, and a delicious aroma that hinted at something made with apples, brown sugar, and pie crust filled the air. Pam retrieved wine glasses from the cupboard and poured each of them a glass of Merlot. Both had offered to bring a dish to the Saturday night planning meeting, but Miranda refused all offers of food. She'd felt the urge to cook. And if they were to devise a strategy for the next day's congregational meeting, good food and, no doubt, good wine would be required.

Miranda couldn't say it to the church women, but the stakes were high for the outcome of the congregational meeting. If the good people of St. Gabe's stood behind Alejandra and showed themselves committed to doing the right thing, then staying in Sparrow would be easy. But if they didn't stand behind Alejandra, if they let her be deported, it would change things for Miranda. Maybe the congregation wasn't what she thought they were. Or wanted them to be. It all came down to how the congregation voted.

"Does this house have a septic tank, or is it on town water?" Ramona asked as she took a sip of her wine.

Miranda had never seen Ramona in anything but her green coveralls, work boots, and Red Sox cap, except for church on Sunday, when she wore black pants and a white button-down shirt every week. Tonight, Ramona wore skinny jeans and a red T-shirt with a gray hoodie zipped halfway up. Her short black hair was slicked back, and she had no makeup or jewelry. It was a look only the sprite-like Ramona could pull off. Ramona reminded her of a wood nymph. Maybe all her flexibility and energy resulted from wriggling in and out of crawl spaces and around people's toilets all day.

"Town water," Miranda said.

Ramona nodded sagely. "Glad to hear it."

Miranda drew a knife across a honing steel. She hated a dull knife.

"I wish my husband would get our leaves raked like this." Pam picked up her glass and walked to the back window. "I told him to stop doing it himself and hire someone, but he won't hear it. He thinks the leaves should stay on the ground—that it's good for the environment. And I suppose it is."

"Careful you don't clog your sewer drains," Ramona said. She leaned across the kitchen island and peered at the array of bowls, dishes, spices, and cutting board. "Looks good. What is it?"

"Spaghetti carbonara," Miranda said. "Which is simple, I know." Whenever people realized she had been a chef, they expected her to whip up something dramatic and complicated. But as any chef knew, good cooking was all about the fundamentals, and simple was often the best.

She opened the refrigerator and removed the paper-wrapped guanciale. She had been pleasantly surprised when the little butcher shop in Sparrow carried the rich, salty Italian meat. The butcher had been thrilled to have a customer who knew what guanciale was and how to use it. They'd had a spirited conversation regarding guanciale versus pancetta and the absolute inferiority of bacon.

"What's that?" Ramona asked, nodding to the guanciale.

"It's a kind of cured pork," Miranda told her.

"Like bacon?" Ramona said.

"No." She unwrapped the meat package. "Bacon is from the back of the pig." She hesitated. Not everyone wanted the details of exactly where pork came from. "This is from the cheek of the pig."

"Oh," Ramona said thoughtfully. "Pig cheeks."

"It's common in Central Italy. In Umbria, mostly." She carved off a thin slice of the guanciale and diced it quickly.

"You chop like Peg types," Pam observed.

"A true compliment," Miranda said, carving off another slice and going at it again with her sharpened knife.

"Would you be offended if I told you that I like little pieces of hot dogs cut up in Spaghetti-O's?" Ramona said.

"Not if you pair it with the appropriate red wine." Miranda stepped back and surveyed the mound of guanciale.

"How long were you a chef?" Pam asked.

"Ten years or so. I started in the eleventh grade when I worked the line at Famous Bill's Burgers. I learned mostly about burgers, fries, and cheesesteak. And how to clean the grill. Then I went to Boston University as a history major and waited tables to make ends meet. I realized how much I liked food service and cooking professionally. So right after BU, I enrolled at Johnson and Wales in Providence. Went straight from school to Pellegrino's."

She cracked three eggs into the bowl, then deftly separated a fourth, adding only its yolk. As she whisked quickly, Ramona frowned.

"Won't that make it like scrambled eggs?"

Pam snorted, refilling wine glasses. "Says the woman who eats cut-up hot dogs in Spaghetti-O's."

Miranda swiped chunks of guanciale into a bowl before pulling a carton of eggs from the fridge.

"The eggs make it rich and creamy—that's why I whisk it into an egg slurry. Not at all like scrambled eggs." She paused and smiled. "Unless I don't do it right, and then very much like scrambled eggs." Miranda put the eggs aside and grated a large chunk of pecorino cheese. Never take shortcuts was her motto, especially with cheese.

"You use interesting cheese," Ramona said.

Pam eyed Ramona over the top of her wine glass. "Please don't tell us your favorite is Velveeta."

"I was raised on Velveeta," Ramona said.

"Me, too," Miranda added. "And truthfully, there's nothing like Velveeta for a grilled cheese sandwich."

Ramona raised her glass in triumph.

They all watched as she dumped the cheese into a large mixing bowl with the egg slurry and quickly beat it into a smooth, creamy mixture, then grated in black pepper. She put the cheesy egg bowl aside, dumped the guanciale into a cold pan, and turned on the stove.

"You need to heat guanciale slowly," she said, her back to the women at the table, who sat breathing in the aroma of the cooking guanciale. "Do you want me to drain off the fat?" she asked. "Are you worried about calories?

"No!" they said in unison.

"Why drain off the best part?" Ramona said.

"Says the Queen of Velveeta," Pam added.

The pot of water on the stove had just started to boil. Miranda fanned in a handful of spaghetti with a generous dash of salt. "I want the water to be *salato come il mare*. As salty as the sea."

When the pasta was ready, she drained the noodles and slid them into the pan with the guanciale. She tossed it until it was evenly coated with the fat. And then she dumped in the egg and cheese.

"Scrambled egg time," Ramona said.

"Not if I mix fast enough." Miranda leaned into the whisk, and to the women watching, the mix was a creamy, yellow blur.

Pam sat back and stared at the stovetop. "Honestly, when you said you were making us spaghetti, I was a little disappointed. But this—this smells—and looks—out of this world."

"Done right, carbonara is heavenly. And—" Miranda twirled the spaghetti in the pan. "Simple."

* * *

The clock in the center of town chimed nine times. The carbonara was a thing of the past, the crusty bread from The Rolling Pin

Pastry down to a final heel, and the salad bowl scraped clean. There was a collective groan when Miranda slid the apple crisp out of the oven.

"I love making an apple crisp. If I didn't make it for you guys, I'd be eating it alone."

"I think all pastors should be chefs in previous lives," Pam said, the most relaxed Miranda had ever seen her. A combination of wine, good food, and the fact that she had turned off her phone and shoved it to the bottom of her purse.

Miranda dried her hands on a dishtowel and followed the others into the sitting room. Ramona flipped on lamps, filling the room with soft light. Pam brought in a tray from the kitchen with a carafe of herbal tea and three mugs.

"Thought we might want something soothing," Pam said, setting the tray on the coffee table. "Chamomile okay with everyone?"

Miranda and Ramona nodded appreciatively as Pam poured the steaming tea into the mugs and handed them around. Miranda could hear Howard scurrying across the bedroom floor. Pam and Ramona had already met him, admired his Hobbit house, and fed him his veggie pellets. He seemed done with company now and was taking refuge under the bed. The three women settled back into the comfortable chairs and couch with a collective sigh.

"What do you expect tomorrow, Pastor?" Pam asked, her sharp eyes turned on Miranda.

"I have mixed feelings. On one hand, I definitely want the church to vote to give Alejandra sanctuary. On the other hand, it is a long arduous road to get her to be documented." Miranda took a sip of coffee. Her secret weighed on her. The chef job offer was hard to keep quiet. She hated hiding things from her friends, especially news that could hurt them.

"Well, I don't have mixed feelings," Ramona said. "I know exactly what I want and I don't care how hard it will be. We need to give Alejandra asylum. And to shelter her until she has citizenship in this country." Ramona slipped off her shoes and put her feet—in bright orange socks with grinning Halloween ghosts—on the ottoman.

"Okay. So maybe my feelings aren't mixed," Miranda admitted. "It's important to me that the church do the right thing." She was mortified that her voice broke. She tried to cover by coughing and clearing her throat. "Of course, that's what I want. But it's a long haul. Giving Alejandra sanctuary will take all the energy, faith, and goodwill the church people possess. Not to mention, a lot of food delivery, laundry, and once the baby is born, diapers."

Miranda tried to smile, but the expressions on the women's faces stopped her. "Alejandra could be at the church for a year or more."

She told the women about her meeting with Carla and Miguel, the representatives from the Council on Immigration. Alejandra and Miranda had met them in the church office the previous day. Both reps had expressed caution about a successful appeal to the Immigration Board. And they were very clear—Alejandra needed sanctuary so that she would not be picked up by ICE and deported, but she would also need a lawyer. They would help find the lawyer, but the church should expect to assume all legal expenses. They also said that the process could easily take one to three years.

The women sat silently as the mantel clock chimed nine times—ten minutes past the town clock tower.

"Your clock is off," Ramona said absently, glancing at her phone.

"I know. I can't seem to fix it. I might have to take it to a clockmaker."

"Are there still clockmakers these days?" Pam asked.

Miranda shrugged. The enthusiasm of the dinner party had plummeted. But maybe a dose of reality was good.

"Look. On the one hand, offering Alejandra sanctuary is going to be hard. More challenging than anything this church has ever done. And I am in my first year as a priest. I'm still learning the ropes. I will admit to feeling as if this is—maybe not a great idea. But then, what are we supposed to do? Let someone be deported because it's inconvenient to us?"

She looked at Ramona and Pam. They were her biggest allies. Filled with vitality and wisdom and faith and humor, they were her team. She needed them if the church decided that Alejandra was to stay. But what would she say to them if they rejected Alejandra and she decided to take Tony up on his offer?

"And anyway," Miranda continued, "we didn't ask for Alejandra to come to us and ask us to help her. It's not like we sent out an invitation."

"We found her making breakfast in the church kitchen," Pam added thoughtfully.

"Climbing through a window to find shelter," Ramona added.

"It's like the parable of the Good Samaritan. A man in need, lying by the edge of the road. Do we walk on by, or do we stop to help?" She looked at them. "Walking on by would be so much easier."

"Personally, I am not walking on by," Pam said in a firm voice.

"I think the congregation will see what we have to do," Ramona said confidently. "They'll listen to Alejandra's story, and I believe they will vote to be the good Samaritan."

"What do you think, Pam?" Miranda asked.

Pam frowned thoughtfully and tossed one of the throw pillows to the side. "I think the vote may be close. And I think Betty Hardacre and her minions will do all they can to stop a sanctuary vote. But this is a good congregation, and I would like to say that they're not going to turn a young woman out into the cold."

"But you're not sure?" Ramona said.

"No. I'm not sure. Not at all." She looked hard at Miranda. "I think we need to be prepared for the worst."

* * *

Miranda stepped into the Youth Room and found Dr. Hazeltine and Alejandra huddled over a laptop. The early afternoon sun shone through the basement window, and she noticed that the room no longer had its typical musty smell. "What's going on?"

Alejandra looked up. "I'm enrolling in a pre-med ESL course at Eastern Maine Community College," she said with a glimmer of excitement in her eyes.

"Wow," Miranda replied, trying to sit up straight in the beanbag. "I didn't know they had a pre-med ESL program. That's great. Good for you."

Dr. Hazeltine rose from her seat, her expression brightening with interest. "Alejandra has a passion for medicine," she said, gesturing to the laptop. "And I think she has what it takes to be a top-notch doctor."

"I have *mucho camino* to go." A long road. Alejandra's expression turned serious as she squinted at the screen. "My *educación* in Honduras, it was always *interrumpido* by the fighting, you know?" Her expression suddenly downcast. "But Dr. Hazeltine says I think is better to start slow. Go at my own *velocidad*, no?"

"*Qué clase estás tomando*?" What class are you taking? Miranda sat up from the beanbag chair to peer at the laptop screen.. "To get started, I mean." College enrollment might also help Alejandra's immigration appeal. Or not.

"*Matemáticas de desarrollo*." Developmental Math? It's online. I enroll now *y después*—after my baby is born, I study *cuando puedo*—when my baby sleep."

"Going slow at first is a great idea. Organic Chemistry and Advanced Histology can wait." Dr. Hazeltine placed a reassuring hand on Alejandra's shoulder. "Those two classes were never my favorites anyway."

Miranda was about to ask who was paying for Alejandra's classes when Dr. Hazeltine spoke up. "I'll cover the cost of the first few classes and then we'll look into scholarships." She smiled at Miranda over Alejandra's head.

Dr. Hazeltine's kindness almost brought tears to her eyes. Miranda made a mental note to remember this moment when she was feeling discouraged by the narrow-mindedness of the Thanksgiving Committee or the short-sightedness of the vestry.

"I think you're amazing, Alejandra," Miranda said. "And with Dr. Hazeltine by your side, the sky's the limit."

Medical school was certainly a possibility. But then, so was getting deported.

CHAPTER TWENTY-SEVEN

Miranda stepped into the pulpit. She felt her fingertips tingle. And this was nervous-nervous. Not nervous-happy. The church was packed, a palpable silence in the air. The congregation looked back at her with a mix of faces. Some were encouraging and open, others closed off and stony. Very few in between.

Margery sat with Alejandra in the third pew on the Gospel side and offered Miranda a smile. Peg, sitting in the back of the church, gave her a small nod of encouragement. *You can do this*, it seemed to say.

Miranda took a deep breath. "Good afternoon, everyone," she said in her most confident pulpit voice. "Thank you for returning this afternoon for our Congregational meeting."

Some returned her gaze with encouragement and a smile, while others looked away, their expressions closed.

"Let us open with prayer." She took a breath and closed her eyes. "Gracious and loving God, we pray that this meeting will truly be a time when this congregation comes together. May we be united and inspired in our shared work of Your Son, Jesus Christ. Amen." There, she thought. Short and to the point.

"And now," she said, forcing her voice to be upbeat, "as is our practice, our Senior Warden, Harry Hopkins, will lead our meeting." She took a seat in the celebrant chair directly behind and to the left of the pulpit.

Harry stepped into the pulpit, reached into the pocket of his tweed jacket, and pulled out a small gavel. They all watched as he held it up, waiting for the gentle thud indicating the start of the meeting. Instead,

Harry hesitated and slipped it back into his pocket. He took his glasses off and polished them with the end of his tie. He put them back on. The congregation waited.

"Now, folks," he said, his voice firm but friendly. "We all know why we're here. We're here to figure this thing out about being a sanctuary church. And I imagine you all know by now that we have a young woman—" he paused. "Stand up, please, if you would, Mrs. Romero." He waited while Alejandra stood.

"Mrs. Alejandra Romero, everyone. She has come to us from San Pedro Sula, Honduras."

Alejandra turned and faced the congregation. She rocked back slightly on the heels of her new sneakers, one hand on the pew at her back and the other on her abdomen. A quiet murmur went through the pews. With her pink oversized T-shirt and her hair pulled back in a ponytail, she looked young, like one of the kids in the youth group.

Miranda noted many looks of concern on the faces of most of her parishioners. A few flushed with anger, though. Betty Hardacre glared openly.

"Thank you," Harry said as Alejandra sat down. "We will hear from Mrs. Romero later in the meeting, but first, I want to lay down some ground rules." Harry paused, peering out over his glasses. "Let's keep one thing in mind. A church is a family. And if we're anything like my family, we're not good at listening."

A ripple of laughter went through the sanctuary.

"But today, we are going to listen." Harry paused again. "I want us to listen to the young lady here. I want us to listen to the experts Pastor Miranda has provided for us, and most of all, I want us to listen to each other."

"Give 'em hell, Harry," a voice called out from the back. This time the congregation laughed openly, happy for the release of tension.

Harry smiled. "Thanks for your support, Joe. But no more comments from the cheap seats, if you please."

"You going to bring this to a vote, Harry?" A voice from the back. Sam Reeves. Miranda wondered where Sam fell on the political ladder.

"Yes, we will vote." Harry squinted over the pews at Sam. "But not until we're ready. And we'll be following Robert's Rules to the letter, so next time you have a question, Sam, wait till you've been recognized."

Sam gave a sheepish nod.

"All right, then," Harry said. "Here's our agenda. We're going to start off with a little Immigration 101 lesson from our experts here. And you can ask them all the questions you want about what 'sanctuary' means. Then we will hear from Mrs. Romero. And at the end, Pastor Miranda."

"And then we vote?" Betty Hardacre said from the middle pew.

Harry blew out his breath. "Yes, Mrs. Hardacre. And then we vote."

Miguel and Carla stood side-by-side behind the pulpit. Miguel was tall and professional in a gray jacket and blue tie, gray hair cut short. Carla was younger and offered a reassuring smile that emanated goodwill.

"First of all," Carla said, "thank you for inviting us to your Congregational meeting. Please think of me and Miguel as an endless source of information. Information is the key to deciding about offering sanctuary. We find that the more the congregation knows, the better the process."

"And so, with that in mind," Miguel said, leaning into the microphone, "let's start at the beginning." He turned and gestured toward Alejandra. "Alejandra Romero seeks sanctuary from this church. What does that mean? First, she is an asylum seeker. An asylum seeker is someone who has fled their home in search of safety and who has formally applied for legal protection in another country.

"But it does not always happen that the country to which they apply offers protection. In this case, Alejandra Romero has received a letter saying that an immigration judge rejected her asylum claim that she made three months ago at the border. Now, Immigration and Customs Enforcement, ICE, has issued her a deportation order."

"How is that our problem?" Betty called out. The congregation rumbled, and Harry started to rise to his feet, his face stern.

"It isn't your problem," Carla said, her voice light. Harry slowly sat back down. "It's your opportunity. As a church, you have the opportunity of offering protection. ICE considers churches sensitive locations. Therefore, if a congregation chooses to, they can shelter immigrants facing deportation."

Miguel jumped in again. "It's a huge step for any church to offer sanctuary. You should be proud of yourselves for even considering it. Proud that you are following the biblical tradition of giving hospitality to the stranger."

"I'm not saying we should send her back, but why can't she just go back to Honduras?" Mike Clarkson asked.

This time Harry stood. "Mike, that's a good question, so I'm going to let you ask it. But from now on, no questions without being recognized."

"This isn't about sending her anywhere," a voice from the back called out. "It's about keeping her here at this church."

"You people must not read the same Bible that I do." Lucy McClain rose to her feet, her voice pitched with emotion.

Harry stood and cut off the rumble from the pews. "Simmer down, everyone." He glared over his glasses at Lucy, who glared back as she took her seat in the pew

"Under U.S. law," Miguel said calmly, "if a person is afraid to return to their home country, they will be referred for a credible-fear interview conducted by an asylum officer. Both Mrs. Romero and her husband, Daniel, were given the opportunity for a credible-fear interview. If the officer makes a positive finding, the asylum seeker is referred to an immigration court where they will have the opportunity to apply for asylum before an immigration judge. If the individual does not meet the credible fear screening standard, they can be deported immediately. In the case of Mrs. Romero, she was referred to immigration court. Her husband, Daniel, was deported in June."

A rustling murmur went through the congregation. Matt Killinger, one of the youth leaders, raised his hand. Harry nodded to him.

"Why would she get asylum, and he wouldn't? From what I understand, they left Honduras together, so how could their experience of danger be that different?"

"Good question," Carla replied. "Things at the border can be very arbitrary. Some people make it across; others don't."

Miguel jumped in. "It is important to realize that immigration isn't what it used to be. Things have changed quite a bit in the past two years."

"Amen to that," came from the far back of the room. A buzz zipped up and down the pews.

"The present administration," Carla said, "has implemented changes which make it much harder to be granted asylum. These new rules have had a particularly harmful impact on survivors of domestic violence, the LGBTQ community, and those fleeing gang violence."

Mike Loeffler rose to his feet. "Not that I want to kick anyone out in the cold, but we have to look out for the reputation of this church." Nods of assent went around the room.

Miranda felt a rising disappointment. Reputation? They were afraid of their reputation, as if they were members of the Sparrow Country Club? Now that was depressing.

"What if people start thinking of St. Gabe's as the immigrant church?" Mike added.

"It would be an honor!" Lily Jenkins, chair of the Climate Justice Committee, rang out.

"Or what if people start thinking of St. Gabe's as the church that helps people?" Ramona added.

Donna raised her hand. "How do we know we won't be arrested?"

"No congregation in the country has been prosecuted for providing sanctuary in the past forty years," Miguel said. "If you offer sanctuary, you do it publicly. You make a declaration as a church. Therefore, you are not concealing anything."

Betty Hardacre rose to her feet. Miranda's stomach tightened. "I don't know if any of you have noticed, but the girl is pregnant. Very pregnant. And her husband is nowhere to be found."

"That's what happens when your husband gets deported, Betty," Margery said. "He doesn't leave a forwarding address."

"Call it what you like," Betty shot back. "But in my day, there was a name for a pregnant girl without a husband."

"She has a husband!" Ramona stood, her face flushed red.

"So she says." Betty's face had turned just as red. "Has anyone met this husband? Seen a letter from him? Anything?"

Harry rose to his feet. "Betty, do you have a question?"

"Yes. And it's the same question everyone in this room should have: what happens when the girl goes into labor on the couch in the Youth Room?"

Before anyone could respond, a clear voice spoke from the side balcony. All necks craned to look up. "Elizabeth Hazeltine, here. Sorry, I'm up on the balcony, but I came late. Though it's a rather nice spot. I'm getting a whole new perspective up here."

The steady voice of Dr. Hazeltine swept over Miranda like a breath of fresh air.

"So that you know, I am prepared to serve as Mrs. Romero's medical doctor. And as long as I have the floor, or, should I say, the balcony, I want to explicitly state that I fully favor offering sanctuary to Mrs. Romero."

A cheer broke out from the pews.

As Dr. Hazeltine sat down, Sam Reeves stood. "I'm not for or against this thing. But since I'm the treasurer, I'll ask the question we're all thinking: Who's going to pay for it?"

"You're right. That's critical," Carla said. "The host congregation will need to cover expenses such as food, clothing, and laundry. Usually, churches do fundraisers, participate in crowdfunding, and apply for grants to defray costs. It's best if the funds come from outside your operating budget."

"Anything from outside the operating budget works for me," Sam said. A small laugh from the congregants.

Harry rose and thanked Carla and Miguel, who took a seat in the front pew. Harry looked at Miranda with his eyebrows raised. She nodded.

"I think," Harry said, "that it's time for us to hear from Mrs. Romero."

Margery stood at the end of the pew while Alejandra stood and stepped into the aisle. Margery hugged her, and then Alejandra came forward, climbing slowly into the pulpit. Harry adjusted the microphone to her height and then stepped back.

"My English is not as good as my Español. But I will try."

Carla stepped up next to her. "May I translate?"

"*Sí*," Alejandra replied. "Thank you."

Alejandra stood behind the oak pulpit and gazed out across the congregation. She looked up and locked eyes with Dr. Hazeltine. There was a long pause, and the congregation seemed to hold its breath.

Finally, Alejandra began. "Daniel, *mi esposo,* we came from Honduras."

"My husband," Carla translated.

"*Para huir de la violencia.*"

"To escape the violence," Carla said.

"What violence?" someone in the front row asked. Miranda noticed that Harry let the question linger.

"In Honduras, *es muy peligroso.* Many people leave in *caravana* because—how you say—they run from violence. The gangs, they control everything, *sí*? They take *dinero*, they hurt people, make everyone scared. *La policía* no help much. *Mucha corrupción.* So people no feel safe, no have hope for *justicia*. They think, *mejor* to risk the journey in *caravana* than stay and maybe die. Is very hard choice, you know? But sometimes, is the only choice."

"What happened to make you finally leave?" Carla waited while Alejandra gathered herself.

"*Mis padres*. My parents. They were—*cómo se dice*?—executed."

The congregation fell silent. Frozen.

"*Miembros de una pandilla*. Gang members." Her voice took on a new edge of strength as if summoned from a distant place. "One night they came. *Las pandillas*." The gangs.

"Where were you that night?" Carla's voice was soft.

Alejandra faltered, the memory stealing her voice, leaving only the weight of the unsaid. "Daniel and I were *en la casa*. In the house. *Con ellos*. With them."

"Why were your parents executed?" Carla said.

"They owe *impuesto de extorsión*. Extortion tax. They could not pay."

"What did you do?"

"Escape. We run all night." No one moved. Or even seemed to breathe. "In the morning —Daniel and I—*la caravana*."

"Caravan?" a voice from the back said. "Like in the news a year or so ago?"

"*Sí, la caravana*. We travel together. To the border."

"Are you saying you walked from Honduras to the Mexican border?" Miranda cringed at the mocking tone in Betty's voice. At least this time, Betty stayed seated.

"Forty days *caminando*. Daniel and I travel together." She met Betty's gaze.

"*Cómo fue para ti cuando llegaste a la frontera*?" Carla asked softly. "What was it like for you when you reached the border?"

"*Si buscas asilo en la frontera, te llevan a*—" Alejandra began, then paused, looking at Carla for help.

"If you seek asylum at the border, they take you into custody. *Si buscas asilo en la frontera, te ponen bajo custodia.*" Carla translated.

"*Sí*," Alejandra nodded. "They did not believe Daniel. *No creyeron que fue perseguido en Honduras.*"

Carla translated the last part: "They didn't believe he was persecuted in Honduras." She looked to Alejandra. "And he was deported?"

"*Sí.*"

"Where is Daniel now?" Miguel interjected.

Alejandra shrugged and shook her head. She leaned back on her heels, her eyes closed, tears seeping.

"Oh, come on," Betty said from her pew. Her voice loud. Angry. "They're not going to deport a man with a pregnant wife. Probably a drug dealer, or something."

"You have no idea what you are talking about, Betty," Ramona said, rising to her feet. Her voice shook. "No idea."

"Take it easy, everyone," Harry said. "This is a friendly discussion."

"You're right," Carla turned to Betty. "There was a time when border patrol would never separate a pregnant woman and her husband. But those days are over."

Miguel cut in. "Daniel can appeal, but that takes months. And he can't live in the U.S. while he is appealing."

"And you've not heard from him?" Harry asked.

"No." Alejandra rested both hands on her abdomen. "*No se donde esta.*" I don't know where he is.

Dr. Hazeltine spoke from the balcony. "I would like to hear Alejandra tell us how she ended up at the church."

Miranda figured that Dr. Hazeltine already knew, but she was grateful the doctor had asked the question.

Alejandra looked up at the balcony, her eyes meeting Dr. Hazeltine's. "I had a friend in Portland and money for a bus ticket," Alejandra said in Spanish. "I slept on her couch, waiting to hear from the immigration court. I finally got my letter." Alejandra took a breath and looked down at the top of the pulpit. "It said, no asylum. I was afraid. I ran. I got on a bus and rode all day. When the bus stopped here, I got off." She looked around.

In English, she continued. "I could see *restaurante* from the bus stop. I was hungry."

"Loretta's." A friendly voice from the middle of the pews.

"I went in, and the lady gave me a meal." Alejandra spoke in Spanish again, with Carla translating. "The bus left without me, but I didn't care. It was dark, and I was so tired. I walked along the street and saw the church. I tried to get the lock to open. But couldn't. Then I saw the basement window was open, and so I came in. I found a room with a couch. I slept."

"So you tried to pick a lock and when that didn't work, you decided you'd break in through a window?" Betty said, her voice hard.

"Would you rather she slept over a sewer grate somewhere?" Linda Darcy rose halfway in the pew and twisted back to glare at Betty.

"I'd rather she went back to where she came from," Betty said quickly.

Bill Meade, the entire bass section of the church choir, boomed out, "For I was hungry, and you gave me something to eat, I was thirsty, and you gave me something to drink, I was a stranger and you invited me in. Matthew 25, verse 35. For me, that settles it."

"Is there anything else you want to add, Mrs. Romero?" Harry said, his voice weary.

She turned her eyes to the rows of people sitting in the pews. "*Gracias por tu generosidad. Gracias.*"

"Thank you for your generosity," Carla said.

"*Te agradezco y mi bebé te lo agradece,*" Alejandra added.

"I thank you, and my baby thanks you," Carla translated and stepped back from the pulpit.

Alejandra returned to her pew, sliding in next to Margery, who clasped her hand and held it.

"I have something to say on this whole issue." Harry stood up, facing the congregation.

"I didn't think the moderator could speak," Betty snipped. "You know, Robert's Rules and all."

"The moderator has voice, and he can vote," Sam Reeves called out. "Of course, there's the fact that no one in this meeting has been following Robert's Rules anyway."

"However, Robert's Rules does require the Presiding Officer to generally remain impartial and avoid taking advocacy positions on pending motions," Sylvia Clacken spoke up for the first time.

"Good grief," Pam muttered, loud enough for Miranda to hear.

"We don't have a pending motion," Sam Reeves thundered. "The moderator can speak all he wants." The room went silent. It wasn't often that the good-natured Sam raised his voice.

Harry cleared his throat. "As many of you know, my mother was a Portuguese immigrant. What you might not know is that she came here as part of the Azorean Refugee Act." Harry removed his glasses and took his time polishing them again with his tie. "There was a volcano on the Azores Island off Portugal's coast in 1957. Wiped out homes, a village or two, people's lives, and livelihoods. My grandparents—" He paused. "They lost everything." Harry put his glasses back on.

"The U.S. opened its borders to anyone affected. My grandparents grabbed the first opportunity. Brought the whole family over. Settled in Portland. My mother was only nineteen. She met a handsome young man on the ship, and they tied the knot on American soil a year later. 1958. I was born in '60 in case anyone wants to do the math."

Harry took a deep breath. "My father, may he rest in peace, told us many times how he stood on the deck of that ship." Harry stopped. He cleared his throat and stared hard at the top of the pulpit for a moment. When he looked up, his eyes swept the congregation. "And watched as the Statue of Liberty came into sight. 'Give me your tired, your poor, your huddled masses yearning to breathe free.' My Dad recited it like it was the Lord's Prayer." Harry let his gaze rest on one person after another. "I said to Marge last night, what would my dad say? What would he say? A pregnant young woman separated from her husband at the border because the husband's story didn't impress the border guards. The same young woman told she would be deported to a country where she fears for her life? And now the life of her unborn child? And the place where she finally finds safety, a church, argues over whether or not they should welcome her or send her packing."

They sat in complete silence while the clock tower chimed four times. Harry turned and nodded to Miranda. She took it as her cue and stepped into the pulpit.

"We have been asked to give a cup of cold water to not the least of Jesus's followers, but to the bravest." She stopped to breathe, her hands finding anchor on the pulpit's edges.

Pam looked straight at her from the third pew, tears falling down her face.

"To the bravest," Miranda repeated, forcing her voice to be strong. "I ask you to offer sanctuary. I know it's a hard decision. It's a long way outside your comfort zone. Mine, too, if I'm being honest. But we are the church. Not a club, or fraternity, or social group. We are the church. And this is what the church does." She stepped out of the pulpit and sat down.

Harry stood and asked for a motion.

"I move." Lucy's tremulous voice rang out. "That we shalt love the Lord, our God with all our hearts and neighbor as ourselves!" Scattered applause from some, others looked away, tight lipped.

"Thank you, Mrs. McClain, but you'll have to be more specific," Harry told her.

"More specific than the Great Commandment, Harry Hopkins? Well, all right, then. I move that we offer sanctuary to Alejandra Romero and do everything we can to get her asylum in a country that was built on the backs of its immigrants!"

"Do I hear a second?" Harry asked, looking out.

Miranda was encouraged when several enthusiastic voices seconded the motion.

The deacons distributed ballots, waited for them to be marked, and then collected them back. All in total silence. Harry and two vestry members left for Peg's office to tabulate the results. While they were gone, Miranda expected the church people to relax and visit with one another. But all that could be heard was the gentle hum of traffic through the open windows.

When Harry returned to the room, Miranda couldn't read his face. He stepped into the pulpit, gavel in hand, but made no move to use it.

"First, let me ask," he said. "Is there anyone here who didn't vote but would like to vote now?"

Not exactly Robert's Rules, Miranda thought.

No one responded. Harry peered down at the slip of paper he held in his hand. "I probably should have asked this before the vote, but did anyone vote who shouldn't have? I mean anyone who isn't a member?"

No movement, silence.

"No one?" Harry stood another moment, looking out. "All right then. One hundred twenty-eight votes were collected. We counted them three times. Sixty-four in favor of offering sanctuary. And sixty-four against. We are officially tied."

A buzz went through the pews.

"According to the church by-laws: in the event of a tie, the decision will be determined by the Church Vestry at its next scheduled meeting." Harry glanced at Miranda.

She started to rise and then sat back down.

"Is there any further business for the good of the order?" Harry looked the congregation up and down, his gavel poised above the pulpit. He waited another long moment, then brought the gavel down with a bang.

"Meeting adjourned."

CHAPTER TWENTY-EIGHT

Peg met Miranda at the office door and handed her a cup of steaming coffee. "I thought it was a double-dark roast morning," her secretary said.

"Believe me, it is." Miranda sank into the Chesterfield chair. "Thank you." She took the cup from Peg feeling the comforting warmth.

"The phone has been ringing off the hook," Peg said. "If phones still had hooks."

"Who?"

Peg picked up her yellow legal pad and adjusted her wire rim glasses. "Dave Johnson wants to know whose idea it was to invite illegals into the church." She looked up. "I think he just woke up and realized it was all happening. I told him about how the window his building committee left unfixed for six months had something to do with it." She turned back to her list. "Anthony Billings wanted to know if he could contribute to a Save Alejandra Fund." She made a check on the legal pad. "I suggested that getting caught up on his pledge would be a more fruitful endeavor."

"I suppose we could do a GoFundMe page or something." But was that really the biggest problem, when the vestry could throw her out after its next meeting?

"A reporter from the *Rockland News* wants to do a story on Alejandra," Peg continued. "The preschool parents' group is meeting to discuss safety issues, and the fire chief suddenly feels the need to inspect the building. And three different church members have called to say that the by-laws do not give the vestry authority over a Congregational vote."

She looked up. "It kills me that members who have never once bothered to read the bylaws are suddenly ecclesiastical attorneys."

Miranda took a quick sip of the hot coffee. Nothing like a double-dark roast. "I wasn't really prepared for this. Not from so many good church people."

"Listen to me." Peg slipped her pen into the penholder on her desk. "I have sat behind this desk for the past thirty years and I've learned a few things about good church people."

"Such as?" Miranda wasn't sure she wanted to know.

"That sometimes, they can restore your faith in life itself. And other times—" Peg paused. "And other times, they will break your heart."

Miranda felt a lump rise in her throat. She stared into her coffee cup willing the tears not to come. "I'm sure you're right." She cleared her throat and looked up. "It's just that welcoming a stranger who desperately needs us seems basic to what we should be about." A car horn honked on Main Street, and a shout came from the preschool play area. "Basic to who we are as a faith community."

Peg peered at Miranda over her half glasses. "I hate to tell you, but in addition to all the phone calls, there has been a—development."

"Oh?" Miranda could barely summon the energy to ask.

"A few Thanksgiving Committee members have organized a—a movement, you might say."

"Movement?"

"A campaign. A crusade, in a sense. Phone calls, mostly. Apparently, in the last few days, they turned people against the idea of sanctuary. Against Alejandra. The Thanksgiving Committee dedicated Saturday to phone calls, warning about the dangers Alejandra supposedly poses to the church. They continued their campaign during Sunday morning's coffee hour."

"So they set the stage for the Congregational meeting on Sunday afternoon."

Peg tapped her pen on her desk blotter. "I just found out. I'm sorry. I got word of it on Saturday but thought I was jumping to conclusions." She leaned forward. "I'll be having words with them." Her voice was clipped. As icy as Miranda had ever heard it.

"The Thanksgiving Committee? They staged a coup against *Alejandra*. All because I didn't want them to wear their Pilgrim costumes? Because they didn't get their way, they want to send a young pregnant woman back to Honduras?" Miranda, her hands shaking, set her coffee cup on the edge of Peg's desk.

Peg walked across the office and shut the door.

"Do Pam and Ramona know about this?" Miranda thought back to dinner on Friday. They couldn't have known this was happening.

"No, they didn't. But they do now. If I understand it, the group elected a new leader. Pam is no longer the chairperson."

"They can't do that."

"Well, they did."

"Who's the new chair?"

"Betty Hardacre."

"Yikes."

"Pam and Ramona want a meeting with you as soon as possible."

"Of all the—wait. What about Linda Darcy?"

"Linda has withdrawn her membership, I'm sorry to say. She told me she didn't join a church to be—" Peg picked up a pink memo slip and read aloud, "—harassed by a bunch of vicious gossips."

"And I had her pegged for senior warden one day." Miranda and Peg stared at each other. "I need a list."

Peg opened the top desk drawer and handed her a pink memo slip.

"Edna, Donna, Betty." Miranda read the women's names aloud, her voice bitter. Three of the most active, long-term members of the church. She slipped the memo slip into her hoodie pocket. Maybe it was time to move on. Do something that had nothing to do with the church. With any church. Reach out to Tony. Pack for Seattle.

★ ★ ★

Miranda sat across from Pam and Ramona and reminded herself that she was the priest here, not the injured party. Which meant that she needed to respond to their needs—not her own. After taking the list from Peg, her first impulse had been to conduct a full-on, scorch-the-earth, come-to-Jesus confrontation with the three women. Instead, she had called Linda Darcy and asked if she would meet for coffee.

To Miranda's disappointment, Linda had politely refused. "It's not that I don't like you, Pastor Miranda. I love your sermons and all that you have brought to St. Gabe's. But I'm not looking for a church that has to ask, 'Should we help someone in need?'"

Miranda didn't say it, but she felt the same.

There was a knock at the door, and with an unprecedented act of hospitality, Peg pushed in backward with a tray carrying three teacups on saucers, a teapot, and a plate piled with cookies. The round, yellow cookies gave off a faint lemon scent. Miranda recognized them from the stash of Girl Scout cookies in Peg's bottom drawer. Peg didn't eat sugar products, but she never refused a Scout selling cookies.

"I thought you ladies could use some sustenance," she said crisply as she left the tray on the coffee table.

Pam poured a cup of tea for each. Her mouth set in a grim line.

"Good heavens," Ramona blurted out. "If I weren't about to snake out Harmon Holbeck's basement sink, I'd say we ditch the tea and reconvene at the Speckled Sparrow."

"A pub is not a bad idea," Miranda sipped her tea.

"It was a coup d'état," Pam informed them. "Betty asked for a special meeting of the committee, which I thought wasn't a bad idea. There were still a lot of loose ends, and I was about to call a meeting anyway."

"And we both thought you had been invited to the meeting, Pastor." Ramona took a cookie from the plate and bit into it. "Hey, this is the new Girl Scout cookie."

"They have a new cookie?" Miranda took one off the plate.

"Lemon-Ups."

"So, you can imagine. When you weren't there, I thought you had a conflict or something."

Ramona broke in. "Then Betty announces that without you at the meeting, they could talk more openly about the Pilgrim costumes."

"And so, I asked, well you did *invite* her, didn't you?" Pam dropped the cookie back onto the plate. "And Betty gets all huffy and finally says she wasn't required to invite you. So I said, look, I'm the chair of this committee, and if the Pastor isn't invited, then there's not going to be a meeting. And that's when Edna told me maybe I shouldn't be the chair anymore."

"Betty jumps in and makes a big deal out of how she would be honored to run the committee," Ramona filled in. "I asked her, what do you think this is—a campaign for mayor? Then Betty asked for a show of hands, and it was three in favor, two against."

Miranda picked up another cookie. "But aren't there seven people on that committee?"

"Linda's gone, and Shirley abstained."

Miranda had noticed that Shirley had signed up to bring food to Alejandra next Friday. Maybe she really was an ally.

"Coward," Ramona said.

"So then Ramona and I walked out." Pam topped off the teacups. "Now I wish we had stayed because I heard they went on a rampage about Alejandra. That's the saddest part of all is that they've twisted the whole Pilgrim thing into an assault against America. And somehow, Alejandra represents it."

"How do you know they went on a rampage if you left?"

"Shirley."

"Double coward," Ramona said, but since her mouth was full of cookies, it came out more like *dubba cowvard*. She took a sip of tea. "I am loving these Lemon-Ups. So, Shirley won't vote but she'll talk behind everyone's back later?"

"Don't be so hard on Shirley," Miranda said. "I think she is trying to do the right thing but not lose her friends."

"A tough place to be, I suppose," Pam conceded. "Apparently, they made a bunch of phone calls asking people if they *liked the direction St. Gabe's was going*. And, of course, let everyone know that they didn't."

Now Miranda understood the visit from the PSRC.

"I am sure the congregation would have voted in favor of sanctuary if those women hadn't campaigned," Pam said.

Miranda wasn't so sure, but she didn't say it.

"How about calling those three in here and reading them the riot act?" Ramona said.

Miranda bit into a cookie as a way of stalling. It hit her that perhaps the remainder of her ministry at St. Gabriel—however short it might be—would be remembered by how she handled things right now. If she did decide to leave and cast her lot with Tony in Seattle, the least she could do was get the church through this immediate crisis. And if she wasn't going to leave, then she needed to make things right. If that were still possible.

"Believe me, I'd love to." Miranda's voice was low and strained.

"So why don't we?" Ramona leaned forward, eyes bright with indignation.

"Because we need to approach this carefully. Acting on emotion alone won't help our cause." The women fell into a thoughtful silence, broken only by the soft clink of teacups against saucers.

"You're right, of course." Pam leaned back in her chair. "We should take some time to plan our next move."

"Exactly," Miranda fought to keep the weariness from her voice. "We have until the vestry meeting. That gives us three days to come up with a strategy."

"I've got some plumbing jobs lined up. But I can make time to meet."

Pam checked her watch. "And I've got Tommy's band concert tonight, but I'm free tomorrow afternoon."

Miranda forced a smile. "Perfect. Let's regroup when we've had time to think. We'll make sure they hear us, but we'll do it right."

After Pam and Ramona left, Miranda collapsed into a wing-back chair. Her mind reeled at the thought of leading a congregation that would turn away a pregnant girl in need. She absently finished her tea, now cold, and ate the final cookie. Despite the warmth emanating from the little brick fireplace, a chill seeped into her very bones—as cold as she had ever felt at St. Gabe's.

CHAPTER TWENTY-NINE

Adam stood with his neck craned upwards, admiring the grandeur of the four-story brick factory before them.

"A work of art, really," he murmured, taking in the segmented arched windows and the intricate corbeled brickwork under the eaves. The faded words, *Barnes Bros. Button Works*, were painted on the factory wall, a reminder of a time when this building had been the lifeblood of Sparrow's economy. Now, it stood empty, a ghost of its former glory.

As he turned to Miranda, his eyes alight, an unexpected warmth blossomed within her.

"It is." Her voice came out softer than intended. She took a breath, willing her pulse to steady. Adam's salt-and-pepper hair, usually so meticulously groomed, was charmingly disheveled today, curling over his collar. She liked this glimpse of a less polished Adam. "How old is it?"

"1897. We don't do construction like this anymore. You know, with such attention to detail and artistry."

"I've often thought that about old churches."

He turned his eyes to her. "People cared more back then, right?"

She looked into his eyes. "I know. Things were so different."

"I'll take you inside. But you'll have to wear this." Adam popped the trunk of the silver Lexus and retrieved two yellow hard hats. "The latest in architectural historian fashion." He handed one to her and plunked the other on his own head.

As she tucked her hair under the hard hat, Adam reached across and adjusted its brim.

She felt a warm flush.

"There," he said. "If it doesn't fit properly, you might as well not even wear it."

"Right," she gulped. *Get a grip,* she told herself. *This is the guy who called you a hearty eater.*

Earlier that morning, when Adam stopped by the church and asked if she wanted a tour of the old Button Factory, Peg had piped up before she could respond.

"Sounds fascinating to me," Peg said. "Pastor Miranda loves history."

"I have a lot to accomplish today," she had said in her most disinterested voice, regretting her choice of pink Converse sneakers and faded jeans. "I'm not sure I can just—"

"What do you have to accomplish?" Peg peered at her over her glasses.

"Well, there's the vestry meeting."

"Two days away." To Peg, that settled it.

"Planning the children's Advent play. Christian Ed wants me to bring ideas to their meeting tonight."

"Nonsense," Peg said. "Sheep, shepherds, and the baby Jesus. What else is there at the Advent play? Go see the button factory. You need the fresh air."

"Sure." She shot Peg a glance. "Let me get my hoodie."

★ ★ ★

"Careful," Adam warned as they entered the heavy front entrance. "Step exactly where I step. I don't want to have to tell Aunt Lucy that I lost her favorite pastor through the floorboards."

Miranda followed Adam into a long, open room and was instantly swept away by its Old-World feel. Weak light lit the scratched wooden floor. At one end, a vast stone fireplace covered almost the entire wall. A heavy wrought iron spiral staircase led to a long balcony stretched along the back of the open room. A flock of sparrows fluttered overhead. The faintest oil smell of machinery lingered in the air.

"This was the main workroom floor. Imagine two rows of cutting machines along the center, and then these huge button-stamping machines over there." Miranda caught her breath as she felt his hand gently press on the middle of her back. He steered her toward the stamping area.

"Look closely, and you can still see impressions on the floor. That's how heavy the machines were." Adam's voice grew animated. He was clearly in his element.

"Amazing to think of all the people who showed up here every day to earn their living, to support their families," Miranda said. She gazed up at the heavy beams crossing the ceiling. She could almost hear the machines' clack and the workers' voices.

"Not much of a living, I am sorry to say," Adam replied. "Factories like this one employed children well into the twentieth century. And for women, it was nearly indentured servitude." Adam dropped his hand from her back.

"We forget how hard life was, only a few generations ago." Alejandra flashed through her mind. "Or maybe not so long ago."

"Want to go up?" He nodded toward the spiral staircase.

"I'm game," she said. "It's safe, right?"

"Why do you think I gave you a hard hat?" He grinned. "Sure, it's safe. I've been up and down all day taking photos." He pointed to one end of the balcony. "The factory boss would stand up there at the railing and watch the workers. You know, make sure no one slacked off during their twelve-hour workday." They walked across the creaking wooden floor to the bottom of the staircase. Adam stepped aside and made a sweeping gesture. "After you."

Miranda grabbed the iron railing and started up. She remembered that Adam worked out at the gym. His muscles had tensed under his button-down shirt when he took his suit coat off that night at her house. She had also noticed that he didn't carry an ounce of fat.

"Doing okay?" Adam asked.

"Oh yeah. I'm fine." The spiral staircase was so steep and twisty that she had to grip the railing and pull herself up with every step. She tried to conceal it, but she was starting to breathe hard.

"You're almost there." He called up.

She finally reached the top, taking a few unsteady steps along the railing. Catching her breath, she realized her daily walk from rectory to church wasn't cutting it as exercise. "Sorry. Those steps are steep," Adam said.

"I'm good," Miranda replied, catching her breath. She looked around. "Wow. I can see why you're intrigued by this place." Miranda loved abandoned old places. A dusty attic or a falling-down barn always gave her the feeling that she could observe life from another era.

"Hungry?"

"What?"

"I was wondering if you wanted to get lunch?"

"Um—sure. Right now?"

Adam removed his hard hat, running his fingers through his hair. His gaze flickered to the brick walls around them.

"Well, I meant when we go back into town." He gestured toward the vast, empty space before them. "Much of the factory isn't safe to walk through yet. But I wanted you to see this big room." His voice softened. "This is where all the women and children worked. I thought you'd—you know, appreciate it."

He shifted his weight, the floorboards creaking beneath his feet. Sunlight from the skylight windows touched his hair. His suit coat, always immaculate, was covered in dust. Clearly, the place made Adam feel alive. Maybe like when she stood in the pulpit and looked out over the pews of people. *This is where I am supposed to be, doing what I am supposed to do.*

She nodded. "Yes. I do appreciate it. What do you plan to do with the factory once it's remodeled?"

"Restored. As an architectural historian, I don't like the word 'remodeled.' Restored indicates that you are bringing the old building back to life—back to its original condition, and into its new life."

"I like that," she said. "You're giving it a new purpose but keeping its integrity." She liked seeing this side of Adam. "And what's its new life going to be?"

"Art studios upstairs and a gallery on the first floor."

"How wonderful for Sparrow. I can think of a few local artists who would probably love the opportunity to showcase their work," she said. The two of them stood together in silence, gazing down at the bustling factory floor below from their perch atop the railing. They stood silent for a moment, looking down over the railing at the factory floor. "I can see why you like doing this sort of thing."

He nodded. "Restoring a place like this—it's kind of my dream job."

She started down the spiral staircase. Dream job. That's how she had thought of St. Gabe's. The stairs were so steep and sharply winding that she didn't talk until they reached the bottom. "And by the way," she said, "lunch sounds great."

They made their way out of the factory and got into Adam's car. He started to press the ignition button, then stopped, reached over, and removed her hard hat. "Maybe you should take this off," he said. "Unless it's a statement on my driving?"

"No. Not at all," Miranda said, smoothing her hair. "I forgot I was even wearing it."

"It looks good on you. Not everyone can pull off hard hat-chic."

She grinned. "Well, I've been told that I look good in hats."

He pushed a lock of hair back out of her eyes, his fingers lingering for a moment. "I think you have perfect hair—for a hard hat."

"I do?" she asked, eyebrows raised and trying to ignore the flush she felt.

"How about me? How do I look in a hard hat?"

"Hmmm." She cocked her head, looking at him. "I think hard hats give you bedhead."

He laughed and backed out of the parking space. "Well, then I hope my hair recovers before we get to Loretta's."

★ ★ ★

"Salad?" Loretta said, eyebrows raised. "You never order a salad."

"It sounded good," Miranda lied.

"I have a nice steak-and-cheese sandwich. Today's special. Thin sliced rib-eye, melted provolone, fried onions. Fresh roll, lightly toasted."

"That sounds great," Adam said, his eyes lighting up. "Can you toss in an order of fries?"

"The pastor here likes onion rings," Loretta said, peering at him, her pencil tapping on her order pad.

"Okay, then, a large order of onion rings." Adam closed his menu. "We'll split it."

"Salad dressing on the side," Miranda said. "No bread."

"I thought you were a foodie?" Adam remarked as Loretta turned on her heel and walked away.

"Why would you say that? Because I was once a chef? People who cook are not necessarily big eaters."

"I didn't say big eater. I said foodie."

"Right. I am a foodie. I just happen to feel like a salad." She hoped it sounded convincing since salad was the last thing she wanted, but Lucy's words were ringing in her head. "Tell me more about the button factory." She tried to get the conversation back to how it was in the car. Carefree, laughing. But all her huffing and puffing up the staircase reminded her that she was in lousy shape—and overweight. Seventy-two-year-old, 142-pound Peg could climb those steps without even noticing.

"Well, first, I want to restore the original brick facade. Some of it is still there, but a bunch has been torn down or—if you can believe it—painted over."

Miranda nodded and stirred her coffee. "Sounds amazing."

"I'm a planner. I like nothing better than to have a project to dive into. Do you have big plans for the church, too? According to Aunt Lucy, you are the best thing that ever happened to St. Gabe's."

That did make her feel better. But only for a moment. "I had some ideas. Plans. Thought we could—" She stopped abruptly.

Adam leaned in. "Could what?"

"It doesn't matter now. It all fell apart."

"Are you okay?" Adam asked. "Sorry, I've been rambling on. Aunt Lucy told me about the Congregational meeting the other day. Sounds harsh."

"It was. But I'm fine. I love hearing about your work." She didn't feel like talking about the church with Adam. He was her opportunity to get away from it all.

"Thanks." Adam suddenly looked self-conscious. "My work means everything to me. Especially when I get to do something like restore an old factory. Factories were the heartbeat of so many small towns. Restoring them is almost like—" He paused, thoughtful.

"Like honoring the people who worked in them."

"Exactly." Adam grinned. "It's obvious that you love the church, but do you ever miss being a professional chef?"

Miranda hesitated. She fought the urge to confide in Adam about Tony's offer.

"I don't miss it as much as I expected," she said. "Ministry and cooking have more in common than you'd think."

"Really? How's that?"

"Both nourish people, just in different ways. And both need careful preparation."

"Like how?" Adam ate an onion ring and tipped the plate toward her. She took two.

She bit into an onion ring and thought for a moment. The sounds of the diner bustled around her. "A good chef doesn't cook to show off. You know, to demonstrate their amazing skill and mastery of the art. A good chef cooks to feed people. That's why I am so into hearty foods like lamb and root vegetables and cabbage and lobster and—well, real food. Not white bread and pizza. My end goal is to provide sustenance. And as a pastor, it's a lot the same. I feed people. I provide them with care and nurture. My favorite verse in the Bible is where Jesus tells his disciples, 'Feed my sheep.' And that's what I do. I feed my sheep."

She sat back and bit into the other onion ring. She seldom articulated it so clearly before, not even to herself.

"I get it. I really do."

"Thanks. Not everyone does."

"And now I understand why you eat so much."

"Excuse me?" Miranda sat back in the booth and laid down her fork.

"You know, I get it now, why you are always eating."

"I'm not always eating."

Adam smiled, oblivious to the path the conversation was taking. "You know what I mean."

"No, I don't. What do you mean?"

"I mean, you like to cook, and you like to eat. Nothing wrong with that."

"Thanks for your approval." She regretted having a mouthful of onion rings when she said it. A tiny piece spit out onto the table. She swallowed hard.

"What's going on? Are you upset or something? So, you like to eat. Whatever."

"Rather a big double-standard, don't you think? You love to eat. And you love to cook. Why is a man allowed to eat all they want, and a woman is expected to enjoy nibbling on lettuce so they will never be called fat." There. She said it. The F-word.

"Is that why you ordered that salad? You're not fat. I never said the word 'fat.'" He picked up his cheesesteak and took an inordinately big bite. She watched him chew and swallow. "Every man knows never to say 'fat' around a woman."

"Oh my God. You did not just say that." Miranda half rose in the booth and then sat back down, staring at Adam.

He swallowed. "Say what?" He put his sandwich down. "You're big-boned. Like my sister. What's wrong with that?"

"It was bad enough that you told your aunt Lucy that I am a hearty eater for a girl?" Miranda leaned in. "And that I don't worry about being thin?"

"Oh my God. Aunt Lucy. That wasn't for you to hear. It's not even what I meant. Or even said. Exactly."

She stared across the table at him. She hated it, but tiny pricks of tears jabbed at the back of her eyes. She willed herself to not let those tears out. It was just so utterly disappointing. Adam seemed different from most guys. And here he was calling her big-boned. Just what every woman wanted to hear from the cute guy she was falling for a little bit.

"Look," she said, sliding out of the booth. "Women are told from birth that they have to be thin. As a child I was always referred to as pudgy. As a teen, I was heavy. Now, I've reached a point in life where I finally feel good about how I look. And yes, I like to eat. But may I point out, you, also, like to eat. Of course, though, that's fine because you're a man."

"Oh, please." Adam tossed his napkin on the table. "Don't you think you're being a little sensitive? I'm just stating my opinion. I like to be direct."

"You might think it's fine to be direct about someone's eating habits and their weight, but it isn't." She slipped on her hoodie to leave. "Sorry if that's too sensitive for you."

CHAPTER THIRTY

Miranda followed the sound of laughter toward the Youth Room. She pushed open the door and saw Dr. Hazeltine and Alejandra sitting across from each other on the purple couch. The early light flooded in through the basement windows.

"Good morning," she said. Just the sight of the two women laughing lifted her spirits. She had barely slept last night, her mind racing with thoughts about tonight's upcoming vestry meeting, her disappointing conversation with Adam, the Thanksgiving Committee, Alejandra, and the sad loss of Samson.

No wonder she often looked like something the cat dragged in. Something big-boned that the cat dragged in.

"Pastor, good morning to you, too," Dr. Hazeltine said. "Glad you're here. You can help translate."

"I'll try," Miranda said, flopping down into a pink beanbag chair.

"I was just saying—or trying to say—how impossible bean bag chairs are when you are nine months pregnant." Dr. Hazeltine said.

"I can imagine," Miranda said. "Gravity works against you."

"I am enjoying all the food from your church people," Alejandra said. "Perhaps too much."

"Good! And how are you doing otherwise?" Miranda looked from Alejandra to Dr. Hazeltine.

"I am *ansiosa*." Anxious.

"I would be *ansiosa*, too," Miranda said. "What's making you *ansiosa*?"

Again, Alejandra and Dr. Hazeltine exchanged a glance. "Alejandra and I are re-evaluating her due date. It might be closer than I had previously thought. She has not had consistent prenatal care for obvious reasons. When she was in Portland, she didn't go to a doctor or clinic."

"If someone saw me at the clinic and *reportó* that I'm *embarazada*, my asylum status would *be en peligro*." In danger.

"But didn't you—" Miranda stopped. She was about to ask what the plan had been when the baby was born. She realized once again that hers was a world of privilege, which meant making plans was the usual way of doing things. But if you were poor or in constant fear of being deported, plans meant day-to-day survival. She really had no cognizance of the world in which Alejandra lived. "Any guesses on the due date, then?"

"The Braxton-Hicks contractions were an indicator that she is getting ready to deliver. I would say that she may go into labor next week or—"

"Or what?"

"Or anytime sooner. When does the vestry meet?"

"Tonight."

"Any possibility that I could attend the meeting?" Dr. Hazeltine asked.

"I should think so," she said. "But I'll ask Harry. Vestry meetings are the territory of the senior warden."

"Will they let me stay in the church, if the baby is here?" Alejandra looked imploringly from Miranda to Dr. Hazeltine.

"We'll think of something. I promise," Miranda said.

Alejandra nodded, her face hopeful. "*Por eso, te agradezco.*" For which, I thank you.

"*De nada*," Miranda answered slowly.

"I have faith that this will all come out right," Dr. Hazeltine stuffed her stethoscope into her black Gucci bag. Miranda noticed the doctor's bag wasn't a knockoff like Sylvia's. "Don't you agree, Pastor Miranda?"

"I totally agree," Miranda said with as much enthusiasm as she could summon. "Absolutely."

CHAPTER THIRTY-ONE

Thanks to Harry, the vestry meeting was mostly without conflict—no outbursts of anger and no calls for Alejandra to be arrested for trespass. Dr. Hazeltine's presence in the room changed the dynamic for the better. She gave a convincing speech in favor of St. Gabriel's establishing itself as a sanctuary church and then spoke passionately about Alejandra and her needs. A few vestry members who had entered the room with unsympathetic faces leaned forward and appeared to listen. Elizabeth Hazeltine could inspire even the most reluctant.

Lucy also spoke in favor of sanctuary. First, she insisted that every vestry member join hands while she prayed. Then she referenced Mother Teresa, Jimmy Carter, and John Henry Newman; finally, she brought down the house with a from-memory scripture recitation that lasted four minutes.

Following Lucy, several members spoke against sanctuary. They cited everything from endangering the church's nonprofit status to the loss of pledges. Which, the treasurer pointed out, had already occurred. Two of the church's largest donors had threatened to withdraw their support if the vestry voted in favor of sanctuary.

Harry called on Miranda as the last to speak before the vote. She stood, took a centering breath, and held eye contact with each person before speaking. Then she launched into a brief but heartfelt statement about why the congregation had a moral obligation to offer sanctuary to Alejandra and how the experience would make them a better church. She ended with the verse from Ephesians: "You are no more strangers and foreigners, but fellow citizens with the saints and of the household of God." When she sat down, Lucy applauded, and Sam Reeves gave a resounding amen. Otherwise, the room stayed silent.

"All right, then," Harry said. "There is a motion on the floor to offer sanctuary to Mrs. Alejandra Romero."

Miranda was struck by the simplicity of the motion. And yet, such an undertaking was perhaps the most complicated role a church could assume.

"Any more discussion?" Harry asked.

No one spoke. The bell in the clock tower chimed, and the faint hum of Colville's vacuum on the floor above. "Speak now or forever hold your peace." Harry paused for a long moment. "All right then. All in favor?" he said, his eyes sweeping the room, counting hands raised.

"All opposed?" Again, a piercing gaze across the room. A moment later, the gavel thudded down.

"Motion fails. Meeting adjourned."

★ ★ ★

"Let's tell her together, Pastor Miranda," Harry said as they walked toward the Youth Room.

"Sure," she said, not trusting her voice to say more.

"I'm sorry. I know this isn't what you wanted."

"Every vestry member who voted against sanctuary should have to look Alejandra in the eye and tell her that she has no place to stay."

"I know." His voice sounded as tired as Miranda had ever heard it. They continued down the hall without speaking. Miranda was shell-shocked, disappointed, and above everything else, wondering how she would ever be able to stand in the pulpit and preach this Sunday.

Muffled laughter drifted from the Youth Room. Harry gave Miranda a sideways glance.

"Whatever you do, tell Marge I voted in favor."

Miranda nodded. "I know you did. And I appreciate it." She paused at the door. "Sounds like Dr. Hazeltine is with them, too. She must have come downstairs after her talk."

"I'm making an executive decision here. We will find her a new place. A new church. But until then, she stays put."

"What about Betty and everyone who wants her out now? Before the baby?"

"I'll deal with them." He paused. "I know you're upset, Pastor. And I don't blame you, but—"

"I'm fine," she said curtly. "Let's just tell her."

CHAPTER THIRTY-TWO

"Get your jacket," Peg snapped, leaning into the doorway of Miranda's office.

Miranda stood up from her desk where she had been sitting, staring out the window. She had avoided the Youth Room since delivering news of the vestry's vote, unable to face Alejandra. At the jingle of keys and zip of Peg's running bag, she grabbed her hoodie and followed Peg into the hall.

"Wait up." She broke into a jog to keep up with Peg's power-walking legs.

"Lewis called. Someone saw Samson. On Main Street."

"Oh my gosh. I hope they can grab him." She zipped her hoodie.

"Last night. In the alley behind Loretta's. Security camera. Lewis is meeting us there."

Miranda noticed that Peg carried the blue leash in her hand. *Dear God, let him be there. Don't let someone as good and caring as Peg be disappointed again.* She jumped in the Volvo with barely enough time to shut the passenger door before Peg peeled out.

They parked behind the diner next to Lewis's panel van.

"Have you seen him?" Peg jumped out. Miranda followed.

"Afraid not, Mrs. Dunbar," Lewis replied. "But that doesn't mean he isn't around. I think he'd come to your voice if he heard it. Poor guy is probably skittish again, living in the rough and all."

Peg walked up and down the alley behind Loretta's, calling Samson's name. Miranda ran out to the sidewalk along Main Street.

"Samson!" she shouted. "Samson!"

The sky was bright, and the air was crisp but not yet cold. The moment held hope.

"Samson! Here, boy." She could no longer hear Peg calling, so she made her way back to the alley. Peg and Lewis stood talking. As she approached, she heard Peg asking Lewis if she could see the video.

"Got it right here," Lewis said. "Loretta emailed it." He swiped a few times on his phone and handed it to Peg. "It's one minute and twenty-two seconds. He finishes off a take-out box of something. I'm thinking fish and chips. And then hightails it out."

Miranda watched the video. It was clearly Samson in the dark shadows and eerie light of 4:12 a.m. At one point, he raised his shaggy silver and gray head and looked right into the camera.

Peg caught her breath and quickly handed the phone back to Lewis. "That's our Samson all right." She cleared her throat.

"He looks healthy," Miranda said. "And happy."

"He always did like leftovers," Peg added, her voice now business-like.

"I say we wait around here tonight and see if he shows up," Lewis said. "Do a stakeout."

"I'm in," Miranda said. She turned to look at her secretary.

"It's just that—" Peg said.

"Just what?"

"Nothing." Peg paused. "Well, I had acclimated to the fact that he was gone. Accepting it, as it were. And now—"

"Then why did you keep his leash in your desk drawer? If you had acclimated?" Miranda countered.

"I didn't say I'd given up entirely." Peg had her resolute look back.

"I think we should show up just before dark." Lewis said, cutting in. "All right with you ladies if I take first shift, say five p.m. to midnight? My wife's a good sport when it comes to dogs, but with getting four kids off to school, she'll want me home."

"Of course, Lewis," Peg said. "Miranda and I will stake out here, midnight till sunrise." She turned to Miranda. "Are you up for that, Pastor?"

"I'll bring the snacks." She liked the energy that had returned to her secretary.

Peg and Miranda said goodbye to Lewis and walked to the diner's front door. Peg wanted to express her gratitude to Loretta.

"I usually don't even watch the video from the camera, but something is digging up my trash. Figured I had a raccoon. When I saw that big dog, I called Lewis. It was only after I called him, I remembered you had lost your dog."

"We appreciate your help," Peg said.

Miranda heard the pain in Peg's voice, and Miranda wanted to take her hand or throw her arms around her. But Peg Dunbar was neither a hand-holder nor a hugger.

"Why don't you ladies take that empty table and have a piece of pie and a coffee. On the house. Mrs. Dunbar, we have a vegan pie this morning, if you can believe it. Chocolate cream. I use dairy-free whipped cream and no eggs, either. And don't worry, no tofu. I won't let tofu in the door."

"How did you know I prefer vegan?" Peg asked. "To be precise, ovo-vegetarian."

"I pay attention," Loretta said. "And the Pastor here," Loretta nodded at Miranda. "Wants a dark roast with cream and a big slice of pie—but the real kind made with eggs, butter, and whipped cream."

A big slice. Was it that obvious?

"I guess it won't set us too far back if we take a short break from the church this morning," Peg said as they pulled out chairs and sat down.

"The church will be just fine." Miranda unrolled the silverware wrapped in a paper napkin. She looked at Peg as nonchalantly as possible. "Do you think I eat too much?"

"Not this again."

Miranda shrugged.

Loretta slid two plates of pie onto the table between them and filled a cup with steaming dark roast for Miranda. She then placed a pot of tea and a mug in front of Peg.

"You'll find that dog," she said. "I know you will."

Making plans for a stakeout while eating in a diner made Miranda feel like a character on an old detective show. Of course, most stakeouts weren't to find a lost and beloved dog. Peg insisted on collecting Miranda at the rectory at eleven-thirty that night. They would park behind the dumpster so Samson wouldn't be spooked, and if he showed up looking for scraps, Peg would get out of the Volvo slowly and call to him. Miranda had already begun praying that Samson would run straight to Peg.

Miranda finished the last bite of chocolate pie just as the door to Loretta's opened, and three men in work clothes and heavy boots walked in. Miranda recognized the older man in the group as one of the contractors who had repaired the church roof last March. She remembered him because he had stopped by her office to apologize for all the noise. She had assured him it was music to her ears. Getting the church roof fixed was a dream come true. She thought for a moment. *Ed Stanton*. She took a small amount of pride in her ability to remember names.

The three men sat on the stools at the counter. After a moment, Ed spun around and stared at her. "Pastor," he said across the nearly empty diner.

Miranda smiled in his direction. "Ed, right? Nice to see you."

"Heard something I couldn't quite believe," he said. The other men snickered and buried their faces in their menus. "Heard you got an illegal hiding in your church."

Peg slowly placed her mug of tea on the table.

"She's not an illegal," Miranda said. Out of the corner of her eye, she saw Loretta step out of the back office.

"Not an illegal? How's that work?" Ed's face had grown red, and his voice slightly louder than necessary.

"She's seeking asylum." She took a centering breath.

"That's what you call it? In my day, she's what you called a—"

"Get out." Loretta's voice was low and furious. She stepped behind the counter. "You're done here." She snatched the menus back from each man.

"You can't kick us out," one of them said. "That's violating our rights."

"My diner, my rules." Loretta tossed the menus under the counter, never taking her eyes off the men.

"Come on, boys, we don't want to eat here anyway." Ed slid off the stool. No one spoke as they crossed the room, the door banging behind them.

Loretta opened the small fridge under the counter and took out a white paper sack. "A piece of pie for you to take to your friend," she said, sliding it down the counter in their direction. "And it's not ovo-vegetarian either. It's the real thing."

★ ★ ★

The early morning sun cast a fresh glow on the front of the rectory, birdsong filled the sea air, and the waves whispered against the shore. But none of it mattered because the stake-out had been a bust. Miranda felt as if one disappointment in her life had just piled onto the next. The vestry vote, Adam, now Samson. She eyed Peg, who was uncharacteristically slumped behind the steering wheel. Neither woman spoke as Miranda gathered her things from the front seat and shoved them in a satchel. Empty coffee thermos, a box of Thin Mints with nothing left but crumbs, and two bottles of water which Peg wouldn't touch since no one should be buying plastic bottles these days.

The night had started out with such optimism. But the hours went by with no sign of Samson. The worst part was that Peg had arranged his dog bed in the back of the Volvo: a fluffy pillow in the dog bed, and on the pillow, a yellow sock with a knot tied in it.

"I need to stop this," Peg said, staring out of the front windshield.

"Stop what?"

"Hoping."

"Why? Miranda said. "You saw him on that camera. He looked right at us."

"I have to let go. It isn't healthy." Peg didn't look at her. "Falling in love with a dog. It's ridiculous." She started the Volvo and adjusted her mirrors.

"Love is ridiculous? Since when?"

Peg snorted.

"He needs you."

"For what?"

"To find his way home."

Peg glanced at Miranda, raising an eyebrow. "You look like you've been dragged through a hedge backwards." The conversation about Samson was clearly over.

"It's haute couture for sitting behind a dumpster all night in a dark alley."

Peg gave the smallest of smiles. "We have work to do at the church. The newsletter is only half finished, and I need your sermon title."

"Sorry, but I'm taking a nap."

"A nap? In the middle of the morning?"

Miranda opened the passenger side door and slid to the ground. "It's hardly the middle of the morning. And I'm exhausted."

"Suit yourself." Peg pressed the ignition button and put the Volvo in reverse. "See you at the office."

CHAPTER THIRTY-THREE

Ministry was feast or famine. On some days, obligations crowded Miranda's calendar: hospital visits, an emergency budget meeting, confirmation class, women's Bible study. Other days, nothing happened. Or at least, if not nothing, then next to nothing. The day after the stakeout for Samson was one of those days. Famine. Miranda stared at her blank document, struggling to write her sermon. How could she address the sixty-four people who had voted to send a pregnant, nineteen-year-old girl back to danger? She sipped her coffee and found herself absently scrolling through social media, skimming diet tips and exercise routines. Catching herself, she closed the app with a frown. Why worry about a few extra pounds? She had more important things to focus on

Finally, she stopped procrastinating and logged onto the Diocesan website, searching for a church that might consider taking in Alejandra. There were two possibilities, both in Massachusetts. She would reach out to their priests today.

But she knew that the real question wasn't if she could find a place for Alejandra, but could she find a place for herself? Miranda sat back and looked around her office. She remembered how happy she had been the day she had moved in. Organizing her desk, carefully placing her ordination certificate on the wall behind her desk, filling the shelves with her books from seminary. She had felt elated, inspired. Finally, she was *official*. A member of the ordained clergy. But her enthusiasm had since worn thin, and she wondered if she were only playing at being a priest. How effective could she be if her parish cared so little for those outside their small world?

She looked up when Peg opened the office door.

"I'm leaving now for my power walking workshop at the Senior Center." Peg's workshops were a big hit with the over-seventy crowd. "Afterwards, I'm taking everyone who remembered their sneakers to the high school track," Peg said, adjusting her vintage Red Sox cap. "I don't expect to be back into the office today."

"Have fun." Peg had so enjoyed power walking with Samson. Miranda felt her throat grow tight.

Peg paused at the door. "You should take the afternoon off. Everything is fine here. Alejandra is learning to cross-stitch with the knitting ladies, and then she's attending chair yoga. Although I'm not sure how a woman that pregnant does any yoga."

"Who's doing her dinner?" Arranging meals for Alejandra had fallen to Miranda and Peg. She needed to shift that responsibility onto the church members. If she stayed much longer.

"The Stonehams. All six grandchildren are coming along. They're bringing spaghetti casserole and *Toy Story 3*."

"And multiple boxes of tissues, I hope."

Peg stood with her hand on the doorknob. "I wasn't going to say it, but you look—"

"Like I was dragged through a hedge backwards?" Again, Miranda found herself on the edge of telling Peg about Tony's proposition. She hadn't yet, but she needed to—soon.

Peg raised an eyebrow. "No. I was going to say you look like you are carrying the world on your shoulders. But now that you mention it." And with that, Peg left.

* * *

Miranda sighed, staring at her unfinished sermon. After another hour of getting nowhere, she shut her laptop and decided to clear her head with a walk. The crisp air and steady pace of her footsteps helped, but she still couldn't figure out what to say.

Miranda's phone rang just as she reached the rectory door. She answered without checking the caller ID, then immediately tensed as she recognized Sylvia's voice. It was so cold, Miranda wondered if you could get frostbite through a cell phone.

"I am calling because the PSRC wants a formal meeting with you," Sylvia stated without preamble.

Miranda sighed, fumbling with her keys. She pushed open the door and stepped inside. Howard grunted from inside his Hobbit house. Her palms instantly prickled with sweat. What did Sylvia mean by a formal meeting? And anyway, Alejandra was leaving. What was there to be upset about?

"When? And why?" She crossed the room and opened the little gate to Howard's enclosure.

"Soon. Day after tomorrow," Sylvia replied. "We've asked Harry Hopkins to attend."

Howard darted out and scurried across the floor and under a scatter rug.

"Harry? Why would you need the senior warden?"

"I am not at liberty to discuss details with you."

Miranda gripped the phone. "If it's about Alejandra, the vestry already voted that—" She swallowed hard. "That we would find her a new place of sanctuary."

"The girl is part of our conversation," Sylvia's voice came cool and crisp through the receiver. "But certainly not all of it."

"I should know the agenda prior to the meeting. That's protocol." A PSRC meeting with the senior warden? She began to pace the small front room, her steps quick and uneven.

The silence on the other end stretched, each second feeling like an eternity. When Sylvia finally spoke, her tone was still glacial. "You'll find out the agenda at the meeting. Friday morning, morning, eleven o'clock. We'll come to you." Sylvia ended the call.

Harry answered on the first ring.

"I'm sorry, Pastor Miranda." Harry's voice sounded strained. "Margery couldn't believe that I didn't tell you. But you had so much to deal with already, well, I hated to pile on with this nonsense. And I thought it might fizzle out after the vestry decision."

"*What* might fizzle out?" This was Harry, she reminded herself. Best senior warden ever.

Howard had come out from under the scatter rug and was snuffling and grunting. She tossed him an insectivore pellet and then collapsed onto the loveseat.

"Let's just say that there are a few members in the congregation—maybe more than a few—who want a Congregational vote."

"On what?"

"You. They want to vote on you. There are some folks—not everyone, by a long shot—who are hoping for a vote of no-confidence."

Miranda felt she'd been punched in the gut. This couldn't be happening. "What would that even mean?"

"Now, don't get ahead of things. I suppose it would mean that—"

"That I would be forced to resign." Miranda's chest tightened, her breaths coming faster. Leaving for Seattle on her own terms was one thing. Being fired was another entirely. "Wait. That's not even proper protocol. Isn't the vestry required to take their concerns to the priest? Or the Bishop?"

"Some people wanted to gauge the congregation's feelings first. See what kind of opposition there is before escalating things."

Miranda bit her lip. "I don't understand. Why would they—?"

"I don't think it'll come to that. It's crazy and Margery here—what?" He paused. Miranda could hear Margery shouting from another room. "What? No, I'm not using that language with the Pastor. Anyway, Margery is furious, and I bet a lot of other people will be, too."

"That's—that's good to hear. I guess."

Harry hesitated. "The other problem is that a very vocal group—you know who they are, I'm sure—want Alejandra out before the baby's born. Betty Hardacre is leading the charge on that one, and, well, let's just say she's gaining momentum."

Miranda's breath caught. "And so we throw her out in the street?"

"Of course, not. Don't worry. I'll handle it."

"Don't worry? It's not like we can just get her a room at the Hilton." Miranda dropped the phone from her ear and stared across the room. She took a breath and let it out slowly. A vote of no-confidence from her first assignment. Packing up her office and leaving disgraced. No real goodbye. *Fired*.

"Pastor, are you still there?"

"I'm here." She put the phone back to her ear.

"Listen. All this nonsense will blow over. It'll be fine. And, Pastor?"

"What?" Miranda closed her eyes, tears seeping under her lashes.

"You know there's a tropical storm heading our way."

She dug a tissue out of her jeans pocket and dabbed at her nose and eyes. "I saw it online."

"Supposed to make landfall late tomorrow. Make sure Colville checks your windows."

"Right. Thanks, Harry."

Miranda tossed her phone onto the loveseat. At the moment, windows were the least of her problems.

CHAPTER THIRTY-FOUR

After a restless night, Miranda called the Bishop's office early the next morning. Usually, it took weeks to get onto a Bishop's calendar, but to her surprise, he was able to meet with her the next day. The diocesan secretary had said that he had an Ecclesiastical Council in Augusta. Did she mind an early morning meeting at the Starbucks across from St. Michael's?

"The Bishop can give you twenty minutes," the secretary had told her in a voice so crisp she could have been Peg's twin sister. "Do be punctual."

"Of course," she had answered.

"You know a storm is moving in? I don't want to put you on his calendar and then have you call off due to weather."

"Not a problem."

"Notify this office if you need to cancel." The secretary disconnected.

★ ★ ★

Miranda heard the new Bishop liked wearing liturgically correct socks. In the quiet coffee shop, she saw them: bright green socks for Ordinary time. The Right Reverend Ethan Whitby sat at a cafe table, his back to the windows, one long leg crossed over the other, wearing black wingtips, khakis pressed to a knife-sharp crease, black clergy shirt, tab collar. He had a cell phone pressed against his ear, and when he caught Miranda's eye, he smiled and waved her over. She had met the Bishop of the Episcopal Diocese of Maine just once before, at a diocesan meeting where she had been one of a herd of Episcopal clergy milling around.

Miranda wound her way through the tables at the nearly empty Starbucks as the Bishop stood to greet her. Tall, slender, impeccably dressed.

"Pastor McCurdy," his voice rang out. "So good of you to meet me."

"Bishop Whitby," she said. "Actually, good of *you* to meet me. I didn't think I would get an appointment with you so quickly."

"Well." He smoothed his tie—green stripes that complemented his socks. "My days are usually packed, but I've got a small window between meetings here in Augusta." He nodded toward the cup of coffee sitting on the table. "Your admin said you like dark roast, with cream. I believe she was quite clear about nothing powdered."

"You talked to my admin about my coffee preferences?" Miranda didn't know if that was considerate or creepy.

"My admin talked to your admin. Mostly it's because you and I have just twenty minutes, and I didn't want to waste any of it waiting at the counter."

"Oh, right. Thanks." She sat down and took a sip. "Perfect."

"Before we begin, I need to clear the air about something." He gave her an open look. "Your PSRC has already reached out to me and—"

"You're kidding? They called you? Those little backstabbers."

"And I was terribly remiss because I failed to contact you immediately. I do not tolerate triangulation, and I do not talk behind the backs of my priests, but then we had an urgent finance meeting, and one thing led to another, and I neglected to reach out. So, when you called the office, I made sure to fit you in right away."

He sat back and smiled, his eyes warm. "My sincerest apologies."

She felt betrayed, again, by her PSRC. A call to the Bishop before they had even talked with her at a formal PSRC meeting was playing hardball. She glanced up as a slash of wind and water hit the windows.

"Here comes our rain," Bishop Whitby said. "Nothing like a good tropical storm, is there? But let's get right to business. What is it you want to see me about?"

Miranda was momentarily speechless. If the committee called him, he must know what she wanted to talk about. "Well. The congregation—at least some of them—are talking about a vote of no-confidence. Did they tell you about that?"

"Oh, yes, they told me all about it, in fact. At great length." He peered at her over his Grande cup, the top mounded with whipped cream and swirled with chocolate. "Did you really tell them that dressing up like Squanto was culturally insensitive?"

"Yes, and—"

"And you told them that the Pilgrims weren't seeking religious freedom as much as economic survival?"

"It's true, and I just thought—"

"And then you told them that establishing themselves as a sanctuary church was what Jesus would want?"

"Of course." She sat back and took a breath. "I did. And it is."

His face lit up with amusement as he set his coffee cup down. "And you indicated that kicking a pregnant young woman out into the cold was not following the Gospel?" Here he stopped smiling and gave her a steady gaze.

"All that, and more. You see, I thought—"

"You thought—" He cut her off. "That it's your job to lead them on a journey that follows in the footsteps of our Lord?"

"Isn't it?"

"Of course! Absolutely on the money." Using a stir stick, he scooped a generous glob of whipped cream off the top of his hot chocolate and popped it into his mouth. "This is so good. You would hardly know it was low-fat." He leaned forward. "Is that all? That you've led them in a direction they don't want to go in? Is that what has brought you all the way to Augusta in a storm?"

She shook her head. "It's more." She took a sip of coffee. "They're a big disappointment. The whole thing is."

"What whole thing?"

"The church. The people. They're racist. Mean-spirited. Not everyone of course, but enough."

He looked out the window at the blowing rain. When he turned back to her, his gaze compassionate. "Tell me, Pastor McCurdy, what is your role? In your own words, please, not some trendy language you learned in seminary."

She answered without hesitation. "My role is to model my ministry after the ministry of Jesus. To love God. And God's people."

"Do you think you have done that?"

"I've tried."

"I would say you have succeeded. You've done it in spades. And the result has been that a small group—and I do believe it is small—of parishioners have decided that they don't like you. And that's, well—that's the way it goes. I wish more of my priests would encourage their people to become sanctuary churches and, please God in heaven, to chuck those hideous Pilgrim outfits."

He took another swipe of the whipped cream and stirred it into his coffee.

"Don't get me wrong. I'm not without empathy for your situation." He paused again and glanced out at the storm. Wet leaves slapped against the pane and then flew off. "You've challenged your people to become better versions of themselves. And they don't appreciate it. Go figure."

Miranda didn't speak for a while. She liked that the Bishop seemed okay with silence. Not everyone was. After a bit, the normal sounds of the coffee shop filled the air around them—people talking, cups clinking, and the espresso machine humming.

"There's something else I should tell you,." she confessed. "But I don't expect you to be able to help."

"Try me."

"It's just this. And I know it sounds horrible. But, if I am honest, I don't love them. And I am supposed to, right? And there are a few people, I truly despise." There. She said it. *Despise.*

"I should hope so." His voice was matter of fact. "They've acted despicably. That PSRC lady—what's her name—Sylvia something?"

"Sylvia Clacken."

"That woman is an Episcopalian version of Cruella de Vil."

"I know, right?" She felt momentarily lightened.

"They've betrayed you."

Miranda nodded. The word "betrayed" was painful to hear yet liberating to acknowledge. Voicing it aloud somehow made it less overwhelming.

"Don't forget, they betrayed themselves and their faith." The Bishop finished off the last of the whipped cream and took a sip. "And at some level, they know it."

"I have a job offer." She blurted it out.

He looked at her, eyebrows raised.

"Before I was a priest, I was a chef in Boston."

"You don't say?"

"The job offer is from my old restaurant. The Pellegrino. Executive chef at a new site—in Seattle."

"That would be tempting."

"I am wondering if all this mess at St. Gabe's is, you know, a sign. That I should move on. Take the job. It's not like I've been very effective as a pastor. Not if they are so willing to deny asylum to a pregnant woman fleeing violence. And now, a vote of no-confidence."

The Bishop sat silently for so long, gazing out the window at the rain. She wondered if she had offended him somehow. Finally, he turned to her.

"Let me ask you, do you feel compelled, driven—*called*—to the chef job like you felt the call to the priesthood?"

"No," Miranda answered without hesitation. "Not even close." The immediacy and assuredness of her response surprised her. She had loved The Pellegrino; it had energized her, challenged her. But the priesthood was something deeper, more profound. The priesthood was her life.

"Well, keep that in mind." He tipped back the last of his cocoa. "I don't know what the right decision is for you—chef or priest or—whatever. But remember this—you're the best thing to happen to St. Gabe's in a long time. I will pray for your decision. Just stay strong. Don't let anyone push you around."

He glanced out the window at the pelting rain. "And get home, before this storm really hits."

CHAPTER THIRTY-FIVE

Miranda stood in the doorway of her office and watched Peg pack her gym bag. Her shoulders ached from hunching over the wheel on the drive from Augusta. Miranda had gripped the steering wheel as wind buffeted her little car and rain hammered down, the windshield wipers doing double-duty.

"I'm leaving early." Peg slid her laptop into the bag. "And you should, too. This weather will get worse before it gets better." She zipped shut the bag and slung it over her shoulder.

Still a newcomer, Miranda didn't think about storms the way Maine natives did. And anyway, it was hard to take seriously a tropical storm named *Patricia*.

"Skip that Thanksgiving meeting this afternoon and let those meddlesome ladies plan their own dinner."

Miranda hadn't been invited to the meeting, but with the Bishop's words in her head, she wanted to let the committee know she wasn't going to be pushed around—or closed out. She planned to crash the meeting. "Do you think the storm will be that bad?" she asked Peg.

"Tropical storm off the coast and moving our way? I should think it will be bad."

"Isn't it supposed to fizzle out before it makes landfall?"

"Where did you hear that?"

"The Internet."

Peg rolled her eyes as she pulled an umbrella out of the top file cabinet drawer. "You need to watch Channel Ten Weather. Josh Likens. Now there's a meteorologist you can trust. If Josh says *batten down the hatches*, I batten down the hatches." She tucked the umbrella under her arm and slid shut the metal file drawer.

"I don't even think I can find the hatches. And I might be all out of battens. Whatever they are."

"You seem like yourself again. What did Bishop Whitby tell you?"

"Keep on with things just as I have. Don't let anyone push me around."

"Hard to believe anyone so sensible could have been made bishop." Peg opened the door, then paused and turned back. She peered at Miranda over her rimless half glasses, her gaze sharp "Batten down the hatches is a term that originates with the United States Navy. One prepared for a storm at sea by fastening canvas over openings—hatches—with strips of wood called battens. It is also a metaphor for one who might be heading into challenging times."

Peg closed the door firmly behind her and a gust of wind rattled the window.

★ ★ ★

Miranda reminded herself that as the priest at St. Gabriel's, she didn't need an engraved invitation to attend a meeting. Yet, as she walked down the hall, her confidence flagged. Hard to crash a party when you know you're not wanted. Also, she was still mad at the women for their actions against Alejandra. And now, Alejandra was soon to be homeless. The Bishop was right; she felt betrayed. Deeply.

She paused outside the door and peered in through the narrow window. Donna, Joanne, and Edna. She remembered that Ramona had called earlier to say she was behind schedule for her plumbing calls, but she would be there with take-out for Alejandra. But what about the others? And wasn't Betty the new chair? She pushed in.

"Pastor Miranda," Edna said, perched on one of the child-size Sunday School chairs. "We're glad you're here." Her voice held a note of worry. Edna's hands were empty—no knitting needles or yarn, which was unusual for her. Donna leaned against the wall in a wet raincoat, water dripping onto the carpet. Joanne stood at the window with her back to everyone, watching the heavy rain. "Where's Betty?" Miranda asked.

"That's the problem." Edna replied.

Donna shrugged off her raincoat and tossed it across one of the chairs. "Has Betty ever told you about her daughter?" She asked abruptly, peering at Miranda.

"No. I thought that Betty and Delmar didn't have children." Miranda took a seat at the table. Coloring book pages of Jesus holding a lamb in his arms covered the far wall. Someone named Annabelle had given Jesus green hair and the lamb, pink wool. She made a mental note to meet Annabelle. Clearly, a kid with potential.

It suddenly hit Miranda that if she left St. Gabe's, she wouldn't watch the Sunday School kids grow up. On the other hand, if the congregation voted against her, it wouldn't matter anyway.

"If Betty isn't here in five minutes, we're going out there to find her," Edna said, her voice determined.

"Out where?" Miranda asked. "Maybe she just got held up or stayed home because of the storm."

"Do you think we haven't called her?" Joanne shot her a frustrated look. "Delmar's home alone. She never leaves him for more than two hours. She told me he starts getting into things. She came home last week, and he'd turned on the gas burner. Said he wanted a cup of tea. The kettle had boiled dry."

"That's why she scheduled our meeting for this afternoon," Edna added. "So she could do her thing and come back and be with friends. And now her friends are—Oh, you people are useless." Edna grabbed her yellow raincoat and yanked it on. She reminded Miranda of the girl on the Morton Salt box. "I'm going after her."

"Wait. Everyone, stop." Miranda said. "First, someone call the Sparrow police and ask for a wellness check on Delmar."

She waited as Joanne picked up her cell phone and slipped out into the hall. "Now, please. Tell me what you mean, so that Betty could do her thing? What thing?"

"Today is October twenty-eighth. Betty's daughter's birthday. Or it would have been. She died thirty-three years ago," Donna said.

Miranda was stunned—Betty had a daughter—*who had died?*

"Hard to believe Cathy would be fifty-three today." Edna sat down in a Sunday School chair, the Morton-Salt-Girl-slicker poking around her like a yellow plastic tent. "Fifty-three," she repeated quietly.

"How did she die?" Miranda's animosity toward the Thanksgiving Committee suddenly took a backseat to her concern about Betty. Betty Hardacre might be a selfish, narrow-minded old woman, but she was still one of Miranda's congregation. The comment she had made to the Bishop about despising some of the church members echoed in her mind. Well, no denying it now, Betty Hardacre topped the list.

The other women exchanged glances as a gust of wind shook the windows.

"Cathy walked into the water down at Holbeck's Point," Joanne said, her voice flat. "The tide was coming in. Harmon saw her from up on his widow's walk and thought she wanted to go for a swim. But then she just kept walking farther and farther. He panicked, called the fire department, and then went after her. They had to drag him back to make him stop diving down to find her."

"The Coast Guard tried to convince Delmar and Betty that it was an accident," Edna said. Her voice caught. "But then, when they got home that night, they found a note on their kitchen table. Underneath the sugar bowl."

"Oh, how awful." Miranda reached across the table, and they grasped hands.

"See, Cathy was gay. Thirty-three years ago. And she was pretty open about it," Joanne said.

"As she should have been," Donna added fiercely.

"I'm not saying she shouldn't have been. But you know how Betty and Delmar are. And it was the 1980s. They never came around to it. They made sure she knew they disapproved. And then one day, when they were downtown, she wrote a note that she was sorry she wasn't the daughter they wanted, and she walked into the ocean." Joanne stopped, her hand at her throat, remembering.

"Betty and Delmar had been in town doing errands. They had no idea what had happened. But when they saw all the rescue vehicles on the beach, they wandered over—along with just about everyone in Sparrow," Edna said. "Can you imagine? Your own daughter—"

Miranda shook her head. Dig a little below the surface of any angry parishioner, of anyone, and there it is, pain carefully hidden but living and breathing like a cancerous tumor.

"Some fisherman spotted her body a few days later, and the Harbor Patrol brought her in," Donna said.

The room was silent except for the wind.

"So every year," Edna finally said, "on Cathy's birthday, Betty goes down to Holbeck's Point at the same time of day that Harmon saw Cathy walk out. And she stands there and stares out. Almost like she's waiting for Cathy to come back." Edna's voice softened. "Betty has felt this pain for thirty-three years. It will never end." She paused, her concern evident. "She's eighty this year. And now she's out there in the storm."

"Used to be, Delmar went with her. Now that Delmar can't, we're afraid—" Donna said.

She and Edna exchanged glances.

"Afraid of what?" Miranda broke in.

"We're afraid she'll walk out into the water herself."

"Has she given any indication that she wants to do that?" Miranda said.

"No, but she's been so angry about that Mexican girl in the Youth Room." Edna gave Miranda a guarded look.

"Honduran," Miranda said.

"Betty said that a girl like Alejandra gets to live, and a good person like Cathy doesn't." Joanne stood up. "I know that doesn't make a particle of sense, Pastor, and you probably think we are all a bunch of old biddies who—"

Miranda cut her off. "Grief doesn't have to make sense. We need to find Betty. You're sure she's not at home?"

"She's not answering her cell. And Delmar doesn't pick up the landline anymore."

A branch slapped against the window just as the door burst open. Ramona, brown coveralls, and Wellingtons. The brim of her ball cap soaked from the rain. She stood breathing hard.

"She's gone, Pastor. Packed up and left."

"Betty?" Miranda said, confused.

"Betty? No. *Alejandra.* All the stuff that church members gave her—jacket, new sneakers, books—are piled up on the couch. Wherever she's is, she's gone with just the clothes on her back."

CHAPTER THIRTY-SIX

They moved in a raincoated huddle across the parking lot to Ramona's panel truck.

"First, we find Betty," Miranda said, shouting above the wind. "We'll head to that spot on the beach, near Harmon's."

"October twenty-eighth at two o'clock, on the dot," Edna shouted, the wind snatching her words. "Stands there and looks out at the water. For an hour."

"That was two hours ago," Ramona said.

"Betty's stubborn. Won't just go to the cemetery," Donna said, opening the van door.

"Pastor, you're riding shotgun." Ramona fitted the key into the ignition.

The other women piled in. The door slammed shut. Rain pounded the metal roof.

"Joanne, what'd you tell the police?" Miranda twisted around and looked at the women in the back seat.

"Said we're looking for a friend at the beach. We'd call if she wasn't there."

"Why would you—?" Miranda began, frustration rising.

"Betty'd kill us for embarrassing her. Beach first, then 9-1-1 if needed."

"This van's seen better days," Edna muttered, squeezing past tools and pipes.

"I'm a plumber, not a taxi," Ramona grunted, shifting gears. She pulled out onto the deserted Main Street.

"She won't even let us go with her," Edna said. "We used to hide up on the rocks to keep an eye on her, but then she found out, and we can't do it anymore. The last thing she said was, 'See you at the meeting.'"

Ramona gunned the engine and headed to the beach. "And what could we tell the police about Alejandra? An undocumented woman needs law enforcement to pick her up?" Ramona sent a glaring look at the back seat.

"Just keep a lookout for Alejandra," Miranda had to raise her voice to be heard above the pounding rain on the metal van roof. "Although I can't believe she would be out in this storm. I'm hoping she found shelter somewhere."

"Why did she have to run away?" Joanne said, her voice plaintive.

Miranda almost went into the windshield when Ramona hit the brakes. She jammed the van into park. Miranda was grateful there was no traffic. Ramona spun around and faced Joanne. "Are you that ignorant?"

"What do you mean? Of course not. It's just that I would think—"

"Thanks to you ladies, the vestry voted to throw her out." Ramona spit out her words.

"But you would have found another church for her, right?" Edna looked at Miranda, her eyes wide. "We weren't going to just throw her out."

"I might have eventually found a church that would take her. But even while she travels from one church to another, she can be picked up and is at risk of being deported."

"Betty said that if she has an anchor baby, the government can't send her back, so it didn't really matter where she was," Edna retorted. "And she won't need health insurance or anything because *those* people get everything for free in America. That's why they come here."

Ramona slammed her fist on the steering wheel. She jerked the van into gear and floored it. "I swear to God, if either of you ignorant racists utters another word about Alejandra, you're walking." Leaves whipped across the windshield in a flash of orange.

Ramona leaned forward, eyes fixed on the road. The van fell silent.

Suddenly, she jerked the wheel. Gravel crunched as they pulled into the beach lot.

There it was: Betty and Delmar's green Chrysler, parked by the boat ramp.

The women piled out, faces grim. Edna wiped the car's window, peering in.

"Her phone," she said, voice tight. "Left it. Typical Betty. In this storm, no phone."

"At least we've talked her into taking a lawn chair. She says she goes over everything in her mind about that last day with Cathy. And then she says a prayer."

"She should be on the other side of the rocks." Joanne pointed down the deserted beach, in the direction of Harmon's house

"Facing down this storm feeds into her anger at herself," Miranda said. "Into her own storm."

"Everybody sticks together and stays close to the embankment. Thank God it's still low tide, or we couldn't do this." Ramona put her head down and strode into the wind, her rain slicker blowing back like a billowing sail.

The women began the arduous walk on the sand. Holbeck's Point was only about a hundred yards away, a leisurely stroll on a sunny day. Today it was like pushing against a freight train.

In all Miranda's encounters with Betty, the older woman had never revealed the pain she carried. Betty always acted tough as nails. Even when it came to Delmar's dementia, she was all business. Every bit of her anguish neatly under lock and key. But, it seemed, on this one day of the year, she flung open the door to her rage and pain. And she opened it to the angry sea—the sea that had taken her daughter.

In that moment, Miranda's frustration with Betty melted away, replaced by unexpected empathy.

They heard a shout from Edna, who was several yards ahead. "Look!"

A lawn chair turned upside down and snagged on a pile of driftwood. Edna turned and started forward. "Come on!" she shouted into the wind. "Other side of the rocks."

The wind nearly knocked them over, as they fought their way across the sand. Miranda prayed silently that they would find Betty sheltering there.

No Betty.

"Maybe she got sensible for once and went home," Donna remarked, raising her voice against the wind's fury.

"Don't be stupid." Ramona snapped. "Why's her car still in the parking lot if she went home?" Miranda squinted against the wind-driven rain. Something caught her eye: a faint glimmer in the wet sand near the water's edge. She trudged closer, bending down to investigate. Her fingers closed around a string of smooth, round objects. Lifting it from the sand, she realized what it was: a pearl necklace with a silver crucifix. Rosary beads.

Edna leaned in and examined the beads. "Alejandra's. She had that necklace in church the day we voted. I remember because I thought if she's so poor, why's she got a string of pearls? Then, I saw her pray with them. I felt bad because she told me later, they'd been her great-grandmother's."

Miranda slid the rosary into the deep pocket of her rain mac. She looked out at the water, salt spray hitting her face. The tide had turned, and the sea thundered toward them.

Batten down the hatches. Too late. The storm had arrived.

CHAPTER THIRTY-SEVEN

"The tide's coming in," Ramona shouted. "We might not make it back to the car, and I'd rather not get washed out to sea. I say that we take shelter at Harmon's."

"He'll never hear us at the door, and even if he does hear us, will the old so-and-so even let us in?" Donna said.

"He will," Ramona said. "He's a good guy. Underneath it all."

"Hard to believe," Donna said.

"Come on. I do Harmon's plumbing. I've got a key to the cellar." She took out a key ring with about twenty keys on it. "And, yeah, Harmon is an old so-and-so, believe me. But when my van broke down, he paid to get it fixed. I tried to pay him back, but no way would he let me."

The women followed Ramona up the sandy embankment to the daunting old house. They stood dripping under the porch overhang, a sudden relief from the wind and pounding rain.

"I'm calling the Coast Guard," Miranda said.

"Let's at least go inside," Donna said. "We need to regroup, and then we call. I just hope to God that she got off the beach somehow."

"Why aren't any of you more worried about Alejandra?" Ramona asked as she fit the key into the heavy door. "It's your fault she ran away. It's *your fault* she's out in this."

"We didn't tell her to go out into a storm. We had the best interests of the church in mind." Donna stepped through the door behind

Ramona. The others followed as Ramona pulled the cord attached to a single light bulb. Cobwebs, old boxes, and broken furniture lay scattered in the dim, cramped cellar. A narrow wooden staircase led up into more shadows. Though dark and a little creepy, it was at least a respite from the elements.

"I've been down here before, working on his water tank," Ramona said. "Give me a minute, and I'll go up and let Harmon know he's got five women in his basement. I'd rather not burst in on him all at once."

"You need to stop saying it's our fault that Alejandra left," Donna blurted out. "You don't think that's true, do you, Pastor? You don't blame *us*?"

Before Miranda could answer, a piercing scream came from the floor above them. Ramona spun around and ran up the wooden steps, her Wellingtons thumping into the cobwebby darkness. Miranda followed behind. She had to admire Ramona. No hesitation, no fear, just racing into the unknown at the sound of someone in distress.

Ramona shoved open the door at the top of the stairs, and with Miranda on her heels, they burst into the middle of a spacious, modern kitchen. The other women followed, clutching each other in fear.

The scream sliced the air again. Miranda followed Ramona out of the kitchen and down a vast hallway. She was vaguely aware of large portraits of old men held in heavy gold frames lining the walls, a long oriental rug beneath their feet. They skidded to a stop in the entranceway of a majestic room with a cathedral ceiling and a fire crackling in the hearth, old-fashioned floral wallpaper, oil paintings hung in ornate frames, and end tables with beautiful lamps and vases. Thick velvet drapes covered the windows.

"Good Lord," Ramona said. "It's Downton Abbey."

Harmon stood at one end of the elegant spacious room, his eyes wide and his face flushed. He clutched a stack of folded towels under one arm while gripping an old-fashioned copper tea kettle. He quickly glanced at Miranda and Ramona, then back at the sofa.

Alejandra lay on a daybed in the middle of the room. And Betty, her sleeves rolled up, crouched as though she was about to catch a baby.

"Push," Betty said. "You can do it, my girl. You're almost there."

With one glance she, too, took in the rain-soaked women standing in the doorway, rivulets of water running off their raincoats, wet hair plastered to their faces.

"Pastor, get over here and hold Alejandra's hand. She's been a trooper like you wouldn't believe, but she's running out of steam."

Miranda shrugged out of the rain mac. She nudged a velvet-upholstered settee to the side of the day bed and sat. She clutched one of Alejandra's hands in both of hers.

"Ladies," Betty barked. "Make yourselves useful. Donna, find some clean blankets. Edna, get Alejandra a glass of water. And Joanne, we'll need something for a bassinet."

"I guess we don't need to call the Coast Guard," Edna said quietly.

"I can't tell you how glad I am to see you, Alejandra. And you, too, Betty, we thought—" Miranda started to say.

"No time for that now, Pastor," Betty said, interrupted by a groan from Alejandra. "Ramona, get on your cell and call Dr. Hazeltine." She turned to Miranda. "Will Alejandra be safe in the hospital?"

"Not likely. Sparrow Community is not a designated sanctuary hospital."

"All right, then," Betty said firmly. "This is a home birth. Nothing wrong with that. I've done plenty."

"You have?" Edna said, returning with a glass of water.

Miranda looked at Betty, her eyes wide. There certainly was more to Betty than she had ever imagined.

Alejandra's scream cut through the room again. Her back arched.

"Come on," Miranda heard herself say. "You're doing great."

She could hear Ramona on her cell. Thank God, she must have reached Dr. Hazeltine. Miranda looked up at Betty just as the wind slammed against the house. "Harmon," she said.

"Right here, Pastor." He stepped over to her, still clinging to the stack of towels and copper tea kettle.

"Do you have a generator?"

"Not one that works,"

"Then gather up flashlights and candles. We could lose power." She was aware of Harmon leaving the room, but the anguished look on Alejandra's face held her attention, tears streaming down.

"*Quiero mi Daniel*," she cried. I want my Daniel.

"I know," Betty said in a voice more soothing than Miranda could have imagined. But not just soothing. Strong. Fierce.

Miranda met Betty's eyes.

"She's been calling for her mother, too. Breaks my heart."

"The doc is pulling in the drive." Ramona burst into the room. "I unlocked the front door for her." Miranda noticed that she was still wearing Wellingtons. "She just got back in town from some fancy awards dinner in Boston. Got halfway there, and they called it off due to the storm. She said unless there's a medical emergency, do not call an ambulance." Ramona paused.

"But she did say something else, and it's a direct quote. She said, 'Do whatever Betty tells you to do.'"

Miranda leaned closer to Alejandra. "Daniel and your mother are not here, Alejandra, and I am so sorry. But you do have us. The most capable women in St. Gabriel's church just came through a tropical storm to find you. You've got Harmon. And you're in a house that has survived a hundred years of storms. And probably more than a few home births."

"You're safe now," Harmon's gruff voice came from behind her.

Miranda wished she could believe it. The sound of high heels clicked down the hall, and suddenly, Dr. Elizabeth Hazeltine swept into the room. Dressed in a formal evening gown and her luxurious hair pulled into an elegant updo held in place with a tiara, she slipped off a sodden velvet coat and tossed it on a nearby chair. "Where are we, Betty?"

"So far, so good. I thought the head was about to crown, but not yet. Mother is doing terrific."

"Mother is amazing," Dr. Hazeltine said. "Betty, do you want a break? I can take over."

"No. Please," Alejandra gasped. "Betty."

"She is the best, isn't she?" Dr. Hazeltine said, kicking off her high heels. She hiked up her floor-length dress and knelt on the other side of the daybed across from Miranda.

"All right, then, Betty, carry on. Harmon, hand me your softest towel, and Edna, be ready with those blankets. One last big push, and we might be there."

The doctor removed her tiara and tossed it like a Frisbee onto a nearby chair.

"The head," Betty said, her voice urgent. "Come on. One more push."

"*La cabeza*!" Miranda clasped Alejandra's hand between both of hers. "You can do this, Alejandra."

Alejandra's eyes locked with Miranda's, drawing strength from her words. She took a deep, shuddering breath. With an anguished groan, Alejandra bore down. Miranda felt Alejandra's grip tighten painfully, but she didn't flinch.

"That's it," the doctor encouraged. "Keep going."

Seconds stretched into what felt like hours. Then, with a final push, the baby emerged. Betty's hands, steady, gently cradled the tiny form.

"It's a girl," Betty announced, her voice trembling.

For a moment, the room held its breath. Then, a piercing cry broke the silence, strong and full.

Dr. Hazeltine moved swiftly, clearing the baby's airways. "She's perfect," she said, wrapping the newborn in a soft blanket.

Miranda felt tears streaming down her face. Her lips moved in a silent prayer of gratitude. Across the room, Edna, Joanne, and Donna huddled together, wiping their eyes. Harmon stood back, pale but smiling.

"You did it," Miranda said. She squeezed Alejandra's shoulder gently. "You did it."

"A lovely little girl." Dr. Hazeltine clamped off the umbilical cord, then Betty handed the newborn to Alejandra. Alejandra gazed at her daughter in wonder, her exhaustion momentarily forgotten. Her fingers traced the baby's cheek with feather-light touches. The baby let out a vigorous cry just as Ramona crumpled to the ground.

★ ★ ★

"It's embarrassing," Ramona said, dunking her teabag into one of the porcelain mugs Harmon had placed on the kitchen table. "I'm super squeamish. One time, I cut my hand using a pipe reamer on Ruby Pendegreen's toilet. I woke up on the floor of her bathroom. Took one look at all the blood on that white tile and passed out again. Good thing she wasn't home because you know Ruby. The story would've been all over town by lunchtime."

"Harmon, sit down. Please," Miranda said. He was hovering over the table, refilling teacups, and looking like a waiter in an old hotel. "We're fine. In fact, we're more than fine."

And they were. Betty had not been swept out to sea. Alejandra and the baby were safe. Or at least safe for the moment, since ICE was unlikely to raid an old sea captain's house in the middle of a Maine tropical storm.

The fury that Miranda had harbored toward the Thanksgiving Committee had given way, for now, to a sense of camaraderie. The kind of bond that is forged through a shared experience of adversity—in this case, a violent storm, a grieving mother in peril, a young woman on the run, and a newborn's entry into the world.

"How long had Alejandra been in labor before we arrived?"

"About two hours," Betty answered.

"When you didn't show up for the meeting, we panicked," Joanne told her.

"Could you start taking your phone with you, for pity's sake?" Edna took a sip of tea, her voice gruff with worry.

"Thank God we could get into Harmon's cellar. Or we would be swimming for our lives right now," Ramona added. "Sorry, Harmon, but I used my key downstairs."

"Glad you did," he said. He had placed the teapot in the middle of the table and stepped back, leaning against the kitchen counter.

"How'd you ever hear Betty and Alejandra at the door?" Ramona said. "I know your doorbell doesn't work."

"He didn't let us in," Betty said, pouring a cup of tea for herself and Miranda. "What do you take in your tea, Pastor?" Betty gave her a searching look. Far more searching than a question about tea would require.

"Sugar. And milk if there is any. Thanks for the hot tea. I'm still damp."

"The furnace is running, but it's hard to get this house warm," Harmon said. "That's why I lit a fire in the parlor."

"Here you go, Pastor." Harmon put a small milk pitcher on the table and pushed the sugar bowl toward her.

"I was on the beach at one o'clock this afternoon," Betty said. "I started early because of the storm." Betty stared into her teacup. Her friends waited. A clock in the hall chimed, and the pipes rattled as forced air traveled up from the furnace.

"I've kept watch during storms before," Betty continued without looking up. "But this year—this time—" Her eyes met Miranda's. "I wanted a storm. I *needed* a storm. Everything has been a storm around me. Delmar." She stopped and gazed across the kitchen and out the dark window.

Donna reached out and squeezed Betty's hand. "Don't think that. Please," Donna said softly. "We would have missed you so much."

"Usually, when my hour on the beach is over, I say a special prayer for Cathy." Betty cleared her throat and took a sip of tea. "And for myself." Her voice stronger.

"Well, anyway, before I could do the prayer, I saw someone. Over by the rocks." Miranda could hear the quiet voices of Dr. Hazeltine and Alejandra in the parlor.

"And I'll admit, it made me mad. This was my moment. My private moment. And then I saw the person fall and I knew I had to go over there, and I'll tell you, that made me even more mad. I didn't want to help anyone. It's all I do, all day long. Help people. Take care of Delmar." She turned to Miranda. "Isn't that awful of me, Pastor?"

Miranda shook her head. "It's very human of you."

"So I went over and there was Alejandra. She was down on her knees, and she had those funny beads in her hands. 'Rosary Rattlers' that's what my dad called them." Betty shrugged in Miranda's direction.

"Sorry, Pastor. I suppose that's not what we say anymore. The girl is down on the sand, crying and praying with her beads. The rain's coming down, she's soaked to the skin. No rain slicker. Tide's coming in." Betty shook her head. "Pregnant as can be."

"Well, I got her up," she continued. "Which wasn't easy, let me tell you, her being nine months pregnant and me being an old woman with arthritis. But I got her on her feet, and she let out a scream, and it didn't take a genius to know she was in labor. We manage a couple of steps forward, and the wind picks up, and I'm thinking, we'll never make it to the car. And then, there's an angel standing right next to me."

"Like a guardian angel?" Ramona said. "I believe in those."

"A guardian angel named Harmon." Betty met his gaze.

"I was up on my widow's walk and saw them."

"You'd go up there in a storm like this?" Ramona gazed at him with a new appreciation. "Are you some sort of storm-watcher or something?"

"Every year on October twenty-eighth, I go up," Harmon said quietly, looking straight at Betty as though no one else was in the room. "And I watch with Betty."

He picked up a folded dish towel, pressed it to his eyes, and then tossed it back onto the counter. "I've watched with Betty every year for a long time now. And when she's safe back in her car, I say my own prayer."

No one spoke. Donna slipped her hand into Miranda's, and Miranda reached across the table and covered Betty's hand with her own.

"I was there that day, too, you know," Harmon said to Betty as if no one else were in the room. "The day Cathy—" His voice trailed off.

"I know." Betty's voice was a mere whisper. "I know."

"I should have gone down to the beach sooner. But I thought Cathy was going for a swim and then, when I lost sight of her—" Harmon shook his head.

"I remember, Harmon," Edna said. "They dragged you half-drowned from the water yourself." Her voice was clear, firm. "You're our hero. No one's done anything as brave in thirty-three years. The fire chief says it. Everyone does." She locked eyes with Harmon. "Don't forget that. Don't ever forget that."

Harmon met Edna's gaze, his jaw tightening. "I'd do it again," he said. "In a heartbeat."

"Harmon and I got Alejandra inside," Betty said. "We set her up on that daybed in the parlor, and then we realized my phone was in the car. Harmon doesn't have a cell phone, and his landline was out with the storm. But things were moving so fast, it didn't matter."

"You seemed like you knew what you were doing in there, Betty," Ramona said. "And Dr. Hazeltine acted as if you were a colleague from the hospital."

"I trained as a nurse in Korea when I was young." Betty gave a half laugh. "Very young."

"Korea?" Ramona asked. "Like *M.A.S.H.* on TV?"

"Not *like M.A.S.H.* It *was* M.A.S.H. The 171st Evac Hospital under Nurse Colonel Ruby Bradley. Colonel Bradley taught me everything I know." Betty cleared her throat and sat up straight. "Recipient of the Florence Nightingale Medal of Honor. There's never been anyone like her, and there never will be."

"It sounds like she might have made you who you are," Miranda said, quietly.

Betty nodded, her eyes glistening. "You could say that. Yes, you could say that." She paused, taking a shaky breath.

The group sat silent for a long time. Finally, Harmon spoke. "The young lady can stay here at my house as long as she wants. Let's not move her to St. Gabe's, only to move her again."

Miranda nodded. "Thanks, Harmon, but unfortunately, she's not safe here. However, I may have found a church that's willing to offer sanctuary. There are two possible churches, and I am fairly sure that one of them will agree to take her. The vestry was hoping to get her relocated before the baby arrived. But obviously, they didn't move fast enough."

"Alejandra is going back to St. Gabe's, and she is staying there until the whole immigration mess is straightened out," Betty said in her commanding voice.

"If you will recall," Miranda said, regretting the edge in her voice. "That course of action is no longer possible. The vestry voted."

Edna and Donna studied the table's surface, unable to meet anyone's gaze.

"Well, you just call Harry Hopkins and tell him the vestry needs to vote again." Betty said. "And this time, they need to get it right."

"It doesn't work that way." Miranda said. "They voted. It's over."

"It isn't over till I say it's over." Betty declared. "That girl is going back to St. Gabe's."

Miranda cocked her head and looked at Betty. "You want Alejandra at the church?"

Betty didn't speak for so long that Miranda almost broke the silence herself.

The clock chimed in the hall, and the wind banged a shutter. Dr. Hazeltine slipped into the room and quietly took a chair. Harmon poured a cup of tea and handed it to her.

"When Cathy was a little girl," Betty finally said, staring out the dark window, rain slashing against the pane. "She would have bad dreams. Like children do. And she would call out for me in the dark, and I would go to her. I would sit on the side of her bed and hold her next to me. I would rest my forehead on top of her head and breathe. I would breathe her in." The only sound was the storm and the murmuring of Alejandra to the baby, from the parlor.

"I have always wondered." Betty held Miranda's gaze. "If she called out for me that day, that day when she—when she realized that she was drowning." Betty looked down and then up again. "When I heard Alejandra call out for her mother today, I thought, here she is, a poor girl alone in the world who only wants her mother, and here I am, an old lady with not many years left. And it hit me, what have I become?" Betty leaned forward, looking from one woman to the other at the table. "What have I become?"

She waited as if expecting an answer. No one spoke or even moved. Betty sat back. "I've become someone that no one can call out to."

★ ★ ★

When Miranda pushed open the door to the rectory hours later, the sky was still dark, but the light of dawn had begun to creep along the edge of the horizon. The waves crashed on the beach, and the rain still pelted the windows, but Patricia's violence had spent itself and blown out to sea.

Miranda fell into the club chair and turned on the lamp. A warm light chased away the shadows in the room. Howard snuffled and grunted inside his Hobbit house, settling in for sleep.

Reaching for her phone, she scrolled to the archived voicemail. She listened as the familiar sound of Jason's voice brought his image back to her. His laugh, his warm green eyes, his sandy blonde hair. Then, the recording ended and all that was left was the steady hum of rain on the slate roof overhead.

Miranda realized that her grief, like the storm, had spent itself, washed out to sea with the waves. That last night in the hospital, the night she watched Jason's body wheeled away, grief had settled in. It hovered, waiting, in the background of her emotions, thoughts, and choices. It pushed in whenever she began to feel contented or optimistic, or adventurous.

But now, with that heavy sadness lifted, would she be genuinely free for new love? If not Adam, as she realized she hoped, then someone else? But she would never find that love if she kept returning to reclaim love long gone. Miranda opened the archive again, and Jason's final voicemail popped up. Without hesitation, she clicked delete.

A message appeared: *Are you sure you want to delete this voicemail?* Yes, she said in a whisper. Yes. She clicked again, and it was gone.

CHAPTER THIRTY-EIGHT

Long tables lined the Fellowship Hall at St. Gabriel-by-the-Sea. In the middle of each table sat a roasted turkey, and the delicious aroma of stuffing, pie and fresh coffee wafted in from the kitchen.

"One more person comes through the door," Sam Reeves noted, "we'll have to set them up with a tray in the hall."

Cheerful conversation bantered across the room, small children ran up and down between the tables, and an unseasonably warm breeze blew in through open windows. Volunteers of all ages and genders hovered at the head of each table, ready to refill empty bowls of cranberries, mashed potatoes, yams, stuffing, and the obligatory green bean casserole.

The members of the Thanksgiving Committee were clad in bright green T-shirts with the words, *¡Santuario no Deportación!* splashed across the front. After a brief discussion, the members of the Thanksgiving Committee had decided that Pilgrim costumes no longer represented genuine welcome. They opted for the T-shirts instead.

The day after the storm, Alejandra had returned to the Youth Room with a new Pack N Play, an anonymous delivery of a hundred diapers, a towering pile of receiving blankets produced during a Knitting Ladies all-nighter, and a very tiny baby named Beatriz Daniela Romero, named for her new godmother, Betty, and her still-missing father, Daniel.

A few days after Beatriz's birth, and with Pam reinstated as chair, the Thanksgiving Committee invited Harry to join them in the first grade Sunday School room. Seated at the story table and surrounded by Jesus coloring pages, they gave Harry his marching orders.

The first order of business was to rename the Thanksgiving Committee "The Hospitality Team," which had been Ramona's idea. Among its tasks would be the annual Thanksgiving Dinner. Still, the group also claimed jurisdiction over all aspects of welcome and hospitality at St. Gabe's, including the official establishment of St. Gabe's as a sanctuary church.

A three-day wait was imposed before Harry could call for a new vestry vote on sanctuary. This gave Alejandra's new advocates—previously known as the Thanksgiving Committee—a window to garner support within the church.

At first, Harry refused. A re-vote was a direct violation of the by-laws since all vestry votes are final. Betty reminded him of the paint fiasco of 2015.

"Oh," he said slowly. "Well. That was a special case."

"What paint fiasco of 2015?" Miranda asked.

Pam explained how the vestry had voted to repaint the Fellowship Hall Frosted Emerald when it had been Eggshell White for as long as anyone could remember. Word had gotten out to the congregation, and the vestry was forced to call for a new vote. Eggshell White had won the day.

"If you can do it for a paint color, Harry Hopkins," Betty said, "you can do it for a homeless girl with a baby."

Next, the women demanded that the PSRC cancel the vote of no-confidence. Miranda held her breath as Sylvia made clear, in her most chilling voice, that the Thanksgiving Committee had no authority over the PSRC.

"Hospitality Team," Ramona interrupted, correcting her.

"Whatever," Sylvia muttered.

"The problem is, Sylvia," Pam said, "we can't call ourselves a welcoming church when we don't even welcome our own priest. And isn't Thanksgiving all about welcome?"

"I thought it was about giving thanks," Sylvia said coolly.

"Giving thanks and welcome," Ramona rejoined. "If you want, we have an awesome video that explains it."

Sylvia checked her phone.

"Here's where the rubber hits the road, Sylvia," Donna said, leaning forward. "If there is a vote of no-confidence taken, the ladies here won't feel up to putting on the Thanksgiving Dinner. And if there is no Thanksgiving Dinner, there'll be no Harvest Fund, and with no Harvest Fund, the annual budget is tanked. I would hate for the congregation to blame the financial demise of St. Gabe's on the actions of the PSRC."

In her most Cruella de Vil voice, Sylvia had responded that she would run it by the committee members. And just like Frosted Emerald paint, the vote of no-confidence was never mentioned again.

★ ★ ★

Margery and Harry sat next to Alejandra at one of the long tables. Linda Darcy sat across from them, holding four-week-old Beatriz in her arms. Two tables over, Dr. Hazeltine had Colville laughing, and next to them, Harmon listened intently to Colville while Lucy, seated across the table, seemed to be enjoying an animated conversation with Edna.

The sight of Lucy made Miranda think of Adam and how she hadn't heard from him in weeks. Good heavens, she thought. *Why should I care? I don't, even if I do.*

As she gazed around the room at the happy faces of her parishioners, a feeling of solitude washed over her. Couples and families surrounded her, laughing and chatting, but she was alone. Church events like this, which she usually enjoyed, seemed to emphasize her single status and the emptiness of having no one to share the moment with. The thought of Adam, who she had once thought might fill that void, brought a fresh wave of loneliness. It was apparent that whatever might have happened with him was not to be, that he would not be her person after all.

The side door opened, and Peg strode in, still wearing her race-day walking gear, gym bag slung over her shoulder. The room broke into applause. Peg had placed first in her age group for the walking portion of the Wobble Gobble that morning. She waved off the applause and took a seat next to Sylvia.

Miranda dismissed an unexpected pang of sadness. After Samson's late night on Loretta's security camera, he had not been seen. Peg suspected the worst. And, by now, so did Miranda. It was such a sad topic that the two women agreed to stop talking about him. However, she noticed that her secretary still kept the blue leash in her bottom desk drawer.

Harry stood up from the long table, let out a long whistle, and paused while conversations dwindled to a hush. He thanked the Hospitality Team for their hard work and reminded everyone of the free-will offering to raise money for an asylum attorney.

"The big coffee cans by the side door. Be generous," he said. "And don't think we won't be collecting for the Harvest Fund. The deacons will pass the offering plates right after the children's choir. I don't need to remind any of you how important that offering is." Harry paused and nodded across the room at Miranda. "Now, our pastor will lead us in thanks."

She led the most heartfelt prayer of Thanksgiving she had possibly ever prayed.

"Almighty and Gracious God, we give You thanks for the fruits of the earth in their season and for the labors of those who harvest them. Make us faithful stewards of thy great bounty, for the provision of our necessities and the relief of all who are in need, to the glory of thy name; through Jesus Christ our Lord, who lives and reigns with You and the Holy Spirit, one God now and forever. Amen."

The room chorused a loud *Amen* and broke out again into laughter and conversation. Platters of turkey passed up and down the tables, along with bowls of mashed potatoes, gravy, yams with tiny marshmallows, cranberries, stuffing, and freshly baked rolls. Miranda had prepared butternut squash ravioli with white-wine sauce while Alejandra had spent the afternoon the day before in Pam's kitchen making her childhood favorite, *Plato Típico* Honduran dish of grilled steak, chorizo, fried plantains, refried beans, cheese, tortillas, and pickled red onions, Harry had tried one and loudly declared the dish delicious.

As Miranda stood looking out at her congregation, the Bishop's words came back to her. "You have challenged them to become better versions of themselves." And they were, she thought.

But more than that, she realized, so was she. She took out her phone, and after typing for a moment, she hit send.

Almost immediately, the phone began to vibrate in her pocket. Too bad, she thought. Tony will have to get over it. As he said, plenty of people would jump at the chance to be his head chef. She wasn't leaving St. Gabe's or the town of Sparrow or Peg or any of them. She belonged here.

Miranda sat with Betty and Delmar at one of the long tables. She had not laid eyes on Delmar for some time, not since he stopped attending church with Betty, and Betty had refused a home visit from the pastor. He was thinner than she remembered, his posture more stooped, his hair white and thinning, wrinkles etched deep into his face. But despite the cloud of dementia, his eyes held a kind expression.

She watched, transfixed, as Betty guided Delmar with a gentle touch. Delmar's face shone as he reminisced about Thanksgivings past, and Betty listened even as he rambled. Miranda felt a new sense of admiration for the woman she had previously underestimated. The love and support that Betty showed Delmar was truly moving.

Miranda vowed to remember this. That people can change, or better yet, that people are not all one thing. They have dimensions. As a pastor, she should always be on the lookout for the kindness a difficult person like Betty might have hidden within them.

As slices of pie were handed out, Miranda walked from table to table, visiting with each church member. The conversation jumped from discussions of being a sanctuary church to how long everyone had already been listening to Christmas music. The atmosphere was light and joyful—a moment of true Thanksgiving.

Just as she was about to return to her seat and claim a wedge of pumpkin pie, a frustrated voice came from outside the open window. "Come on, you mangy creature!"

A moment later, the side door banged open, and a thin and lanky dog with a silver-gray coat burst through, waving its feathery tail and dragging Adam McClain at the end of a long leash. Before anyone could react, a clear, crisp voice rose above the din.

"Samson!" Peg stepped away from the end of her table. "Samson!"

The dog stopped instantly, frozen for one moment as his eyes fell on Peg. He lunged.

Adam dropped the leash before he was yanked off his feet, and Peg went to her knees. She opened her arms, and Samson nearly knocked her over with his exuberance. Within a moment, though, Peg regained herself. As she stood, the room fell silent, as mesmerized as the dog.

She snapped her fingers and said, in a voice matched only by the Dog Whisperer, "Sit."

And Samson sat, his eyes filled with pure love, gazing up at Peg.

"Good boy," she said. "Good boy." The room cheered, and then folks turned back to their pie.

"Don't you want to invite your young man to stay?" Harmon said, walking over to Miranda.

"He's not my—" Miranda looked around. "He's left anyway. So I guess he didn't want to stay."

"My dear." Harmon gripped her hand in a brief squeeze. "Don't spend your life waiting and watching. I can say from personal experience, you'll regret it."

Miranda squeezed his hand back and quickly slipped out the side door. Adam sat on the stone bench under the maple tree, its branches bare, the orange leaves long gone. He hadn't left after all.

Their eyes met.

"Adam," she said, relieved, and surprised at how calm her voice sounded.

"Miranda." He stood, the breeze ruffling his salt-and-pepper hair and lifting his burgundy tie. "How are you?"

"I'm fine," she managed to say. "How are you?"

"I'm good. Working in Boston."

"No more Button Factory?"

"Funding dried up for a while, but I think we're back on." He paused. "I hate giving up on something so worthwhile."

"I know, right?" She stopped and took him in. Blue button-down shirt, camel jacket, black wingtips. And for once, dog hair on his trousers.

He cleared his throat. "And you're good?"

"I'm good." She laughed and came over to the bench. They sat. The sleeve of her clergy shirt brushed against the sleeve of his suit coat. After thinking about him so much for the past weeks, sitting next to him felt surreal. And her fingertips were tingling unbearably.

"I have something that I need to say." Adam cleared his throat as if to make a well-rehearsed speech.

She started to interrupt him, but he held his hand up and stopped her. "Please—let me say something which I should have already said. I'm sorry. I mean, really sorry about the whole food thing. You are an amazing, incredible, beautiful woman."

"Thanks. I just wanted to—"

He cut her off. "And you're not a hearty eater."

"I am." She grinned.

"Well, okay. But I will never bring it up again."

They both laughed. She loved Adam's laugh.

"I told my brother about you."

"Aaron? What did you tell him?"

"I told him that I had met this terrific woman who was smart and beautiful and, well, adorable. But I had ruined things."

"What did Aaron say?"

"To get over myself and go do something to prove to you that I'm not a complete and total—I won't use the word he used."

"He thought you needed to prove yourself?"

"Didn't I?"

"A little bit. Maybe. Is that why you brought Samson back? To prove yourself?"

"Of course. I mean who can resist a man who rescues a big, slobbery, badly behaved dog?"

"Some men would have sent flowers."

"Brilliant. Didn't think of it."

"And for future reference, I also like chocolate."

"Again. Brilliant."

"How'd you ever find him?" She loved how Adam's hair had grown a bit longer and curled above his collar. And how his eyes crinkled when he laughed. She hadn't actually forgotten all his cute little details but had pushed them away when he disappeared from her life.

"It struck me as odd that Samson never returned to the alley behind the diner. And then it hit me. Delivery trucks pull up in that alley all the time. What if he had jumped on one and taken a ride somewhere? So I put his photo on the Facebook page of every dog shelter up and down the East Coast. Two days ago, I heard from a shelter in Newburyport that had taken in a young Irish wolfhound with a collar that said Samson. I called the shelter, and the dog they found sounded exactly like him: exuberant, gigantic, and impossible to control. Our Samson had hitched a ride in the back of a Pepperidge Farms truck. I knew finding him would make Peg happy, too, and well, that would make you happy."

"And you found him for us? For me?"

"It was the one thing that was certain to make you happy."

A brown leaf drifted from the maple tree, perhaps its final one. Miranda watched it float down and alight on Adam's head. Her heart quickened as she reached up, and as she did, he took her hand in his, his touch sending a warmth through her arm.

"You wanted to make me happy," she said, her voice barely above a whisper.

"I did." Adam's eyes met hers, filled with a mix of hope and uncertainty.

"Why?"

"Because there's something between us. Don't you think? I mean, I think there is." He spoke haltingly, a flush creeping up his neck. "And I want to know if you feel the same. Tell me that you don't, and I will go away and leave you alone forever. I'll stop chasing runaway dogs, attempting to bake sourdough bread, and obsessing over your adorable laugh."

Her pulse raced. Could he really feel the same way she did? "You've been baking sourdough?"

"Trying." His grin made her melt a little inside.

"And you're obsessed with my laugh?"

"Let's just say that your laugh is more addictive than my failed attempts at bread-baking."

"Good to know," she whispered, her body gravitating toward his. As she leaned in, the world seemed to slow.

Their lips met, soft and tentative at first, then with growing certainty. The kiss deepened, and she felt as though she were floating. As they parted, breathless, the sound of the children's choir reached her, and the soft breeze touched her flushed cheeks. In that moment, everything felt right with the world.

Enjoy more about
Widow's Walk: A Novel

Meet the Author
Check out author appearances
Explore special features

ABOUT THE AUTHOR

JANE WILLAN is the author of the heartwarming yet delightfully mysterious *Sister Agatha and Father Selwyn Mystery* series, where faith, community, and murder intertwine to create captivating cozy mysteries. As the pastor of Plantsville Congregational Church in Connecticut, Jane brings authenticity and warmth to her storytelling, drawing inspiration from her experiences in ministry and her love for the church's rich liturgical traditions.

With degrees in Religion and History from Hiram College, theological studies Vanderbilt Divinity School, and graduate degree in Biology from Boston University-- Jane's background is as varied as the characters she creates. Her stories reflect her passion for weaving intricate plots with humor, heart, and suspense, offering readers both a mystery to solve and a world to savor.

Jane's upcoming novel, *Widow's Walk*, is a heartwarming tale of resilience and second chances set in the quaint coastal town of Sparrow, Maine. Featuring Miranda McCurdy, a former Boston chef turned priest, the story explores community tensions, sanctuary, and the transformative power of connection.

When she's not writing or preaching, Jane enjoys exploring the beauty of New England, biking scenic rail trails, and spending time with her husband, Don, and their rescue dog, Ollie. Her website, www.janewillan.com, offers readers a glimpse into her books, reflections on the intersection of faith and fiction, and insights into her creative process.

Through her ministry and her novels, Jane invites readers to embrace hope, community, and the unexpected joys of new beginnings.

ACKNOWLEDGMENTS

Thanks to all the wonderful people in my church community over the years who have shown me unwavering loyalty, love, grace, and understanding. Your laughter, encouragement, and inspiration have brought to life the good people of St. Gabriel-by-the-Sea. Your steadfast support has taught me the true meaning of community, and, like Miranda, I strive to serve with the same spirit of dedication and care.

A heartfelt thank you to my ever-fantastic agent, Stephany Evans, for your constant support and sharp editorial insights. Those wonderfully encouraging smiley faces you sprinkle into editor's notes are often exactly what I need to keep going—you've been a guiding light throughout this journey.

To my friends, Jane Gardner and Anne Nafziger, thank you for your unwavering belief in my stories. Your encouragement and refusal to let me give up have been a constant source of strength and inspiration—I am endlessly grateful for your support.

Thanks to the incredible women at Sibylline Press. Your passion, creativity, and dedication have been a dream come true for this author. You are truly the best team I could have ever asked for.

And, of course, to my husband, Don: Thank you for being my support, my rock, and my steadfast companion in all things. You've walked beside me through every twist and turn, celebrated every success, and encouraged me through every challenge. Your love and belief in me have made this journey possible.

STUDY GUIDE QUESTIONS

1. The role of tradition is a recurring theme in the novel. How do characters like Betty Hardacre and the members of the Thanksgiving Committee demonstrate their adherence to tradition? How does Pastor Miranda challenge these traditions? What does the novel suggest about the importance and limitations of tradition, particularly within a religious community?

2. The character of Miranda McCurdy undergoes several changes throughout the story. How does her initial resistance to small-town life and the expectations of her role evolve? What are some key moments in the story that highlight her growth as a pastor and as a person?

3. The conflict surrounding the Thanksgiving celebration reveals deep divisions within St. Gabriel's congregation. How does the debate about the Pilgrim costumes highlight differing views on history, race, and social justice within the church community? What does this conflict suggest about the challenges of creating a welcoming and inclusive community?

4. Peg Dunbar's character is complex and multi-layered. How does her relationship with Miranda evolve throughout the story? What does her care for Samson and her sharp wit reveal about her personality?

5. The theme of sanctuary is central to the novel. How does the congregation's struggle with whether to offer sanctuary to Alejandra reflect the broader issues of immigration, compassion, and religious responsibility? How do different characters, like Betty, Harry, and Lucy, react to the idea of sanctuary?

6. How do the settings of the story (the town of Sparrow, the church, the beach) contribute to the overall atmosphere and themes of the novel? How does the natural environment mirror the emotional and spiritual struggles of the characters?

7. The ending of the novel resolves many of the conflicts but leaves some open for interpretation. What does the final scene at the Thanksgiving meal suggest about the future of St. Gabe's and its members? What message is the author trying to convey about forgiveness, growth, and community?

Sibylline Press is proud to publish the brilliant work of women authors over 50. We are a woman-owned publishing company and, like our authors, represent women of a certain age.

ALSO AVAILABLE FROM
Sibylline Press

Other People's Kids: A Novel
By Kim Culbertson

FICTION
392 pages, Trade Paper, $22
ISBN: 9781960573438
Also available as an ebook AND AUDIOBOOK

After a violent incident at her prestigious Bay Area school, English teacher Chelsea Garden returns to her rural hometown seeking refuge and a fresh start. There, she reconnects with a burned-out principal and an old flame, both working at the local high school. *Other People's Kids* follows three educators at different stages of their careers as they navigate second chances, personal crossroads, and the risks of starting over.

Collateral Stardust: Chasing Warren Beatty and Other Foolish Things
By Nikki Nash

MEMOIR
280 pages, Trade Paper, $19
ISBN: 9781960573421
Also available as an ebook AND AUDIOBOOK

Raised in a chaotic, bohemian Hollywood household, teenage Nikki Nash becomes fixated on a bold mission: meet and win over Warren Beatty. With determination and a detailed plan, at eighteen, working in a restaurant near the Beverly Wilshire, her long-shot dream collides with reality. While Warren remains ever present in her life, this is really the story of one woman navigating Hollywood as a producer, comedian, and actor in the eccentric fringes of L.A., brushing up against fame, danger, and dysfunction.

Seeds of the Pomegranate: A Novel

By Suzanne Samuels

HISTORICAL FICTION
416 pages, Trade Paper, $22
ISBN: 9781960573445
Also available as an ebook and audiobook

After illness derails her dreams of becoming a painter in Sicily, Mimi Inglese immigrates to New York, only to be dragged into her father's criminal underworld. When he's imprisoned, she turns to counterfeiting to survive, using her artistic gift to forge a path through Gangland chaos. As violence closes in, Mimi must risk everything to escape a life built on desperation and reclaim the future she once imagined.

You Could Be Happy Here: A Novel

By Erin Van Rheenen

FICTION
280 pages, Trade Paper, $19
ISBN: 9781960573476
Also available as an ebook and audiobook

When Lucy loses her mother and discovers her real father may be a man from her childhood summers in Costa Rica, she sets out to find him—and herself. But the village she returns to is no longer the paradise she remembers, and her search raises more questions than answers. *You Could be Happy Here* is a story of identity, belonging, and redefining home in a world that no longer fits the past.

The House of Cavanaugh: A Novel
By Polly Dugan

FICTION
248 pages, Trade Paper, $18
ISBN: 9781960573469
Also available as an ebook and audiobook

In 1964, Joan Cavanaugh has a secret affair that leads to the birth of a daughter whose true paternity she takes to her grave. Fifty years later, when 23andMe unearths the buried truth, the foundations of two tightly connected families are deeply shaken. *The House of Cavanaugh* is a gripping story of hidden pasts, unraveling loyalties, and what it really means to be family.

Reviving Artemis: The Making of a Huntress
By Deborah Lee Luskin

MEMOIR
280 pages, Trade Paper, $19
ISBN: 9781960573759
Also available as an ebook and audiobook

At sixty, longtime writer, gardener, and teacher Luskin feels a wild new calling: to leave the safety of her garden and learn to hunt deer. *Reviving Artemis* follows her late-in-life transformation as she confronts fear, embraces the forest, and reclaims a primal connection to nature. Blending humor, vulnerability, and myth, it's the story of a woman choosing to age on her own fierce terms.

 For more books from **Sibylline Press**, please visit our website at **sibyllinepress.com**

www.ingramcontent.com/pod-product-compliance
Lightning Source LLC
Jackson TN
JSHW021328130925
90972JS00002B/3